"Isabella? Are you okay?"

She opened her eyes and raised them ever so slightly. If Gabe thought he'd been stabbed through the heart when they'd first met, seeing the pain-filled expression in her dark eyes this time was far worse. Her pain had risen to the surface and was stark and immediate.

Moments later, he realized her fingers were flexing almost madly in the woolly coat of the lamb she'd been trying to feed. *The limp body of a now-dead lamb.*

"Oh, Isabella," Gabe murmured as he tried to remove the lifeless animal from her arms. "It's not your fault. You did your best to save him."

She snatched her hands back so fast, Gabe was left grasping air. Still without words, Isabella cradled the creature to her breast and began a distraught keening. It was a tortured, gut-wrenching sound. Gabe didn't know how in God's name to help her.

Instinct said that someone who hurt this badly needed holding. Considering the distance she always maintained between them, Gabe didn't know if he should be the one to offer comfort. But right now there was no one else.

He wrapped her and the lamb in a gentle embrace. And he rocked her from side to side, crooning nonsensical words close to her ear, just loud enough for her to hear him over the sound of her distress.

She shivered violently, yet he knew it was warm enough in the b̶ ̶ ̶ ̶ ̶ ̶ ̶ ̶ ̶ ̶ ̶ ̶thing. Clearly, Isabella's ̶ ̶ ̶ ̶ ̶ ̶ ̶ ̶ ̶ ̶ ̶ ̶ ̶ ̶ ̶ ̶ her. From the very de̶ ̶ ̶ ̶

Dear Reader,

As has so often been the case with the books I write, Gabe and Isabella's story began with a news article I cut out a few years ago and stored in my files. Some articles cry out for a happy ending. If there can be happiness (and there should!) for good people who have bad things happen to them, then it should come in the form of a love like Gabe Poston's. (You may remember meeting him in *Wide Open Spaces*.)

I selected Isabella Navarro to be the recipient of a tragedy no woman should ever have to endure. To ease her heavy burden, I gave her Gabe's love; for good measure, I tossed in a large, loving family—part of a tight-knit Basque farming community in eastern Oregon.

Everyone should have the privilege of attending a Basque wedding. There's lots of great food and wine, dancing and laughter, and it goes on for days. The memories have stayed with me. Yet even with such delightful events to offset Isabella's sadness, I discovered this wasn't an easy story to write. So I hope you'll think I've done right by her and also by Gabe. I finally felt comfortable leaving them in each other's care.

Sincerely,

Roz Denny Fox

P.S. I enjoy hearing from readers. You can get in touch with me at P.O. Box 17480-101, Tucson, AZ 85731 or via e-mail (rdfox@worldnet.att.net).

Books by Roz Denny Fox

HARLEQUIN SUPERROMANCE

Someone To Watch over Me

Roz Denny Fox

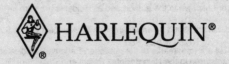

HARLEQUIN®

TORONTO • NEW YORK • LONDON
AMSTERDAM • PARIS • SYDNEY • HAMBURG
STOCKHOLM • ATHENS • TOKYO • MILAN • MADRID
PRAGUE • WARSAW • BUDAPEST • AUCKLAND

ISBN 0-373-71108-5

SOMEONE TO WATCH OVER ME

Someone To Watch over Me

CHAPTER ONE

AS WEDDING RECEPTIONS WENT, Gabe Poston rated Colt and Summer Quinn's better than most. Held outside on a large covered patio, this gathering at least didn't leave him feeling strangled for air. But after a gazillion introductions to people he'd probably never see again, Gabe was still desperate to escape for a while.

He carried his dirty plate into the kitchen, where caterers were too busy keeping food platters generously filled to care that one guest had slipped out the back door of the Forked Lightning Ranch house.

Hands tucked deep into his suit pants pockets, Gabe set out along a winding graveled road that led past a series of fenced pastures. He paused at a point where two fences intersected and propped the toe of one spit-polished black dress shoe onto the bottom rail. Preoccupied with his thoughts, it took him a while to appreciate the solitude and the scenery. A distant, purple mountain range, whose peaks were dusted gold in the warm spring sun, eventually had the calming effect he'd been seeking.

To better appreciate the panorama spread before him, Gabe removed the wire-rimmed glasses he needed only for reading. When, he wondered, pocketing his glasses, had he started craving seclusion?

And why? He used to want people around.

But apparently he hadn't been totally successful in leaving the party behind. Raucous voices and high-pitched laughter reached him on a sighing breeze. Or had *he* sighed—again? Gabe had caught himself doing a lot of that in the past few weeks.

As if anyone gave a damn. Certainly not the livestock munching contentedly on the lush green grass. Gabe's personal strife had no effect on Colt's new crop of Morgan horses. They frolicked across the pasture and on the other side of the fence Summer's curly-coated Belted Galloway calves did the same.

Lucky beasts. They lived the good life.

Ha! Most people would say Gabe Poston lived the good life.

Out here, communing with nature, he was able to admit that his odd melancholy could have something to do with turning thirty-eight yesterday, rather than the fact that Colt had opted out of SOS to marry the woman of his dreams.

No, Gabe didn't begrudge Colt his happiness.

Breaking off a piece of tall grass, Gabe stuck it between his teeth. His fortieth birthday breathing down his neck wouldn't bother him at all if Colt's marriage was the only sign of the old gang breaking up. But two other members of the original "fearless foursome," who'd forged ties in the Marine Corps, announced that they were also cutting loose from SOS, the land conservation agency where Gabe had found them all lucrative jobs. Save Open Spaces had provided Marc Kenyon, Reggie Mossberger and Gabe with a much-needed haven after a private rescue operation went bad. One that ended with Colt's capture by South American rebels.

Gabe knew that incident had hit him harder than it

did Marc or Reggie. After all, it'd been his bright idea to leave the Corps and sell their services in the private sector. The money offered to liberate kidnapped corporate travelers promised to make them millionaires. Shoot, it *had* made them millionaires. Except for Colt. He'd sunk every last cent into a horse ranch that his first wife had sold out from under him during the time he was held captive.

What a debacle that was. Although…back then they'd all feared Colt was a goner. None more than Gabe. Life sure could change in the blink of an eye. But Colt had escaped, and now he'd found real love with Summer.

Money didn't seem so important to any of them now. Not like it did when they were young and thought cash was a cure-all for everything.

Personally, Gabe had invested enough to let him do just about anything a man might dream of doing. *If only he had a clue as to what that might be…*

Maybe that was what bugged him. His buddies had their lives mapped out. Not so long ago, they'd all been footloose and loving it. Now, three of the four had announced plans to abandon SOS. According to Marc, they'd gone into nesting mode.

What the hell was nesting mode?

Oh, Gabe knew, but he didn't really understand it.

Tossing aside the piece of grass, he rested his chin on fists propped on the top rail. The view out here sparked an odd longing inside him and he acknowledged an emptiness he hadn't stopped to examine in years.

Clearly, Colt had found his dream here in Eastern Oregon with Summer and her son, Rory. Love. Colt said he'd found true love. *True* and *love* rarely went hand in hand in Gabe's estimation.

Loving your work, now that concept he understood.

Last week, when Reggie Mossberger phoned to say he was leaving SOS, his reason made sense. Moss had worked his butt off to finish veterinary school. It'd been a dream that had driven him to come out of the Corps alive.

Gabe had barely digested Reggie's news when Marc called to say he'd met someone special on his last trip to Utah—a woman he wasn't anxious to leave for months at a time as his job with SOS demanded. Add that to Colt's defection and it left Gabe working alone for Marley Jones. In all honesty, he didn't want to be the only guy on the team.

A shadow blocked the sun, breaking his concentration. A flash of blue caused him to raise his head.

It was a woman, hurrying toward an area where wedding guests had parked. Gabe idly followed her progress and saw her open the back door of an aging white van. He realized then that he'd seen her earlier, navigating the crowded patio with trays of hors d'oeuvres. Something in the way she walked grabbed a man's attention.

Classy was a description that came to mind. It probably had to do with the way she carried her tall, willowy body. She sort of…floated. That must have been what caught his eye, since he hadn't really seen her face.

Or maybe the way she wore her gleaming dark hair contributed to his first impression. So black it appeared almost indigo, and silky in the afternoon sun, her hair was parted in the middle with the sides scooped up into a complicated crown of braids. Gabe couldn't recall ever having noticed before how any woman arranged her hair.

Staring, he imagined the dark tresses flying loose and wild in the wind. *How dumb was that?* She didn't have so much as a hair out of place, even though she'd obviously been dashing in and out of a hot kitchen all afternoon.

Indulging in a long second glance, Gabe saw that outside of her incredible hair she was largely unremarkable. Most of her blue dress was covered by a white bibbed apron. Less-than-attractive shoes were undoubtedly comfortable but not in the least flattering. And compared to the gauzy spring dresses worn by most of the female wedding guests, her attire would be termed drab.

Not by him, though. The woman had…something Gabe couldn't quite put his finger on. As he continued his perusal, he saw her slide a large board holding a four-tiered cake out from the cavernous interior of the van.

Surely she wasn't going to try and carry that? He lifted his foot from the fence but he hadn't gone two steps in her direction when he saw Reggie ambling down the path. So were two women and three brawny cowboy-types who soon overtook Reggie. Those five made a beeline for the white van. One man in the quintet shouted, "Wait! We've come to help carry the cake."

Gabe checked his forward motion in time to see the cowboys take up posts on either side and behind the cake board. They retraced their steps while their female companions, plus the black-haired woman, began hauling cases of champagne out the van's side door. They wasted no time following the cowboys with the cake.

It was obvious they'd all reach Reggie long before Gabe got to the van.

Still compelled to offer assistance, he called to the last of the three women. "Is there anything else you need carried? If so, my friend and I have brawn to spare." Laughing, Gabe jerked a thumb toward Reggie. He'd stepped aside to let the men lugging the heavy cake pass.

"Moss, don't stand there like a statue. Help the lady with those bottles."

Lean, lanky Reggie Mossberger had probably never moved quickly in his entire life. Nor did he now. He managed a U-turn at a snail's pace—or so it seemed to Gabe.

The caterer, focused on the fate of her cake, cast a furtive glance at Gabe before turning to Reggie, who was closest. "I'm, uh, fine. But thank you," she said in a dark, smoky voice that affected the pit of Gabe's stomach.

"Really, I've got things under control," she reiterated, as Reggie tried to take the box. "There's nothing left in the van. But…if one of you gentlemen could close the side door, I'd appreciate it." Without waiting to see if either did as she asked, she walked away from them.

Stopping, Gabe swore under his breath. The woman's eyes, darker than coffee, lacked so much as a tiny spark of life. Gabe frowned. He'd seen such eyes before—in the hopeless, vacant stares of children in third world countries. For a moment he felt knocked off stride.

"Help. Don't help." Throwing up his hands, Reggie swung around to face Gabe, who, being nearer the van, jogged back to comply with the woman's request. As he slid the door shut, he took a moment to read the hand-painted logo sprawled across the side of the vehicle.

Isabella's Bakery, written in flowery script, curved around the silhouette of a birthday cake topped with a firestorm of lit candles. A local phone number and address were neatly stenciled below that.

Obviously it was where his sad goddess worked. Gabe donned his glasses for a closer inspection. Below, in smaller script, it said the bakery provided full-service catering for all parties and weddings, with their specialty being authentic Basque foods.

Straightening, Gabe turned that over in his mind. During his military travels, he recalled having eaten at a Basque restaurant in the Pyrenees region of Spain. Great food. The Basques were a proud, independent people, if he remembered correctly.

"Who was that?" Reggie spoke from directly behind Gabe.

"I don't know." Gabe straightened slowly. "She's obviously part of the catering crew handling Summer and Colt's reception."

"Oh. So why are you out here messing in her affairs? Marc and Trace have been hunting you for half an hour. The babelicious blonde—the one who's been dogging you all day, said you'd bolted out the back door. Dang, Gabe, what would possess you to run out on such a hot babe?"

Gabe scowled. "If you're referring to Megan Ward, who waits tables at the Green Willow Café, half the reason I ducked out was to dodge her."

"No way! Not unless old age is making you go blind." Jabbing Gabe with his elbow, Reggie threw back his head and laughed.

"Oh, so I'm old because you and I don't agree some woman's a babe?"

"Yeah. Used to be the four of us could walk into any bar and we'd all zero in on the hottest babe in the whole place."

"In the old days, you and Colt only had eyes for a sound horse. And Marc was usually too busy polishing whatever car he'd blown his money on to know women existed. In case it's skipped your pea brain, Colt's the one getting hitched for the second time. And Marc's sounding alarmingly serious about some woman named Lizzy down in Utah. Which leaves you, my friend. Because I'm damn sure not in the market for a woman." Gabe stabbed a thumb at his own vest. "If you'd like an introduction to Megan Ward, I'll be more than happy to oblige."

Reggie stared longingly at the crowd milling around the patio they were approaching. "Can't. I've sunk every cent I have or will have for the next five years into buying out a vet in a dinky Idaho town. As well as being stone broke, I have nothing to offer a woman like Megan. Or any woman, for that matter."

"Did you take a good look at the main street when you and Marc hauled into Callanton? Post office, general store, café, a boarding stable, two bars and a motel. Oh, and a professional building that houses a lawyer and two people docs. Megan said she's lived here all her life, so she must like small towns."

Hooking his thumbs over his belt, Reggie slowed his pace even more. "This conversation is pointless. Anyway, I came out to drag you inside. Colt and Summer are almost ready to cut their cake. Tracey's been tapped to deliver a toast. He wants your help writing something. The kid said if he'd known he'd have to make a speech, he never would've agreed to be Coltrane's best man.''

Both men grinned at that truth—each privately thankful it was Tracey stuck with the chore, and not them.

A visibly nervous best man grabbed Gabe the minute he set foot on the brick patio. "Did Moss tell you I need your brain, Gabriel? I've never been a best man before.''

Gabe smiled crookedly. "What makes you think I can help? I do my best to avoid getting roped into attending weddings.''

"C'mon, you're a lawyer. Everybody knows lawyers have silver tongues.''

"I'm an accountant who happens to have a second degree in finance law, kid.''

"Yeah, and I'm a wrangler, not a kid. I also quit college after one semester. Give me a break here, will you?''

"Okay, okay. For Pete's sake, get up off your knees. Everybody's staring.'' Gabe awkwardly yanked the young man—who topped his own six-foot height by several inches—to his feet.

Smirking in satisfaction, Tracey whipped a pen and crumpled envelope from the inside pocket of the short tux jacket he'd teamed with well-pressed jeans.

Gabe snatched the items. "Give me those. Folks who are being asked to hold off drinking their bubbly like toasts to be short and sweet. How about you say, 'Here's to Summer and Coltrane, who rose from the ashes of their pasts and now stand ready to embrace whatever new opportunities lie ahead.'''

"That's it?'' Tracey gaped at Gabe, then at the single sentence written on the envelope Gabe had thrust back into his hand. "I stewed for an hour and I've only gotta say one line?"

Gabe clicked the pen again. "Here, I can stretch it to a paragraph or two if you'd rather. You never said you wanted ten minutes center stage."

Tracey ripped the pen from Gabe's hand. "Funny! Blow it out your ear, Poston." Backing up, Tracey almost upset a tray of full champagne glasses carried by a woman wending her way among the guests.

"Oh, gosh. Sorry." He righted the tray, then shifted the pen and envelope to one hand in order to relieve her of two glasses. Trace passed one flute to Gabe with a flourish. "Thanks a bunch. You know good and well you saved my sorry ass."

Chuckling, Gabe accepted the champagne. He couldn't help wishing the tray-bearer had been the dark-haired caterer. Then he'd have leapt to her rescue.

Shocked by that revelation, Gabe almost drained the beverage he should have saved for the toast. Lowering his glass abruptly, he swept a furtive glance around the room in search of the woman. She was at the front table, preparing Colt and Summer for the cake-cutting ceremony.

As Tracey was summoned from that same table, Gabe fell in at his heels, his primary objective being to get a second look at the caterer. Maybe he'd only imagined her somber eyes.

Perky blond Megan Ward broke away from her circle and took Gabe's arm in a light yet oddly possessive manner. "Hey, hi there again. Did your friend find you? A tall guy with really short, sandy hair?" Megan said when Gabe ground to a halt and stared at her blankly. "I don't know his name," she admitted. "Gina worked the bar last night at Colt's bachelor party. She said the Ichabod character came and left with you and Marc. He's the one Gina's been drooling over these last two days.''

"Ichabod?"

"No, silly, Marc. Gina's hot for Marc Kenyon."

Normally quicker on the uptake, Gabe could make little sense of Megan's chatter. "Excuse me," he said, pulling from her grasp. "I see Reggie in the cake line." Gabe had to rise on tiptoe to locate Moss, even though his friend, at six-five, stood head and shoulders taller than all men at the party except for Tracey Jackson. Gabe hesitated after sinking back on his heels. "I'll be happy to introduce you to Moss."

"Who?" Megan blinked her big blue eyes.

"Reggie Mossberger. Tall guy standing behind Marc. Reggie said he'd like to meet you." Gabe began elbowing a path through a crowd, which had again closed.

"But…but…why me?"

"Reggie's kinda shy."

"Pu…leese!" Megan snatched Gabe's left wrist. "He's the one Gina nicknamed Ichabod. As in Crane," she said, stopping suddenly, thus checking Gabe's forward momentum. "You know—because of the odd way he walks." She broke off speaking in the wake of Gabe's fierce glare. "Goodness, haven't you heard a word I said? Gina's interested in Marc Kenyon. *He's* the hottie, not the other goofy guy."

"Reggie limps because he took a butt full of shrapnel saving me and some other Marines in a firefight. I owe him my life," Gabe said right before he left Megan standing openmouthed while he muscled his way to where his friends stood.

The bad thing about stopping to set Megan straight

was the fact that the caterer he'd wanted to see again had disappeared by the time he reached the front row.

Marc clinked his glass lightly against Gabe's. "Glad you hung around. Knowing your aversion to gigs like this, when I couldn't find you, I figured you'd split."

"Nope. I went outside for a last look at Quinn's ranch."

"This is country to die for, isn't it? Old Colt's done okay for somebody who, two years ago, didn't care if he lived or died. So, Gabe, any idea where Marley's sending you next?"

Gabe shook his head. "He's not sure. Said he's had several properties under review. But with the downturn in the economy, a lot of big contributors have pulled back on funding the program."

"What about land conservation projects currently in the works? I promised to stay with SOS until we close on that Utah deal near Heber City."

"So you're really going to do it?"

Marc lowered his glass. "Do what?"

"Bail out on the team?"

"I don't call it bailing out exactly." Mark fiddled with his glass.

"What do you call it?" Gabe shot back.

"Look, Gabe, I thought I already explained myself. I'm tired of the gypsy life."

"I know what you said. It's just…all so sudden. First Colt. Then Moss, and now you. Hell, you guys are like family. The only family I've got," he said gruffly.

Reggie broke into their conversation. "The house that comes with the veterinary practice I bought in Idaho needs sprucing up. But it's got two passable bedrooms and a bath with hot and cold running water."

He offered a shrug and a toothy grin. "Might do you good to take out your frustration with hammer and nails. What do you say, Gabe? The invitation's on the table for an extended visit."

"Thanks, but I work with my head. I'm not so good with my hands."

Marc unleashed a belly laugh that drew some attention. "That's not the word we used to get from your dates, Gabriel, old friend."

Gabe socked him on the shoulder.

"Hey, pipe down." Reggie nudged them both. "Colt and Summer are about to smash cake in each other's faces. Trace is gonna do his thing. Then we can get to the good part. Eating cake and drinking this high-octane stuff," he said, wagging his glass.

Gabe craned his neck, hoping to catch a glimpse of the elusive caterer. He saw another woman, similarly dressed, topping off champagne glasses. The woman with the braided hair seemed to have vanished. Gabe hoped she hadn't left the party. Releasing the breath he'd been holding, he massaged the back of his neck. Something must be wrong with him to be mooning over some woman he'd never even met.

The newlyweds went to stand behind the tiered cake. The local sheriff and a rancher Gabe had met the last time he was in town were doing a bang-up job of heckling the couple. His mission then had been on behalf of Save Open Spaces. Through their efforts, Summer had not been forced to sell this historic ranch to a crooked developer commissioned by her equally unscrupulous ex-husband.

The three friends fell silent. But it meant everything when Colt's roving gaze sought each of them out. He smiled and mouthed *semper fi*. A hole opened in

Gabe's chest again. Damn, he was going to miss these guys. Marc might've figured he was kidding, calling them family. But the unvarnished truth was that no one else on earth gave a damn about Gabe Poston.

Not a soul since he was twelve, anyway. That terrible morning in Texas when his mom's body washed up in Baytown on the shores of Galveston Bay. All the neighbors whispered she'd have died anyway. Shooting heroin off a dirty needle killed her, some said. Russ Poston, a long-haul trucker, claimed he couldn't, or more likely wouldn't, raise a kid he'd never believed was his. Gabe's grandparents backed their son's claim. And his mother's folks lived hand-to-mouth on public assistance. They couldn't afford to feed the eight kids they'd already produced, let alone take on another. In a blink he was made a ward of the Houston court.

But Gabe had always been good at taking care of himself. Or so he thought, until at seventeen he ran afoul of the law and a cop invited him to join the Marines or spend more than four years behind bars. He'd made the wisest choice, it turned out.

So what in heaven's name was wrong with him now?

Blinking to clear a vision gone cloudy, Gabe did his best to work up enthusiasm for watching Summer and Colt trade promises along with bites of cake. He raised his glass with everyone else. He even prompted Trace when he stumbled and got flustered during his one-line toast.

The icy champagne tasted good going down, but Gabe declined a second topping off of his glass. After setting his empty flute on one of the trays situated around the patio, he let himself be swept forward with the boisterous crowd, all bent on hugging and backslapping the happy couple. Gabe attempted to veer off the moment he saw that the caterer with the haunted eyes had returned to finish cutting the cake. But the other revelers were too determined, and Gabe soon found himself pressed into a corner with the blushing bride.

"Gabe, hi." Summer inched farther backward, letting Gabe's broad shoulders conceal her from the crush of well-wishers. "Hey, block for me a minute, will you, please? I've been hugged so many times my ribs are all but cracked. Just until I catch my breath," she added, holding Gabe in place.

"No problem. Especially as you're just the person to answer a question for me."

"You have a question?" Summer smiled. "Colt calls *you* the answer man."

"Afraid I'm out of my depth on this one. See the woman cutting your cake? Who is she?" Gabe spoke in a rush because he was bumped from behind.

Summer dipped her head to look beneath the arm he'd anchored to the wall. "Izzy, you mean? Isabella Navarro." Summer straightened, lowered her voice and frowned at Gabe. "We've got a large Basque population living east of Callanton. She's from their community."

Gabe didn't say anything. He made it obvious that he was waiting for more information.

Summer grudgingly gave a little. "Granted, Izzy's beautiful, talented and about as nice a person as you'd ever hope to meet. She's also in the midst of a horrible personal tragedy, Gabe. I'll gladly introduce you to any other of the unattached females at our reception, since you seem to be put off by Megan. Oh, look—over near the grape arbor. It's Maggie Fitzgerald and Dawn Cunningham.'' Summer physically turned Gabe's head in the direction she wanted him to look.

He couldn't pretend interest in either the flashy redhead or the petite brunette who chatted with Jesse Cook, owner of the Broken Arrow Ranch. Gabe had met Jesse weeks ago and liked what he'd seen of Summer's nearest neighbor.

''Tell me more about Isabella,'' he murmured, returning his gaze to the cake table.

Summer pursed her lips, first studying Gabe, then slanting a worried glance toward her friend.

Colt Quinn elbowed his way into their corner and slipped an arm possessively around his wife. ''Go find your own woman, Poston. This one's mine.'' Bending, Colt pressed a kiss on Summer's mouth. As their kiss ended, Colt started to move Summer out of the corner.

''Hey, hold on.'' Gabe caught at her lacy sleeve. ''I'm serious about wanting to know why a beautiful woman has such soulless eyes.''

Summer's voice dropped even lower. ''I'll tell you because you're Colt's best friend. But Izzy's my good friend, too, so listen up and then forget about this fascination you have with her, okay?'' Clearing her throat, Summer said tightly, ''Ten months ago, not long after she won a bitter divorce, Izzy got home late from work to find her ex in *her* garage—sitting in his car with the motor running.''

Gabe shifted uncomfortably. ''God,'' he exclaimed. ''You're telling me the SOB killed himself at her place?''

Summer squeezed Gabe's forearm. ''Julian Arana was unconscious but alive. The same wasn't true of their two beautiful kids. Five-year-old Antonia and three-year-old Ramon died of carbon monoxide poisoning. Izzy...well, she's making it through day by day."

Gabe's body jerked spasmodically. The champagne he'd just downed threatened to come up again. Of all the scenarios he'd conjured up after glimpsing the woman's eyes, none compared to the horrible truth.

Colt Quinn wrapped his wife in the protective shelter of his arms. "I know that's why you gave Isabella our catering contract instead of going to the Green Willow like your family always did. But, honey, this isn't good wedding conversation." He glared at Gabe.

Gabe immediately backed off. "You've gotta believe that if I'd had any idea, I would've kept my mouth shut. Go on you two, enjoy what's left of your big day."

"Are you sticking around a while?" Colt clapped Gabe on the shoulder. "Marc and Moss are taking off for the airport within the next hour to catch their commuter flights. We've said our goodbyes. You drove, I know. I saw your Lexus SUV outside."

"I haven't decided exactly when I'll check out of the Inn. They're still skiing at Sun Valley, and I've leased out my condo until the season ends. Maybe I'll stay here a week or so and see if Marley wants me to close on Marc's Utah project."

"Great. You guys aren't all taking off on us at once," Summer said. "Promise you'll come to the ranch for dinner one night before you go. Coltrane, call him tomorrow and set a date. Oh, excuse me, please. I see Rory helping himself to a second piece of cake. That little scoundrel will be sick as a dog tonight if I don't call a halt." She left her husband's arms to dash off and intercept her son.

Colt had difficulty taking his eyes off her as she

threaded her way through the guests, who stood in small groups, talking and eating cake.

Gabe experienced a vague surge of envy as Colt finally stirred.

"You've been awfully tight-lipped about any plans you might have if Marley's source of funds for the agency dries up. You got something cooking on a back burner, Gabe?"

Gabe shook his head.

"Callanton needs a good accountant. Or, hell, if you can hang on for a year, Summer and I will hire you to handle the Forked Lightning accounts exclusively. We've already talked it over. We just can't swing it this year."

"In other words, I'm not the only one having a hard time watching the old gang scatter?"

Colt gave a short laugh. "Dumb, isn't it? Four grown men like us. It's not as if we don't all have the means to visit one another, no matter where in the world we decide to sink roots."

"We all have the means, but will we make the time?" Gabe shrugged.

"You've nailed what's been bothering me. Ranching's a three-hundred-and-sixty-five-day-a-year job. I kinda figure being a vet's the same. And who knows about Marc? He said Lizzy's dad owns three car dealerships, and the old boy's planning to retire. You know how crazy Marc's always been about cars. I can see him practically living at a dealership, can't you?"

"Yeah. Haven't we been friends too long to lose touch now? Go enjoy your party, Coltrane. I'm gonna nab me a slice of that cake before it's all gone."

"Uh, Gabe. I couldn't help noticing that you're still

zeroed in on Summer's friend. Whatever's on your mind, it's probably a bad idea.''

Gabe glanced away, trying to hide his guilt. "I don't know what you're implying. Cake. That's all I'm after.'' He spun and walked off.

As he picked up an empty plate, Gabe tried putting himself in Isabella's shoes. But his mind refused, and his gut churned. How could a person go on?

Damn, he'd always wanted kids someday. Gabe knew firsthand how fast life went to hell when a child lost his parents. He couldn't begin to fathom what it'd be like for a parent to lose two kids. He'd studied law, but it didn't take a law degree to determine that Isabella Navarro's ex was seriously wacko. Too bad the SOB didn't die with his kids.

Approaching Isabella gingerly, Gabe extended his plate for a piece of cake. He had no idea what, if anything, to say to her. Something innocuous, he decided, smiling automatically as she looked up. "I closed your van like you asked,'' he blurted. "That was me in the parking lot. Remember? I suggested my friend and I help you carry the champagne?'' Gabe hiked a thumb over his right shoulder to where Reggie and Marc were moving inside with the crowd.

The caterer paled as she set a wedge of cake in the exact middle of his plate.

"The name's Gabe. Gabe Poston. I'm a friend of the groom. I watched you unload this cake from your van and I thought it was too pretty to eat.'' Lifting a fork to his mouth, Gabe raised his eyes to hers. "Um. I was wrong. Tastes great. All the food did. Tasted good, I mean.''

Isabella inclined her head in deference to his compliment.

Gabe knew he should let it go at that and move on. But again the deep shadows in her eyes wrenched his heart. "I'll bet it's not easy handling a party of this size. You made it look simple, though."

ISABELLA NAVARRO REFOCUSED and really looked at the handsome stranger who devoured his cake while trying to draw her into conversation. She couldn't admit she'd performed her services here today by rote. Work took her mind off…other things. She'd accepted this job for the money. She'd need extra to get her through the time she'd have to take off once Julian's trial began. Her brain rarely moved past that point. And she needed to keep her attention—all her attention— on that goal. Too many people thought Julian had simply gone off the deep end. Even the media implied he was insane.

She knew better. And someone had to be an advocate for her kids. Isabella intended to see her bastard of an ex-husband held accountable for his actions. She wasn't letting anything get in her way.

Yet here was this poor man. A virtual stranger who obviously didn't know he was hitting on a woman whose heart had turned to granite. Isabella couldn't find the words to break it to him, either. Not without crying. And she wouldn't. Cry. Not one tear until her mission was accomplished.

CHAPTER TWO

THE MAN'S EYES BORED straight through Isabella, leaving her feeling exposed. The hand holding the cake knife faltered. Why was such a knockout guy attempting to engage *her* in conversation? The self-proclaimed friend of Colt Quinn's wore an impeccable gray pinstriped suit, which brought out gray flecks in otherwise lake-blue eyes.

Isabella stood five-nine without shoes. She had to look up to meet Gabe Poston's eyes. That made him as tall as her brothers, all of whom were over six feet. Poston's healthy tan spoke of someone who worked out of doors, especially as his light brown hair was also sun-streaked. Yet his hands told a different story.

The men in Isabella's family—her dad, three brothers and two brothers-in-law—all carved a living from the land. Their occupations ranged from apple farmers to grape growers to sheep men, which meant that their knuckles were permanently scarred and chapped. She loved them all dearly, but she couldn't help noticing that not one ever had fingernails as clean as the man standing across from her now. Men who looked like Gabe Poston passed through Callanton, but they never stuck around.

That at least came as a relief.

So, the larger issue that loomed on the horizon, beyond his fine physical attributes, was why he'd singled her out. Especially when Summer had invited a score of eligible searching-for-a-mate females to her reception.

She could only assume he hadn't heard about her. Even folks Isabella had known most of her life avoided speaking directly to her now. Not because they were uncaring but because they didn't know what to say. Truthfully, what could *anyone* say?

But this stranger not only spoke, he looked her squarely in the eye and forced her to pay attention. Now that she had, surely he'd see her utter misery, and he'd leave her alone with her pain—like everyone did. Like she wanted them all to do.

Isabella hurt down into the deepest parts of her soul, and she needed to feel every ounce of that rawness. Otherwise she might not have the strength to continue the fight to put Julian Arana behind bars for the rest of his natural life. That was all she lived for. Julian's lawyer bragged that he'd won a huge victory when the judge ruled out asking for the death penalty. Only the state's prosecutor and Isabella's family knew she'd never favored putting Julian to death. Death was too easy an out for a person who had committed his sin.

Her hands shook harder and her stomach knotted just thinking about Julian and the case. Either Poston had no sensitivity, or he was simply the oblivious sort. For whatever reason, he was still smiling at her. A disconcerting smile that revealed tiny laugh lines around his eyes.

"I seem to be your last customer." Gabe gestured with his cake plate. "The other guests have all gone inside. Presumably to dance. At least I hear the combo that arrived a while ago tuning up their instruments. They have a nice sound, don't you think?"

Isabella hadn't seen or heard a band. Of course, she'd ignored everything going on around her except when it pertained to her catering duties. But it was clear that if she didn't say something, this guy would pester her all evening. "Feel free to take your plate inside. There are TV trays for empties set up near the dance floor."

Gabe averted his eyes long enough to study the profusion of plates and glasses left strewn about the patio. "Give me a second to finish this, and I'll help you clean up the mess out here." He gestured with his plate.

"I…ah…" His offer stunned Isabella. Yet she hated the blush she felt creeping up her neck. Finally, she summoned a grouchy tone. "I have a clean-up crew. You, sir, are a guest."

"I'm a friend—"

"—of the groom. I know. You already said that. Oh, look. Here are my helpers now." Isabella cast a relieved glance over Gabe's right shoulder.

Turning, he saw the two women who'd helped carry champagne in from the parking lot. Both were shaking out large empty trash bags. "Those bags will be heavy once they're full. Where are the cowboys who carried in the cake for you? You seem to have lost them."

"Cowboys?" Isabella frowned slightly. "Oh, you must mean my brothers. They went home. They aren't part of my crew. They're ranchers."

"So, they only came to carry in the cake?"

Isabella sighed. Apparently Gabe Poston was a talker. "Most wedding receptions I cater are in town, which means I can slide the cake board out onto a cart and wheel it inside whatever hall the bride's rented. Logistics here at the Forked Lightning necessitated a change in my usual routine. Really, thank you for offering, but my sisters and I have everything under control.'' Closing down again, Isabella set the cake knife aside, then deftly skirted the table, and joined the two women.

Taking time to scrutinize their features, Gabe did see a vague family resemblance. But he thought she was by far the most attractive of the three. If not for eyes filled with pain and shadows, he'd call her beautiful.

Gabe continued to eye the trio while he finished his cake. As he forked up the last bite, he suddenly saw two of the women returning his frank stare. It took a minute for him to tumble to the fact that he was being discussed by them.

He strained to hear but couldn't make out what they were saying, as they weren't speaking English. He knew Basques didn't speak Spanish, although a word or two sounded familiar. *Caliente* meant hot, didn't it? This didn't seem to be a reference to the weather, however, since it wasn't hot on the patio. The late-spring sun had already dipped behind the mountains and a stepped-up breeze seemed downright chilly. Probably why Summer and Colt had planned to have the dancing inside.

Gabe considered edging closer to the sisters in hopes of deciphering more of their conversation, only Marc Kenyon opened the screen door leading from the house and called out, ''Yo, Gabe! Moss and I need to get back to the Inn to collect our bags. If you'd rather stay and dance, Tracey said he'd drive us to town, then on to the airport.''

''I'll take you. Who knows when I'll see you two again.'' Backtracking to the cake table, Gabe set his empty plate atop a stack of others.

Marc moved out onto the patio and peered around. "Why are you out here all by your lonesome? I swear, Gabriel, you've been acting weird all weekend."

"Is it weird to eat cake like a civilized human being instead of swallowing a chunk whole like you guys did?"

"So now your friends aren't civilized." Marc grabbed Gabe and knuckle-rubbed his head as he dragged him inside via the sliding glass door.

FROM THE PATIO, the three sisters watched the byplay. "Like I already asked you once, Bella, who's the hot guy? The one wearing the gray suit." Sylvia Oneida, Isabella's twenty-nine-year-old sister, left off speaking in Euskera, the language of the Basques, to badger her in English. Most of the family called her Bella; friends were more prone to shorten her name to Izzy.

Trinidad Navarro, known to all as Trini, was twenty-five, and very involved in the local dating scene. She'd long since checked out all the single men at the reception. "According to Megan Ward, his name is Gabriel Poston. He was a Marine, along with Summer's husband. And he's an accountant plus lawyer. There's speculation that he's got a fat bank account. Oh, Megan also said hands off."

"Trini," Sylvia gasped. "It's mercenary to care more about a man's wealth than his personality."

Isabella, who'd already begun scraping plates, paused with a plate held over the trash container. "Lawyer? What kind? Is he opening an office in Callanton? The prosecutor assigned to Julian's case is too busy to answer my questions. I wouldn't mind having someone I could retain to help me understand all the legal jargon."

The younger sister, still pouting over the scolding she'd received, answered Bella nonetheless. "He and Marc Kenyon, the guy who just came and got him, both work for Save Open Spaces. That's the agency Summer's husband recently left. Oh, and there's a third friend. Sylvia and I passed him on the road when we helped you carry in the champagne." Trini gave a disgusted groan after a blank expression crossed her sister's face. "Honestly, Bella, you've gotta snap out of it and start noticing what goes on around you."

"Ignore Trini," Sylvia said briskly. "She doesn't mean to be callous. It's another stage she's going through, I think."

"I am not." Trini flung her arms around Isabella. "I'm sorry, Bella. We all loved Antonia and Ramon. I hate Julian for his selfish, heartless stupidity. I just can't bear seeing you so…so consumed. I think the fact that a Rob Lowe look-alike singled you out is the perfect opportunity to get your mind off the tragedy. Even if it's only for an hour or two."

Isabella aimed an awkward pat at Trini's back. "I know I'm not pleasant to be around. I hope you know I couldn't have survived without my family. I want you to find a good man, one who'll make you happy, Trini. But please don't expect me to get on with any type of normal life until after I see the state lock up Julian and throw away the key." Her voice caught, and pulling back, Isabella blinked dry eyes. She never understood why she couldn't shed tears when she hurt clear to the very bottom of her soul.

Sylvia cast furtive glances at the door through which the men had disappeared. "He's gone. Maybe for good, Bella. I heard the one who came to get him say something about an airport. At any rate, Trini isn't going to mention his name again." She shot a warning at the youngest member of the large Navarro clan.

It was well known that Trini had a stubborn streak a mile wide. Snatching up a garbage bag, she announced, "Gabriel Poston is a hunk. Furthermore, he smells yummy. It's too bad our Bella caught his eye first. If he does hang around town, you can bet if I get an opportunity I'll bring him home to meet Mama and Papa."

As always—unless their oldest sister, Ruby, was around—Sylvia had to have the last word. "Who cares how he smells? You bring home a man who's twelve or thirteen years older than you, some ordinary Joe Sixpack at that, and Mama will send you out to cut a willow switch that sings through the air like she did when we were kids who'd misbehaved."

"Oh, your husband's exalted just because he's Basque? He grows grapes, makes wine and smells like yeast, for pity's sake. Ruby's husband and Papa come home smelling like sheep dip. Why *shouldn't* I want a man in my bed who smells nice?"

"Our men are all good and hardworking. Papa never should've sent you off to college in California, Trini. You came home with the idea that you're too good for any of our local boys."

"Stop, you two." Isabella stepped between them. "What if a guest hears us bickering? You know my business depends on word-of-mouth referrals."

Bella's sisters both wore guilty faces. Isabella gave each one a bracing hug. "Let Trini spread her wings, Syl. I know for a fact that being born Basque doesn't guarantee a good man. If community pressures and expectations hadn't been what they were, I might not have married Julian. I shouldn't have married him."

"Oh, Bella!" Sylvia's brows drew down in distress.

"I'm not after sympathy, Sylvia. I hate the pity I see on people's faces. If anything, that's the one nice thing about Mr. Poston. He didn't avert his eyes when he spoke to me."

Audrey Olsen, Summer Marsh's longtime house-keeper, poked her head out of the kitchen. "There you ladies are. I wanted to let you know I cleared a place in the freezer for the top layer of Summer and Colt's cake. She insists they're going to eat the stale thing on their first anniversary. Beats me why anybody would want year-old cake. Summer said you provide a special box, Isabella?" The last was more a question than a statement.

"A tin. It's airtight." Isabella left her sisters to make her way across the uneven brick. "Most brides save the smallest layer of their wedding cake to celebrate their first anniversary. I designed these tins to seal in as much freshness as possible." She handed the older woman a silver canister trimmed with white wedding bells. Her bakery's name was printed neatly on the side. The couple's names adorned the top.

Audrey took the tin. "Well, isn't this nice? I suppose Summer told you I offered to fix food for the reception. After seeing all the work, I'm so grateful she decided to hire you, Isabella. Land sakes, weddings are sure more involved now than in my day. Virgil and I just drove down to the county courthouse and said our *I dos.*"

"I cater anniversaries, too," Isabella said casually. "Summer said you and Virgil have a fiftieth coming up in a few months."

Audrey laughed. "I was fifteen when I set my sights on that man. The day I turned eighteen, I followed him out on a round-up. He'll tell you he couldn't shake me so he married me. We've stuck together all these years, but neither of us makes any to-do over anniversaries. They're just days that come and go.''

"Fifty years living with the same man is something to crow over in my opinion." Isabella eased a business card out of the pocket of her blue cotton dress. "I can go simple for family and a few close friends, or hog-wild feeding half the town like we did today. Thanks to good friends like Summer, my weeks are getting booked fairly fast, so if you change your mind, phone me next week. I promise I'll work up something that won't threaten Virgil's masculinity."

Audrey grinned and read the card in her hand before sliding it into the pocket of her slacks. "You'd better start eating some of the goodies you fix, Izzy. Goodness, girl, you're wasting away."

Isabella raised an unsteady hand to rub her throat. She found it almost impossible to make herself eat, ever since her children's deaths. And now she couldn't force a response past the lump that seemed to stay lodged in her throat. When would the mere thought of losing Toni and Ramon quit causing her problems with swallowing and breathing? Molly, her psychiatrist, said it would eventually ease.

"Oh, darlin'. Shut my mouth. I didn't mean to remind you...of..." Audrey clamped her lips closed. "I, uh, maybe I will throw a little party to commemorate fifty years with that old buzzard." Outwardly flustered, she hurriedly withdrew into the kitchen again.

Isabella felt bad. She drove people away. And that hurt, too. But she couldn't help it. Molly said the mind was an unpredictable thing.

As Isabella soberly went back to her work, she urged

her mind down a different road. She tried to picture what her life would be like fifty years from now. She didn't particularly like the vision she conjured up—a wizened, skeletal version of the unhappy woman who gazed back at her each day from the bathroom mirror. Trini was right. They were all right. She couldn't go on as she was. But how could she not be the spokesperson for her silent children?

Her icy lips formed the mantra she began and ended each day with. "When I see Julian properly punished, I'll worry about getting my life back."

GABE SETTLED back into the soft leather seat of his luxury SUV and let Marc's and Reggie's endless talk swirl around him. They knew each other so well, Gabe could almost predict the path of their conversation. Reggie would talk for a while about the injured livestock he'd healed. Then Marc would jump in and expound on the virtues of the latest sports cars out on the market. Once they'd exhausted those subjects, their interest would undoubtedly veer toward women.

He grinned when their conversation did exactly that.

Moss, who'd changed from his suit into worn jeans and a short-sleeved plaid shirt, stretched his lanky frame across Gabe's middle set of seats. "So, Marc. Are you really serious about tying yourself down to Lizzy Woodruff?"

Marc darted a quick glance at Gabe before he turned sideways in his seat to see both his friends. An oddly dreamy expression softened his pewter-gray eyes. "Lizzy's the woman I want to spend the rest of my life with."

"How do you know?" Gabe jerked his eyes off the road long enough to frown at Marc.

From the back, Moss guffawed. "You said it your-self, Gabe, when you pointed out that little Lizzy's daddy owns a string of car dealerships."

Marc bolted upright. "That's a dog-faced lie! Granted, I met Lizzy at one of her dad's dealerships, where I went to scope out a car. But cars have nothing to do with why I'm going back to Utah to take our relationship to the next level."

"I'm serious, Marc," Gabe said. "How do you know Lizzy's *the* one and only?"

"How did Coltrane know Summer was it for him?"

"I have no idea." Gabe smacked the steering wheel. "Especially since he bombed completely back when he married Monica."

"Now, she was a piece of work," Reggie said.

"Yeah. But I remember envying Colt back then. Hell, we all did."

"Our priorities were different, I guess," Marc mut-tered.

Mossberger jumped in again. "In the Corps, we had stuff to prove. But even then we had each other. When Colt married Monica, it was like we lost something." He shook his head. "Before he was captured in that operation that went bad, we thought we were invinci-ble. Suddenly we were ordinary. Men with shortcom-ings. That changed us."

Marc's brows drew together over the bridge of his nose. "Jeez, Moss, you make us sound like a bunch of losers."

Gabe sneaked a peek at Reggie in the rearview mir-ror. "I think Moss is trying to say that when we were faced with our own mortality, we woke up. On some level, we all knew Monica was a user. But tough guys like us were supposed to bag a trophy wife."

"Yeah. Two by two is nature's way. All God's species come in pairs."

"Spoken like a veterinarian," Marc jeered. "This conversation's getting too deep for me. Lizzy's nothing like Monica. She works and she takes care of her grandmother. Best of all, she has a great sense of humor."

Gabe grabbed Marc's arm. "Wait. Maybe Moss is onto something. Guys usually get along when we hang out together. Once the pack breaks up and we're shuffling around on our own, loneliness forces us to start searching for a mate. Someone to keep us company."

"Marriage is about more than companionship," Marc said. "Don't either of you ever think about having kids?" he ventured hesitantly.

Leaning forward, Reggie planted his bony elbows on his knees. "I do. The old vet I trained under worked closely with the area elementary schools. He kept a petting zoo where city kids come to learn about animals. Some kids, well, they got to me, ya know? You guys'll probably laugh me out of the car, but...I've been thinking about adopting. Not a baby. An older kid. I don't have any prospects for a wife, but I ask myself, do I need a wife to make a home for a kid who has nothing and no one?"

Gabe tugged at his ear. "I'm not gonna laugh, Moss. Growing up, I kicked around the streets fighting hunger in my belly too often. After Russ Poston threw me out, a home like you're talking about would've seemed like heaven."

"Still, if you'd had your druthers," Marc argued, "wouldn't you have preferred having a mom *and* a dad? I sure want a kid of mine to have both."

"Aha! So when's the wedding?" Gabe drawled. At

the same time Reggie whooped and said, "Is Lizzy pregnant?"

Marc turned bright red. "It's not like that with us. She, uh, we aren't sleeping together…yet," Marc qualified, growing ever more crimson.

"Whoa! I believe our ol' buddy is dead serious about this little gal." Moss slumped again. "Man, before long I'm gonna be the only one of the fearsome foursome who's still single."

"When did I get booted out of the club?" Gabe asked.

"You think I didn't see you making cow eyes at that babe today?"

"What babe?" Marc's flush subsided and a gleam flickered in his eyes. "What'd I miss? Gabe's yanking my chain over Lizzy when he's hot for some Callanton babe?"

"It's true," Moss declared over Gabe's vociferous denial. "You mean you didn't see him stalking that tall, black-haired caterer with his tongue hanging out?"

"Keep it up, Reggie," Gabe warned, "and you'll be out on the roadside hitching your way to the airport."

"I see! You can razz me, but *your* woman's off limits? No fair! Give with the details, pal." Marc wasn't about to let it go.

Gabe clammed up as he curled his hands around the steering wheel and kept his eyes on the road.

"She served us cake at the reception," Reggie supplied for Marc's benefit.

"I don't remember even seeing her. You might've tipped me off," Marc grumbled to Reggie. "So what's her name?"

"You won't drop this, will you?" Gabe blew out a stream of air, watching both men lean toward him.

When they only continued to leer owlishly, he reluctantly supplied her name. "Isabella. Isabella Navarro."

When nothing but silence followed his admission, Marc gave another nudge. "How long have you two been dating? Jeez, Gabe, talk about *me* working fast. Colt said you were in and out of Callanton in a matter of days when you closed the agency's deal on Summer's ranch."

"I'm not dating anyone." Gabe's head snapped around. "I...find her...attractive, that's all. She gave me the brush-off. Now enough's enough."

"So what's wrong with her?" Reggie queried. "She engaged or something?"

"Yeah, what's wrong." Marc echoed. "Women never brush you off, Gabriel."

"She has good reason, okay?" Stalling, Gabe finally capitulated, and in fits and starts relayed the awful thing Summer had told him.

"Holy shit!" Marc and Reggie chorused, their voices laced with horror.

"Exactly. So now you see why it'd be plain stupid for a guy to even try and get anything going with her."

"Why do I have a feeling you're gonna do it anyway?" Reggie shrugged. "Otherwise, you'd have packed your bag and come to Idaho with me."

"Naw," Marc insisted, frowning at Reggie. "Gabe's got more brains than any of us. You'll be driving back to Sun Valley tomorrow, right? To kick back and get in a little spring skiing before Marley needs you to close my deal in Utah."

"Well...this is great country. Maybe I'll hang here until Marley phones."

Reggie smacked a hand down hard on the back of

Gabe's seat. "I knew it. You're gonna make a play for the caterer."

"Am not."

"Are too," Reggie shot back.

"No. But I may stay a few days. Maybe see what kind of ranch property's come on the market since Coltrane thwarted those developers and arranged for SOS to save Summer's ranch." Gabe winced at what sounded like a lame excuse even to him.

Naturally, Reggie jumped right on his friend's statement. "Hell, Gabe, you're a banker. What do you know about ranch land? Or ranching, for that matter. I'll bet you don't even know which end of a horse to bridle."

"I'm not a banker, you idiot. I'm an accountant."

"Close enough. Shoot, I just can't picture you mucking out stalls."

"So? Land's always a good investment."

That statement seemed to appease Gabe's friends for the time being. They moved on to talk of other things until Gabe parked at the small yet bustling airport.

Marc and Reggie were booked on the same flight to Boise. From there, each would go his separate way. With the new heightened security, sans luggage or a ticket, Gabe wasn't allowed to accompany the men beyond the passenger terminal. As the three longtime friends prepared to part, it again became evident that their lives were changing. No one wanted to say what all were patently aware of—this might be a more lasting goodbye. All cleared their throats awkwardly.

It was Gabe who finally threw up his hands. "Hell," he growled, dashing at a sheen of moisture in his eyes. "Moss, take care, buddy. And phone."

"And you e-mail me. I wanna know where you end up if you decide to chuck the job with SOS."

Marc punched Gabe's upper arm in manly fashion, but he'd grown strangely quiet.

Gabe, always the leader, grabbed first Reggie, then Marc, and gave them fierce short hugs. "Kenyon, I'll see your ugly mug whenever Marley transfers funds for me to deal on that Utah ranch. Plan on me taking you and Lizzy to dinner someplace nice."

Not waiting for Marc's response, Gabe jammed his hands in his pants pockets, lowered his head and stalked out into the inky night. Dammit, hadn't he learned by the age of two that tears made a man weak?

Both Reggie and Marc stepped to the entrance and hollered after Gabe. He tossed off a backward wave and hustled out to his vehicle, fast. This felt like an ending. But of what? An era? A good one to be sure. So, why did he feel as if he'd been cut adrift? Was it because his friends' lives had seemingly fallen into place while he floundered back at square one?

That wasn't true, either. He had money in the bank and two college degrees. And three staunch friends who'd lay down their lives for him. He had contacts in business if he wanted to make a career move. Last time he'd been at square one, he'd been a street punk living by the seat of his pants. It so happened that his proficiency with math came at an early age. By ten he was making book on the back streets of Houston. Successfully, too. Although in those days he'd lived with a permanent empty hole in his stomach.

At thirty-eight, he'd come too far and gone through too much to still feel like that scared kid with a big chip on his shoulder. Gabe thought back to the walls he'd scaled since. The motto he'd learned to live by flashed in his head. *Forgive and forget.*

His steps faltered when the next image that popped up was a sad-eyed Isabella Navarro. He hadn't lied to his friends. A woman like her should be avoided at all cost.

Except…her haunting image lingered as he clicked the remote to open the doors of his Lexus. Nor did he shake the vision as he rolled down the driver's window and breathed in the loamy scent of new-tilled fields as he drove back to his empty room at the Inn. Isabella's face followed him to bed.

Gabe knew, long before sleep claimed him, that he would make the effort to see her again. And in spite of his own good sense and the unspoken agreement of his friends that she was trouble with a capital T, he planned to see her soon.

Tomorrow.

Surprisingly, his stomach felt better when he'd made that decision.

CHAPTER THREE

GABE LEFT HIS LODGING the next morning armed with the address to Isabella's Bakery. He'd been eating a hearty breakfast at the Green Willow most days, but had at some point during the night made up his mind to forego steak and eggs in favor of coffee and a doughnut. And an opportunity to see if, in the light of morning, he still felt attracted to the baker herself.

He finally located her bakery on a hidden side street, two blocks off Callanton's main drag. He wondered how he'd missed it before, painted as it was in eye-popping orange. Luckily, in Gabe's estimation, a large portion of the storefront was taken up with a plate glass window. That color was godawful.

A bell tinkled overhead when Gabe entered the shop. At once he was struck by homey scents of cinnamon, nutmeg and spicy sausage. There didn't seem to be a soul around, although twin display cases brimmed with freshly baked pastries.

Gabe stood alone, studying available choices for several seconds, before the louvered café doors that led to a back room crashed open. Isabella Navarro, dressed in a style similar to what she'd worn at the reception, rushed out. Flour streaked her face and hair.

She stopped dead in the act of wiping a powdery substance off her buttery fingers.

"Oh...uh...may I help you?" she murmured, a note

of wariness creeping into her voice the instant she recognized the man standing at her counter.

Gabe felt as though he'd been slammed in the stomach. No, he needn't have wondered if the attraction had faded overnight. Even in her disheveled state, he found this woman more compelling than ever.

She approached him cautiously. "Did Summer send you all the way into town to return the leftover plastic dinnerware? I told her that wasn't necessary. After all, she paid for that many."

Gabe realized he'd continued to stare at her without responding. "What? Oh, no. I stopped by for coffee and maybe a doughnut for breakfast."

She processed that news, thinking it must be nice to have a job where you could stroll in for breakfast at ten o'clock. Everyone she knew, herself included, had breakfast finished by five. But why kid herself? Gabe Poston didn't just *happen* to wander into her out-of-the-way bakery. Unless she was mistaken, he had a purpose for everything he did. And for some reason, she'd become his current purpose. The thought sent a long-dormant flutter of sexual awareness to her lower abdomen. It was accompanied by a swift punch of fear.

Gabe rubbed a hand over the back of his neck as he walked up and down past the gleaming display cases. "I'm afraid I don't see anything quite as simple as a doughnut. Care to offer a recommendation?"

A slight smile played at one corner of her lips. However brief, it was the first positive emotion Gabe had witnessed. Best of all, along with the tiny smile, he thought he saw an ever-so-minute spark come into her dark eyes. Gabe knew then that he wouldn't be satisfied until he heard her laugh. Or better yet, saw that spark flame with…desire.

"For my clientele," she was saying, "I stock mostly Basque pastries. If you want something warm I have *polvoróns* due to come out of the oven in—" she glanced at the clock hanging on the back wall "—less than a minute," she said, beginning to edge backward toward the café doors. "Coffee's on the sideboard there to the left of the door. Regular, decaf and two specialty blends. Help yourself. Takeout cups and lids are on the shelf above if you want your food to go," she called over the squeaky door hinges.

"I'd planned to eat here," he informed her loudly, sauntering behind the display case in order to peer at her over the still quivering louvered doors. "What's a *polvorón?* Is that what smells so good?" he asked.

Donning oven mitts, Isabella grabbed a spatula as she opened a wall-mounted oven and pulled out a tray filled with steaming round biscuits. "*Polvoróns* are cakelike biscuits made from finely ground almond and icing sugar. They sort of melt in your mouth. Especially when they're hot."

"They aren't very big," Gabe said, sounding more uncertain after seeing the first batch set out on cooling racks.

"Ah." That one word held a wealth of meaning. "I'll bet doughnuts aren't your normal morning sustenance." For some reason, conversation seemed easier this morning than it had yesterday, although his apparent interest in her was still puzzling.

Knowing he'd been caught, Gabe tried to cover a sheepish look. He managed a rueful shake of his head; she was more observant than he would've suspected.

Now Isabella was quite sure this man had reasons other than food for showing up at her shop. She should probably confront him with that very question. Except that, deep down, she didn't want to know his reasons. She just needed to keep him at arm's length. Once Julian had pursued her, too, and she'd been flattered. She'd been so wrong about him. For six interminable years, she'd tried every way possible to fix their marriage. Now, every day she was faced with knowing she should've tried harder. If she had, maybe Toni and Ramon wouldn't have paid the ultimate price for her weakness in giving up and walking out on Julian.

Her eyes stung as they always did when she thought of her children. Her hands shook so hard, she almost dropped the hot pan of *polvoróns.*

Gabe saw, hoping his presence wasn't the cause of her distress. He cleared his throat, endeavoring to sound nonthreatening. "It was after midnight when I got back from driving my friends to the airport. I overslept and figured it was too late to indulge in a big country breakfast. The clerk at the Inn said I might be able to get something light here." And his nose might grow a foot for that big fib.

"I'm afraid the only breakfast dish I have left is *migas.*" Isabella managed to gain control of her emotions. "I can add a thick slice of *jamón* if you like. It'll cost you four-fifty total. The unsmoked imported Jabugo ham I use is costly, but once you taste it, I guarantee you won't ever settle for less again."

"Terrific." Gabe refused to show his ignorance, even if he didn't have a clue what *migas* might be. *Jamón,* he deduced, was ham. A thick piece would definitely tide him over until lunch.

"Find a table. I'll bring it right out," Isabella said, wanting him to stop hanging over her kitchen door. Something about Gabe Poston unnerved her, and his smile sent shock waves to her already jittery stomach.

In an attempt to still the butterflies, Isabella rubbed her belly. The next time she looked up after warming the breadcrumb, herb, hot pepper and tomato mixture she'd cut into generous squares, he'd disappeared from her doorway.

Thank heavens. Otherwise she might not trust herself to slice the ham with the meat knife her brother Rick had sharpened to a razor's edge just last night.

Gabe smiled hugely when she delivered his piping hot meal. "Since you aren't brimming over with customers, how about joining me for a cup of coffee? I'm sure you've already eaten, or I'd offer to share my breakfast."

"But…I couldn't. Just because I don't have customers right now doesn't mean I'm not busy. I'm catering a business lunch for the Apple Growers' Association. There's only me to assemble sandwiches until my sister Trini gets out of her class at eleven-thirty." A mask slid over her features as she turned away from Gabe's table.

"Okay, suit yourself." He picked up his fork and dug into his food as if her refusal was no big deal. In case she glanced back to check his reaction, he made a show of calmly spreading out the morning paper he'd bought at the Inn. Once he knew she was gone, he stared blankly into the murky depths of his coffee instead of popping that first bite into his mouth. Gabe called himself all kinds of fool for going to such trouble to befriend a woman who clearly would rather he take a flying leap off a short pier.

So why was he expending the effort? Had his recent birthday precipitated some major life crisis? Not wanting to fully examine his intentions toward Isabella Navarro, Gabe swallowed his first forkful of the still-steaming *migas.*

He gasped. His tongue felt on fire. His eyes watered. Sweat popped out on his forehead. Yelping feebly, Gabe attempted to haul in a deep breath, which only increased the burning. Gagging, he stumbled toward the kitchen, hoping to beg a glass of water.

He exploded into Isabella's kitchen, which sent the swinging doors crashing into the walls. One hand was outstretched; the other he'd wrapped around his throat.

The minute she caught sight of his red face and bulging eyes, she dropped the carving knife with which she'd been cutting thick slices of home-baked bread. "What's wrong? Is it your heart? Are you choking?" She reached for the wall phone.

"H...ot!" Gabe managed to get a word past his blistered vocal cords. He stood there dancing from foot to foot, pointing repeatedly at her sink. Isabella finally got the message. She grabbed a glass from the cupboard, reached into the fridge and poured him a tall glass of milk. "Here, drink this. Slowly. It'll coat the inside of your mouth and throat."

Once he'd done that and the pain had subsided, letting his tense features relax, Isabella chewed nervously on her lower lip. "I'm really sorry. We Basques throw Rocoto chiles into practically everything. They're not even at the top of the chile heat scale. You are okay, aren't you?"

"Yeah," he croaked. But he downed the rest of the milk and held out his glass for more. She filled it again, this time in full control of her shaking hands.

"I think you fed me a ball of fire on purpose."

"No. I swear." She frowned faintly. "I didn't know what was wrong with you. But if you could've seen the look on your face…'' She broke off, tightly hugging the gallon milk container.

In a remote portion of his brain, it registered with Gabe that he'd finally broken through her shell. He'd probably presented quite a sight barreling through the swinging doors like a lunatic.

Conciliatory again, Isabella waved a hand toward the door. ''Go on back and eat before your food gets cold. I'll bring a pitcher of milk to your table.''

''Somehow I doubt that stuff's gonna get cold anytime soon,'' Gabe muttered. ''So, milk is better than water to put out the fire?''

''According to chile tests, yes. Although the burning sensation rarely lasts more than a minute.''

''Says you. Seemed a lot longer.'' At the moment Gabe wasn't up to sparring with her on the subject of chiles. He retreated with his glass of milk and as much dignity as he could scrape together. He said nothing when she arrived at his table bearing milk and more information he didn't care about.

''The Rocotos are the small, dark-red pieces in the *migas*. You should have no trouble picking them out. Habanero and Santaka chiles are several times hotter,'' she said, setting the cut-glass milk pitcher on top of his newspaper.

Gabe shook his head. ''Don't most restaurants put triple stars or something on the menu to flag food that's extra spicy? You need a fire truck painted next to this stuff.'' With that, he moved the pitcher and began separating sections of his newspaper. He'd bought it because he wanted to relax over a cup of coffee and take a gander at the real estate section.

Isabella took the hint, and slipped his bill under the

pitcher. After a last worried frown aimed at his bent head, she returned to the kitchen.

Damn, but his tongue still felt numb. Picking up the fork he'd dropped at the start of his fool's dance, Gabe prodded the innocent-looking side dish. He wondered about Isabella's impression of him and decided he must've come across as a complete jerk. He grimaced at the thought.

Gabe dug into his *migas* with a new determination. If Isabella and her family ate five-alarm stuff like this regularly, he was damn well going to choke it down with a straight face.

It took him half a pitcher of milk, but in time he cleaned his plate. Well, except for three big chunks of pepper. And boy, had she been right about the ham. Terrific stuff.

Full and mostly satisfied, Gabe pushed his plate aside. He settled down to read the paper, raising his head only briefly when the outer door opened. Seeing four elderly women, not one of whom he knew, Gabe dismissed them with an impersonal smile.

They, however, stopped their chatter to scrutinize him curiously.

But he'd found something interesting in the ads. Reading soon claimed his attention again. Two large farms, plus a ranchette, were listed for sale within the boundaries he'd learned made up the Basque community. The Inn's clerk had circled the area on Gabe's map after he'd made a few casual inquires this morning. The lonely clerk loved to talk. She was more than happy to educate him on all the local lore. The primary fact of interest to Gabe was that the richest soil in the area lay within the Basque territory.

If he bought a farm—although Gabe wasn't at all

sure he should—he'd want it to pay. His friends teased him by calling him *the banker*. It wasn't really a joke; his attitude was that of a banker. A successful one. He was financially cautious, always sought as much information as possible and only took judicious risks. Gabe noticed the guys didn't complain when he'd steered them toward investments that made them rich.

In the middle of checking the last column of ads, it became apparent to him that Isabella's customers, who'd been yammering in the background in both English and Basque, had suddenly begun to whisper. Cocking an ear, he soon suspected he was the topic of their hushed conversation. What could they be saying about him?

Jeez, maybe men didn't frequent Isabella's bakery. Afraid he might be breaking some local taboo, he quickly folded his paper and tucked it under one arm. He gave the women huddled around one of the display cases a wide berth as he extracted his wallet. Dropping his cash and the bill next to the cash register, Gabe acknowledged the now-silent group with a nod. Then he beat a hasty retreat.

QUITE FRANKLY, Isabella was overjoyed to see him leave. She'd grown weary of fending off the questions from her Aunt Carmen's friends. They weren't accustomed to finding a strange man seated in her bakery at midmorning when they came in to do their daily shopping. Yet when she started to punch Gabe's payment into the cash register, she saw he'd left a ten-dollar bill to cover a four-fifty meal. "Wait!" she called to his disappearing back. "Mr. Poston. Gabe…you forgot your change."

He stopped, one foot already out the door. "You didn't bill me for the milk."

"Goodness, you didn't drink anywhere near five dollars' worth of milk."

"Call the remainder a fee for teaching me how to douse a chile fire." He couldn't suppress a grin. The doorbell tinkled merrily as he closed it.

Dolores Santiago, the next-door neighbor of Isabella's Aunt Carmen, announced, "He's exactly the way Trini and Sylvia described him to Carmen. Deny it all you want, Bella, the man is clearly smitten with you."

"And he's a big spender," Nona Baroja pointed out, tapping the ten-dollar bill with a brightly polished fingernail.

Isabella jerked the money aside with a stern expression as she shoved the cash in the till. "Nonsense." She slammed the cash drawer closed. "Not five minutes ago you were all ready to sic my brothers on the poor man. None of which is relevant, anyway," she said, giving a curt wave of her hand. "As I'm sure Aunt Carmen told you, Gabe Poston is employed by the environmental agency responsible for saving Summer's ranch from a resort developer. He's only in town for his friend's wedding. He'll be gone soon."

Nona shook her head so vigorously she loosened the ornate silver clip holding back her gray-streaked hair. "That one's not leaving anytime soon. Am I the only one with sharp eyes? He was circling real estate ads in the Callanton paper."

The bell over the door jingled. They all glanced up guiltily, apparently assuming that the man they were heatedly discussing had for some reason returned. But Isabella's younger sister breezed in. She carried two bouquets of spring flowers and her face was flushed with excitement.

"Bella, was the man I just saw pulling away from the bakery your admirer at Summer's reception?"

Isabella pursed her lips tightly.

Dolores answered in a roundabout way. "Nona thinks he's planning on settling in the valley."

"In our valley? Or somewhere near Colt and Summer?" Trini handed her sister the bouquets and watched as Isabella placed them in cans and set them in a nearly empty upright cooler.

"Nona doesn't know that he's buying anything," Isabella rushed to say. "He was reading the real estate ads. So he happened to open that section. So what?"

"I saw what I saw," the short plump woman insisted. "He had a red pen in his hand, and he'd already circled at least two ads. One said *acreage for sale.*"

"Interesting," Trini drawled. "I wonder if he'd like some suggestions on where to find the best land?"

Two of the shoppers who'd remained silent up to now both pounced on Trini. "You know very well Luisa and Benito want you to marry Paul Cruz," the elder of the two said. "You wouldn't catch Paul languishing in a bakery midday."

"Paul Cruz is a jerk."

"If you don't trust your elders' judgment," the skinny woman sniffed, "ask Claudia Durazo and Teresa Castillo what it's like trying to fit into a foreigner's way of life. Our great-grandparents didn't come all this way to dilute our bloodlines through intermarriage. You should respect your parents' wishes, Trinidad Lucinda."

Isabella saw Trini make gagging motions behind the women's backs. "Trini shouldn't marry to please anyone but herself. If she doesn't love Paul, she needs to keep looking until she does fall in love.''

''Love can come slowly.'' Dolores wagged a finger. ''Sometimes you need to live with a man and work shoulder to shoulder with him to appreciate his good qualities.''

''And sometimes he doesn't have any good qualities,'' Isabella insisted just as doggedly.

''Bella, Bella,'' cried Nona, flapping her work-worn hands. ''Don't judge poor Paul based on your experience with Julian. Even his dear mother said Julian's mind snapped after you filed for divorce.'' Nona didn't actually say that Isabella bore some responsibility for Julian's terrible deed, but it was implied all the same.

The Navarro sisters drifted closer together for support, and Trini immediately came to Isabella's defense. ''Julian was a horse's patoot long before Bella woke up and decided to dump him.''

Dolores Santiago muttered and crossed herself. ''The Church counsels couples on working through personal problems. It's common knowledge that Bella stopped going to counseling, while Julian continued on alone for over a month.''

Few in their tight-knit village knew of Julian's long-standing history of jealousy and sick possessiveness. The local Catholic priests should have seen through him. Still, Isabella couldn't condemn them. Father Sanchez and Father Achurra had been as hoodwinked by Julian as everyone else. He was a master when it came to hiding his emotional deficiencies from everyone but his wife. Although Isabella found it hard to believe Julian's parents didn't have some inkling, too.

She wiped her hands on her apron. ''I have a lunch

to cater. The Apple Growers' Association meeting,'' she added, preparing to go back to the kitchen.

''Trini, would you mind bagging the ladies' baked goods? I still have half a dozen sandwiches to make. Then the boxes will be ready for napkins, apples and cookies.''

Trini ducked behind the counter. ''I'll finish here so they can be on their way. Then I'll be right in to help you. Oh, Mama sent a messa—'' She frowned. ''Never mind. I'll deal with this.'' She telegraphed a warning to her sister that said *don't ask any details*—or at least not while their aunt's best friends were in the shop.

''Thank you for shopping here,'' Isabella remembered to say belatedly. ''Nona, the *suizos* were fresh-baked this morning.'' Isabella stopped to fill a bag with the currant buns she knew were a favorite of the Baroja family. As she handed it to Trini to ring up and then continued on into the kitchen, she wondered what her mother might want. If it was important, why hadn't she phoned?

She turned on the faucet to wash her hands and discovered they were shaking again. Some days she doubted she could hang on till the trial. It was difficult enough to read the garbage spouted by Julian's lawyer. She shouldn't have to deal with censure from family friends, as well. Thank goodness there were only a few in the community who suggested she fell short as a wife and mother. She couldn't bear it if people she dealt with every day sympathized with Julian.

Granted, they had a male-dominated culture. Which didn't matter as a rule, because the men were good and decent. Men who loved and provided well for their families. According to stories handed down, Isabella knew it hadn't been easy on the first wave of Basque immigrants. Few spoke anything but Euskera or Eu-skera blended with Spanish. They knew the land and the sea, and were fiercely independent. That meant they kept to themselves, so the townspeople often viewed them as antisocial.

Summer Marsh's great-grandparents and many of the Paiute horse-breeders who lived along the Malheur River were kind and understanding, or so the tales went. By the time Isabella and her siblings came along, they were accepted as equals. Each new generation seemed more comfortable working and socializing to-gether than the last. But some older members of the Basque community still balked at the idea of intermar-riage.

Trini stormed through the café doors the way she stormed through life. "Aunt Carmen sicced those old busybodies on us today. I should never have told her about Gabe Poston." She smacked the heel of her hand against her forehead several times. "You'd think I'd learn to watch my mouth. I just don't understand why they can't mind their own business."

Isabella deftly assembled the last sandwich on the board. After setting it in one of the white boxes, she opened a cupboard and took out a stack of paper nap-kins. "Wash, please. Then grab a tray of red apples from the pantry. I'll bag the cookies. We can have this done in a jiffy."

"I wish I could be more like you, Bella. You never let a thing they say get to you." Trini jammed her fanny pack into a deep drawer with Isabella's purse, then scrubbed her hands.

"They get to me, Trini. But arguing and giving them more fodder to complain about is a waste of energy. Energy I'll need to get through Julian's trial."

"Which reminds me. Mama took a call from the prosecutor." Trini entered the walk-in pantry, leaving Isabella's stomach in a knot as she waited for her sister to return with the apples and complete the message.

"Why didn't James phone me here?" Isabella asked the moment Trini reappeared. "He has this number, and I've been here all day."

Trini shook her head, making her short curls dance. "James Hayden doesn't care about your case, Bella. I wish there was a way to fire him and get someone else. Mama and I are positive he didn't have the guts to tell you he lost the appeal to keep the trial in Burns. It's been moved to Bend because the judge doesn't think people in this county can be impartial enough."

"What? When?" Isabella dropped the cookie she was holding. It broke into a million pieces when it hit the tile floor. "No!" she cried, feeling the thread that held her nerves together unraveling. "The drive alone prohibits the whole family from attending."

"I'm sorry, Bella." Trini became instantly sympathetic. "Old Gutless said it was either Bend or La-Grande. He chose Bend because it's a few miles closer."

"It's still a long drive. I'm barely making ends meet and putting aside some money for my time away from the bakery as it is. This means I'll have to stay in a motel. Trini, what am I going to do?"

"You can let Papa help."

Isabella was already shaking her head. "I won't have him and Mama dipping into their retirement savings. And please stop calling the state prosecutor gutless. He's busy, that's all."

"Sorry, I calls 'em as I sees 'em."

"I'll list the house." She'd tried before, but it hadn't

sold and the real estate agent had told her that was because of the stigma attached to it. "I'm never setting foot inside the place again, anyway. Do you think enough time has passed that the stigma will have disappeared?"

"If it's someone who blows in from out of town and knows nothing about the case. No one around here could ever forget what happened there, Bella."

She mumbled something indistinguishable as she knelt to wipe cookie crumbs off the floor.

"Hey, maybe Gabe Poston fits the bill if Nona Baroja's right and he's checking out real estate."

"Don't take Nona's ramblings as gospel. Even if the man *is* house-hunting, why would he buy a place with four bedrooms?" Isabella's voice wobbled as she recalled decorating two of those rooms for her kids. She'd used a ballerina theme for Antonia's and had hand-drawn colorful trains on one of Ramon's walls to match curtains and a bedspread she'd sewn.

"Erase that. Every time I open my mouth I upset you, Bella. Here, the apples and napkins are done. I'll help you pop in the cookies, and then I'll take the boxes to the van. Don't be in a rush to deliver them, okay? It'd do you good to get out in the fresh air. The lilac trees are beginning to bud. Roll down the van's windows—the scent alone is bound to perk you up."

"Trini, you aren't the reason I'm upset. Who moved out of my old bedroom and let me have it back when I slunk home to Mama and Papa? I'd gladly have made do with the smaller room. But I'm indebted to you for giving me the room with the corner window. I...hate feeling closed in."

"I know." The younger girl gave her older sister a quick hug. "I did it for you, but for Mama, too. She never wanted Papa to remodel the house after you, Sylvia, Ruby and the boys got married and left. I was the one who badgered him to combine the bedrooms. So, it's only fair that I sacrifice a view. Enough of this. While we stack these boxes, give me a rundown on what needs to be done for the rest of the day.''

"I'm starting a wedding cake in the morning. And Audrey Olsen phoned to order an anniversary cake.'' She listed the supplies she wanted Trini to buy. "I will take some time while I'm out,'' she said afterward, "to take the flowers out to the cemetery.''

"Do you want company?'' Trini's eyes glossed with tears. "I saw the pinwheels you tucked under the counter. You're...uh...taking them out there, aren't you?''

Isabella got a firm grip on her emotions. Still, all she managed was a brief nod.

Trini turned away and clamped her hands over the edge of the sink. "On second thought, Bella, I can't go and watch you plant those pinwheels.'' She whirled to face her, looking stricken. "I'd remember how the kids loved to race down our driveway holding pinwheels on a windy day.''

"I know, Trini. I know.'' Dismissing Trini to begin loading the van, Isabella collected the flowers and gave her sister a few minutes to deal with her tears. She felt hollow inside, just as she always did.

Getting out in the fresh spring air did allow Isabella some breathing room. She blessed Trini five times over as she drove along the sun-dappled street where the lilacs already emitted their wondrous perfume. In November and December, Isabella had seriously doubted she'd survive the harsh winter. But the Lord saw fit to give her courage to get through a day at a time. There'd been plenty of setbacks. At least now, from the sound of James Hayden's call to her mother, they were moving closer to a court date—even though the venue had been changed. Later, she'd call Hayden to see if he'd heard when they might start selecting a jury.

Thank goodness she had several events scheduled for the next couple of weeks. And lambing would begin at the end of the month.

Isabella didn't think she could handle the trial without assurance that at least part of her family would be with her.

Lost in thought, she parked at the rear of the Arrowroot Inn. The inn had two conference rooms, which they rented out for meetings. The Apple Growers were using the end unit today.

Head down, arms loaded with boxed lunches, Isabella couldn't see where she was going. But she could make this run blindfolded. She was startled to bump into something solid the minute she stepped up on the sidewalk.

"Oh," she cried, just as a deep male voice murmured, "Whoa there!" Attempting to see around the teetering stack of boxes, she met concerned blue eyes staring back, and shivered as strong male hands slid up her arms to steady her.

"You?" Lurching sideways sent her load rocking dangerously again. "What are you doing here?"

After making sure she wasn't going to collapse on him, Gabe Poston relieved Isabella of most of her burden. The mere feel of her skin left his heart pounding like a kettledrum. He took his time answering. "I live here," he finally got out. "Well, for the time being. These are no lightweight boxes. Where's that cart you said you use in town?"

"For a big cake. These are sandwiches for a group of hungry apple growers who'll stampede out that door any minute headed for the rest room in the main building." She was babbling, something she rarely did. "My goal is to deposit this load inside the conference room before I'm mowed down in the rush."

Gabe straightened the stack, which he'd shifted to one hand so he could open the door. "Which room? A or B?"

"B," she said in a tone indicating she neither wanted or needed his assistance. But he barged in without knocking. Isabella knew she'd have knocked first and then been made to wait while the meeting wound down.

Rollie Danville, the man seated at the back of the room actually appeared to welcome their intrusion. Most of the others remained attentive to the speaker.

Rollie wore typical farmer's garb. Bibbed denim overalls and plaid flannel shirt. He drew out his wallet as he approached them. Then, not wanting to disturb his colleagues, he motioned her and Gabe outside.

"Thanks, Rollie." She accepted the check he handed her without looking at the amount. "I have more lunches in the van. And a cooler full of soft drinks. How's the meeting going? Are apple prices up or down this season?"

"Up," he said with a smile. "Your brother Rick is a good haggler. He negotiated well for us at the buyers' bidding in Wenatchee. We should've elected him three years ago. Do you need a hand carrying the cooler before we break?" His gaze strayed to Gabe even as he posed the question.

Gabe stepped forward. "I'm Gabe Poston." He returned Rollie's handshake. "I'll bring the cooler in for Isabella."

"You're the SOS money man? I thought you looked familiar. Someone pointed you out at Summer Marsh's wedding. You fellows dickering on another one of our local ranches?" The door behind them opened, and as Isabella had predicted, a stream of men poured out, all hotfooting it toward the lobby.

She'd turned back to the van intending to collect another load. Interested in Gabe's reply, she slowed her steps.

He laughed openly. "News travels. I met with a man this morning who wants to sell his place. This deal is strictly personal and has nothing to do with SOS."

Rollie stuck out his hand again. "So I guess a 'welcome, neighbor' is in order."

"Not quite." Gabe didn't accept Rollie's hand this time. "I made an offer. I expect he'll counter. Excuse me, sir. I said I'd help Isabella." Leaving Danville, Gabe rushed over to Isabella's van.

"I'm used to making deliveries alone. Don't let me keep you from more pressing business."

"You're not." Ignoring her prickly attitude, Gabe lifted out the heavy cooler.

They unloaded in silence until the van stood empty. Once the last boxed lunch had been deposited inside the conference room, Isabella returned to the sunshine and, with a shade less reticence, thanked Gabe for his assistance.

He shrugged, dropping his sunglasses over his eyes. He casually tucked his thumbs under the leather belt circling his narrow hips as he said, "It's straight-up noon. Even shopkeepers have to eat. Let me buy you lunch?"

"Why?" Isabella pulled her head out of the van. She'd reached inside to the passenger seat to rearrange the flowers Trini had bought. They were belted in to steady the cans.

"Because we both have to eat."

"I can't. I have…an important…ah, errand." Her gaze veered again to the bouquets. Unconsciously she fingered the points on a pinwheel.

"To the cemetery? I'll ride along and keep the flowers from tipping over."

Isabella licked her dry lips and dug in her purse for her sunglasses. She put them on, then raised them again to study this man—a near-stranger who offered to do what even her family shied away from. There was still no sign of pity on his face, nor any in his tone.

"I promise I won't crowd you once we get there," he said softly. "It's not a journey anyone should have to make alone."

Unable to get a word past the sudden lump in her throat, Isabella tried three times to step up into the van. It wasn't until she felt Gabe's cool fingers latch firmly onto her elbow that she felt a hairline crack in her tightly banded control. She managed a simple nod. If he saw her response, fine. If not, she'd make the trip on her own.

But Gabe did see. And he noticed how ragged her nerves were. Quickly rounding the vehicle, he unbuckled and lifted the cans. He sat and closed the door. If asked, he couldn't have said why he was sticking his neck out. Any moment he expected to have his head lopped off.

CHAPTER FOUR

AT FIRST, Gabe Poston's presence in the van set Isabella's teeth on edge. She'd made the drive to the cemetery so often over the past ten months that each winding turn in the road was indelibly stamped on her brain. Normally, she drove in silence, needing the time to prepare herself for a visit that never got any easier.

Isabella especially didn't feel like chitchatting with a man she barely knew.

But they'd driven a mile and Gabe hadn't spoken a word. He didn't toy with the flowers he held on his lap, nor did he fidget like Isabella's brothers were prone to do. Up until a few weeks ago, by tacit agreement forged out of her hearing, the family always discreetly freed up one member to make this trip with her. Today, even before Trini had backed out, she'd been determined to go alone.

But, if truth be known, she wasn't ready. It was comforting to have someone with her, sharing the lonely journey.

"Less than a handful of people would do what you're doing," she said unexpectedly, her voice hoarse.

"Holding flowers doesn't seem like such a hard job."

"You know what I meant. It's fairly obvious you know a whole lot more about me than I do about you."

Gabe turned slightly, resting his back against the door. "I'm thirty-eight. *Just,*" he felt compelled to add. "At the moment, I handle closings on land acquisitions for a non-governmental agency, Save Open Spaces. I have no family to speak of. I find this area..." He paused, as if unable to find the proper word.

"Interesting? Picturesque?"

"Partly. It's difficult to put into words."

"Try harsh, moody or erratic. Unless you've never spent a winter here."

"I came last winter to wind up the custodial deal on Summer's ranch. But winter storms aren't new to me. I own a condo in Sun Valley."

"Oh. Then why aren't you there? Why are you here? And don't say again that it's to hold my flowers."

Gabe twisted his lips to the side, chewing absently on the inside of his cheek. "Honestly? I don't know," he said after a lapse.

His answer threw Isabella for a moment. "You told Rollie Danville you'd made an offer on land. Is your agency fighting off another developer?"

"In other states. Not here. Now, enough about me. Tell me about you."

Isabella immediately clammed up.

Gabe saw how fast her interest had fled. He watched her slender fingers flex repeatedly as she tightened her grip on the steering wheel. A private person himself, Gabe respected that right in others.

Shifting in his seat, he again gazed out on the landscape that slid rapidly past. It had been an unusually long, cold winter according to Colt's wife, who'd lived in the area all her life. Now spring seemed ready to erase the last traces of snow. The deciduous trees were sprouting new growth. Tender, lime-colored tufts of needles formed on struggling young pines. But a cold wind still blew out of the north.

Isabella rounded a bend in the climbing road, and buttercups lent a splash of color to a meadow off to Gabe's right. He barely had time to appreciate the dappling of afternoon sunshine when Isabella made a hard left and braked the van. An underlying tension raised the fine hairs on his neck.

"We're almost there," she informed him.

He'd visited a few cemeteries in his thirty-eight years. After his mom's, most were military burials. Arlington, Calverton in New York, and Hawaii's so-called Punch Bowl. All were rolling green hills intersected with rows of white crosses as far as the eye could see. Very formal, but gut-twisting all the same. Gabe didn't know what to expect of the spot he was about to see. Nor did he know what to expect of the woman seated next to him. He'd comforted a few widows. Wives of buddies lost in the Gulf War. He liked to think he'd understood their grief and their need to grieve in different ways. At the very least, he thought Isabella would get teary simply being here.

She didn't. He watched her slowly steel herself before she climbed down from the van.

Gabe started to open his door.

"Stay," she said, reaching across her seat for the two bouquets he held. He felt the cans leave his nerveless fingers.

"Let me carry them for you."

"I've got them." She bent and picked up a trowel and another sack. "If you'd care to grab some fresh air, it's a short walk to a stream that follows the base of this hill. It flows through that stand of cottonwoods.'' She inclined her head ever so slightly to the south.

Gabe remained focused on her stark white face. If it had crossed his mind a moment ago to accompany her regardless of her protests, that thought died. She was hanging on to a fragile composure. But she *was* hanging on.

He released his breath. His fumbling fingers found the door latch, and he felt it give way. The next time he was in a position to see Isabella, it was only a view of her too-thin frame as she trudged up a grassy knoll. At the very top stood a pine tree whose bottom branches spread wide. Gabe figured the tree had to be a century old. Who knew, really, how long it had stood guard over the loved ones entrusted to its care?

From the hodgepodge of headstones, this looked to be an old cemetery. The pine served as a focal point. A solid, reassuring sentinel.

Suddenly feeling every bit the outsider he was, Gabe jammed his hands in his pockets and meandered in the direction of the stream.

The minute he crossed the gravel road and stepped into the shade afforded by willowy cottonwoods, his breath caught in his throat. Standing opposite him, across the stream, two elk lifted dripping muzzles and froze in place. Man and wild beasts gaped at one another for what seemed to Gabe like longer than the split second it probably was. The larger of the two elk blinked, then of one accord their hindquarters bunched, and both disappeared upstream into thick underbrush.

Rarely had Gabe been treated to such a heart-stopping sight. It struck him hard then. This was where he belonged. He'd done the right thing tendering an offer on a very overpriced property within ten miles of this stream.

Time drifted as Gabe absorbed the sights, sounds and odors around him. His training in military special ops had helped cultivate senses the vast majority of people no longer relied on for survival. Those same keen senses let him appreciate nature's bounty—and had him crouching and spinning almost before Isabella set foot in the copse of trees.

"I didn't mean to startle you," she said, her voice husky, possibly because Gabe's fierce expression alarmed her.

He relaxed instantly, all sign of his panther-like stealth dissolved. "I saw two elk. One with fuzzy antlers, one without." His joy was reflected in his wide smile.

"Elk? Probably not, city boy. Not this low in the hills. It's too late in the season. Any elk herds would've moved on to higher feeding grounds by now. It was probably someone's range cattle gone astray."

"Who are you calling *city boy?* I can tell an elk from a cow, I'll have you know."

Tilting her head to one side, Isabella let herself really look at him for the first time. Oh, she'd given him a fast inspection at Summer's reception. Now she studied him feature by feature. Broad shoulders. Solid chest. Flat stomach hidden by a knit, short-sleeved shirt. Narrow hips still encased in slacks rather than blue jeans. And polished loafers, mud-spattered from his recent trek.

"You look like a city boy of the highest order," she said without inflection.

"Looks can be deceiving." Although as the words fell from Gabe's lips, he doubted their truth, especially in Isabella's case. With her ravaged, empty eyes, she looked like hell. He'd wager that assessment was pretty accurate.

"They were elk," he said with firm assurance. "I take it you're ready to drive back to town?"

"Yes." She turned to lead the way. A hundred or so yards upstream, near a bend where sprinkles of sunlight filtered through the trees, Gabe's two elk lumbered out of the trees, as if on cue. Coats dark against the backdrop of gray trunks, they lowered their magnificent heads to drink from the stream. Isabella stopped on a dime. She drew in a deep breath of awe and grabbed Gabe's arm to keep him from stepping on a broken branch that lay in their path. For several seconds they stood beside each other. Their shoulders might have even brushed.

"Your range cows," he murmured so close to her ear that his warm breath sent a shiver up Isabella's spine. The pale skin beneath her fringe of bangs wrinkled faintly as she frowned at him. The slight turn brought her lips into very close proximity with his smooth-shaven cheek. Flustered, she jerked her hand back, and quickly took two giant steps away from Gabe.

Her foot landed squarely on the branch. Its crack in the quiet glade sounded as sharp as if a rifle had fired. Once more the elk bounded into the thicket.

When Gabe tore his eyes from the spot where the animals had been, Isabella had widened the gap between them. In fact, she'd moved into the clearing, head down and steps determined. He had to run to catch up.

In normal circumstances, Gabe would have needled her until she verbally acknowledged that he'd indeed seen an elk. The minute he noticed the array of head-stones fanning out beyond the silhouette of the van, he was reminded that no relationship with this woman could be classified as normal. He watched her climb inside the van, then walked slowly to the passenger door.

But again she surprised him. He felt her gaze on him the whole time it took him to buckle his seat belt.

Her voice somewhat muffled by the growl of the van's engine, Isabella said, "I'll retract my hasty judgment of you, Poston. You may dress like a city boy, but you do know an elk from a range cow."

"Thank you. I hope it didn't cost you too much to admit that."

She didn't bother to respond.

As she jockeyed the van around a small graveled area in order to head back down the narrow road, Gabe pressed his nose to the side window to see where she'd placed the two bouquets. He spotted them right before she succeeded in completing her turn. Three-fourths of the way up the hillside, not quite in the shade cast by the big pine, two splotches of bright color jumped out at him. The flowers were small, nestled in the middle of a double headstone. On either side of the stone, two tall pinwheels whirled in the breeze. One blurred in shades of red, white and blue. The other spun out every color of the rainbow.

Queasy without warning, Gabe shut his eyes, and kept them shut until he felt the hot pressure behind his eyelids abate. Totally shaken, he was amazed to realize that Isabella showed no sign of crying. Or maybe she had no tears left. He knew she wasn't without feelings. The ever-present bleakness in her eyes couldn't hide the truth. So how did she cope? What was Isabella

Navarro all about? More than ever, Gabe wanted to stick around and find those answers.

Opening his eyes, he saw his breath had steamed the cooler window glass.

"That drop-off on your right isn't as steep as you might think," she said, completely misreading why his forehead remained against the window. "I've been navigating these country roads since I was sixteen, in case you're worried that I'll send us over a cliff."

Gabe swallowed hard several times. "No, ah…I noticed the pinwheels."

Sorrow washed over Isabella, leaving her pupils dilated wide. "Papa used to buy them for his grandchildren at the county fair," she said haltingly. "My nieces and nephews broke theirs within days. Toni and Ramon loved…the colors. They took such good care of them."

Gabe touched her face. A gentle tracing of one finger against her cheek. She seemed to understand it wasn't sexual but meant to connect him to her grief. She was able to regroup and concentrate on her driving when his hand fell to his lap.

Nothing else of a personal nature passed between them on the drive back to the Inn. And darned few generalities, either, Gabe thought after she pulled up and stopped in almost the exact place they'd stumbled upon each other shortly before noon.

Neither one of them quite knew what to say when it came time to part. It hadn't been the kind of journey he could thank her for. In silence Gabe opened his door and prepared to exit.

After a brief awkward moment, she took matters into her hands. "I appreciated your company," she said, not fully meeting his eyes. "I didn't expect to, but…well, I did."

Gabe dug into his reserve for a lightness he didn't feel. "I owe you. If I hadn't invited myself along, I would've missed the elk. I'd like to repay you by taking you to dinner. Tonight," he clarified.

"Not necessary," she said, clearly impatient now to be on her way.

He shrugged. "I didn't think you'd accept. Take care," he said quietly. "I'll see you around." Stepping to the ground, he carefully closed his door, then deliberately set out for his room. Which was where he'd been going when he'd run into Isabella. Two hours ago, he saw now as he glanced at his watch.

ISABELLA DROVE AWAY, her mind jumbled with thoughts of the man she'd just dropped off. Gabe Poston must have gotten his fill of her on the drive. He'd taken no for an answer easily enough this time. But was it any wonder?

In any event it made him the opposite of Julian, who used to push and push and push until she agreed to go out with him. That ought to have been her first clue that Julian Arana would turn out to be far too possessive.

Flipping back through memories she'd spent months trying to block, Isabella admitted the signs were there from the outset of their relationship. Because they'd grown up together, she'd dismissed many of the traits that had ultimately become problems in their marriage. A siren should have gone off in her head when Julian convinced her folks not to let her go away to college. She'd always dreamed of owning a bakery and catering service, but she'd planned to get her degree in business first. It was Julian who convinced his papa to ante up seed money for the store. Julian had never let her forget it was a debt she owed him. Now his parents made that point around town.

Thank heavens Trini did get the degree Isabella longed for. Now, whenever she could grab an extra minute, Isabella picked her sister's brain; she also studied her business textbooks. That way, when Trini finished her Master's and left the bakery for other pursuits, the business would sit on a firm foundation. With careful bookkeeping, maybe she could repay the elder Aranas one day.

Much as Isabella loved owning the bakery, she'd give it up in a minute to turn back the clock. If only she'd fought harder against letting Julian share custody of Toni and Ramon. But she'd been over and over that *if only* so many times, it felt as if her head would split apart. There was no turning back. She had to live with that for the rest of her life.

Why had she started thinking about the past, anyway? *Gabe Poston.* Because she'd found him easier to be with than she'd ever have guessed.

Men. She didn't need another in her life.

When Isabella's mind launched into overdrive, as it did now, she found work the only solution to curbing the memories. So, instead of heading home as Trini had suggested, she drove straight back to the shop. Might as well get a jump on starting Estrella Aguirre's wedding cake.

Five minutes later she parked on the street rather than behind the building.

Trini let out a little screech of fear as Isabella opened the back door with her key.

"Land sakes alive! Scare the heck out of me, why don't you?"

"Sorry. I realize you weren't expecting me, but you

know how restless I get after a trip to the cemetery. You go on home, Trini. I have some demons to exorcise, and work's the only way I can do that.''

''Was the trip to the cemetery responsible for your demons? Or is it the person who went with you?'' Trini lounged against a counter, one eyebrow raised, her arms crossed.

''What?'' Isabella shot upright from stuffing her purse in a drawer.

''Oh, come on Bella. The phone's been ringing off the hook. Did you think in a town the size of Callanton no one would notice? Everyone's speculating as to who he is. My bet's on Gabe Poston.''

Isabella sagged against the wall. She covered her face with her hands. After a moment she straightened and rubbed her temples. ''It was…him. I don't know what got into me, Trini. He's staying at the Inn. I ran into him accidentally. He saw the flowers and seemed to know why I had them. He invited himself along, but I should've told him no.''

''It's okay, Bella,'' Trini said soothingly.

''But what are people saying? You know as well as I do that Julian's attorney would love to find any dirt on me.''

''So a man rode with you to the cemetery. Until the third or fourth call, I told everyone you must've run into Joe, Rick or Manuel in town.''

''Rollie Danville saw us leave together.'' Isabella began pacing around and around the work island.

''Oh. Out of curiosity, Bella, why did Gabe go with you?''

Isabella threw up her hands. ''I think he mentioned he'd heard the story from Summer. He…he told me no one should have to go alone. It was more *how* he said it, Trini. Not dripping with pity but just…concerned. Oh, damn, that's no excuse. But…how else do I explain my sudden lack of backbone?''

Trini caught her sister's arm as she paced around the island for about the tenth time. ''Stop beating yourself up. I think it's nice. It shows chivalry isn't dead.''

''I'm afraid that's not how others will see it.''

''Who cares?'' Trini waved her fingers in Isabella's face. ''Anyway, whose business is it except yours?''

Isabella rested her elbows on the table and again buried her face in her hands. ''It's not that simple. Thanks to the news coverage of this case, every aspect of my life is under a microscope until Julian's trial is over and he's sentenced. Nothing is more important to me than being Ms. Model Citizen until then. Nothing!''

''I know. I know. But you two were divorced, after all. I can't see the harm in being seen with another man.''

''Technically, that's true. But I don't want to give them anything they could use as ammunition. And yet…'' She sighed. ''I swear, Trini, my mind is so muddled I can't think straight. Whole days, sometimes weeks, pass in a blur.''

''And people ought to understand. If they don't, the heck with them.''

''You're right. You're absolutely right. And today was probably the first and last time we'll be seen together.''

''Really? Why?''

Color rose in Isabella's cheeks. ''He…ah…invited me to dinner. I turned him down flat. He said he hadn't expected me to accept. Then he walked away.''

''You should've gone.''

"And send our entire community, to say nothing of Callanton, into total apoplexy?"

Trini snickered. "You've gotta admit it's tempting."

"For you, maybe. Not for me." Isabella smoothed back a stray lock of hair. "Please, Trini, go home and try to douse the fires for me. I'll start on Estrella's cake."

"Okay." Trini ripped off her apron and retrieved her purse. "Promise you won't get so involved you forget to come home tonight."

Isabella drew an X over her heart. "Tell Mama to leave a plate in the warmer oven." She trailed her sister to the door. "And tell her not to load it up. I can't eat half of what she dishes out. I hate throwing food away. It's wasteful."

"You need to eat. Or buy new clothes in a smaller size. Otherwise Julian will take one look at you in court and he'll see he's won."

Isabella's face fell, prompting Trini to give her an extra hug before she left.

GABE FLOPPED ON THE BED in his room. He wished Isabella had accepted his dinner invitation. Eating with people made it easier to pry information out of them. And there was so much he wanted to know about her.

He turned on the TV, but snapped it off after a run-through of the channels didn't produce anything interesting.

The phone rang. Gabe jumped for it. The caller turned out to be John Campos, who owned the ranch Gabe had made an offer on.

"Hi, John. Guess you've talked to your sons in Spain. How do they feel about my offer?"

Gabe listened to the old man talk.

"I'm sure they do want you to come over there."
John had said they'd gone to visit their grandparents
and then when his father died, they'd stayed and taken
over his fishing business. "It's easy to see how much
you miss them."

Campos agreed. In the next breath he said his sons
wanted him to stay put until he got his full asking price.
Apologizing, he stammered out a goodbye.

"Wait a sec. Let me run the figures again." Damn,
but Gabe wanted that property. Shoving his glasses on
his face, he grabbed a calculator and punched in the
price per acre John had first named. Gabe cringed when
he hit the multiplier. No doubt about it, the price was
too high. The house needed work, and Campos had
already sold his livestock. Gabe had no idea what he'd
have to pay for lambs or sheep or whatever it took to
make wool a paying proposition.

He was one breath away from thanking Campos for
his time when Gabe heard himself say, "You drive a
hard bargain, but you've got yourself a deal, John."

The line went dead and Gabe thought he'd lost the
connection. "John? Oh, so you're still with me? Did
you hear me say I'll meet your price? Shall we get
together at your bank to draw up a contract? Tomorrow
at ten? Good. Good. See you then." Gabe hung up,
aware he'd just made the worst deal of his life. Why,
then, did he feel like celebrating?

Unearthing his cell phone, Gabe called Marley
Jones, his boss at SOS. "Marley, it's Gabe. This may
or may not come as a shock, but I've decided to leave
the agency after I close the Utah project. What? No,
I'm not following in Colt's footsteps. Well, sort of. I'm
not getting married, though. But I am trading in my

suit for blue jeans. I've bought a ranch on the outskirts of Callanton.''

Gabe winced as Marley's voice boomed across the wire. "You're one hundred percent correct. I don't know jackshit about horses or cows, Marley. That's why I'm buying sheep. Sheep. You know, those docile, woolly creatures you count whenever you can't fall asleep?''

Jones laughed and laughed. He finally said that if Gabe ever came to his senses a job with SOS would be his for the asking.

"Thanks. I liked what we did. This venture of mine may well turn out a flop. I've been a nomad in one form or another most of my life. Maybe it's a mistake to try and settle down in one place.''

Gabe wiped sweat from his forehead as Marley said he had to go. "Okay. Call me on my cell when it's time to close Marc's deal. Depending on how long it takes the guy I just bought from to move, I could be in my own home in less than two weeks.''

Two weeks! After he clicked off, Gabe panicked. It was obvious that Marley thought he'd lost his mind. A spur-of-the-moment transaction *was* unlike him. Unlike any deal he'd made in his entire life.

Wanting validation, he quickly punched in Marc's number.

Good old Marc.

Ten minutes later, Gabe cut Marc off. He hadn't been half as tactful as Marley. His good buddy and colleague had suggested Gabe get a brain transplant.

So Gabe punched in Reggie's number. That conversation ended abruptly with Gabe swearing. Reggie couldn't seem to stop howling with laughter long enough for Gabe to finish describing his purchase.

"Well, hell," he muttered, standing up and yanking his leather bomber jacket out of the closet. Colt and Summer had said they weren't going on a honeymoon. They had livestock to feed, and Summer's son, Rory to look after.

Slamming out of his room, Gabe climbed into his SUV. If the Quinns didn't show some semblance of happiness for him, he might have to rethink the whole proposition.

His mind preoccupied, Gabe arrived at their ranch in too short a time.

Coltrane threw the door open wide and called out to Summer as he dragged Gabe inside. ""Hey, buddy, great to see you!"

Summer appeared in the kitchen arch. "Gabe, hi." She was shoved aside by her son and his lop-eared dog, who'd been banished to the barn during the wedding reception. The dog, a spaniel-terrier mix, came to inspect Gabe's shoes.

"Rory, take Lancelot outside, please. Gabe doesn't want the polish licked off his dress shoes," Colt instructed him.

His stepson, who'd been crazy about Colt from the first time they met, obeyed with no sign of complaint.

"Can you stay for supper?" Summer asked. "It's Audrey's night off, but I make a mean pot of chili. It's simmered on a back burner all day. I was about to dish it up."

Gabe hesitated, remembering his experience with Isabella's *migas*. "How hot is the chili?"

Summer shrugged, clearly confused.

"I don't mean how warm, I mean did you use chiles that'll burn the skin off the roof of my mouth?"

Colt chuckled. Summer did better hiding her grin.

"I grew up loving Basque food," she said. "Not all of their dishes are spicy hot. Gabe, you should've listened when I said not to hit on Izzy. Next time, stick with the food at the Green Willow."

"I didn't hit on her. You're steering business her way. What's wrong with me dropping some cash in her bakery?"

Summer eyed him the way she would Rory—as if she doubted the truth of what he'd said. "Okay," she finally muttered. "But I'm telling you, she's had enough grief to last a lifetime. I don't want our friends causing her more."

"How about a beer before dinner, Gabe? Let's walk out to the barn," Colt suggested. "One of my mares foaled early. I'd like to check on her again while it's still light."

Gabe nodded. Considering the way Summer was acting, it'd probably be best not to discuss his latest acquisition in front of her.

Taking the hint, Summer ducked back into the kitchen and came out holding two frosty beers. "I'll give you guys fifteen minutes. Then supper's on the table. Either be in here to eat it, or when Rory and I finish, Virgil's hogs get the rest."

Grinning in the face of her feigned gruffness, Colt bent and kissed her, a sound and lingering kiss.

Gabe gazed at the hall ceiling. Not that he hadn't kissed his share of women. It was more that he tended to do his kissing in private.

Colt finally came up for air. He unhooked his jacket from the brass coat tree and handed Gabe the beers to open while he donned his Stetson.

The two old friends made small talk on the short trip to the barn. Both mare and foal were in excellent health. Not only that, lights blazed the full length of the barn. Gabe wasn't surprised when Colt turned, clinked their bottles together and asked bluntly, "So, what's really up with you, Gabriel?"

"I bought a three-thousand-acre sheep ranch a few miles southeast of here today. From John Campos. It's in the heart of Basque country," Gabe blurted.

Colt, who'd taken a big swallow from his bottle, spewed beer all over the place, barely missing Gabe. "Whoa. Hey for a minute there, I misunderstood. I guess you mean you closed on a place for SOS. I didn't realize Marley had his eye on partnering another property in the valley."

"He didn't. Doesn't. It's mine—lock, stock and ramshackle farmhouse."

Coltrane scratched his thumbnail at the paper label on his bottle. "No offense, Gabe, but sheep don't come with little bow ties and vests. They're filthy, smelly, really gross creatures. Never mind," he said with a sigh because he'd seen Gabe stiffen, "I doubt you drove all the way out from town to have me tell you that."

"In boot camp, did you ever see me slack off from a tough, dirty job?"

"Nope. Never. And later, Captain Poston never asked any man to so much as dig a foxhole he couldn't have dug faster and deeper himself."

"Damn right. Armani suits are just the trappings for my current job."

"I'll give you that, buddy. Tell me, though, have you ever met anyone who raises or raised sheep?"

"No." Doubt crept into Gabe's determined eyes. "I learn fast. Do you have a suggestion on where I might start my education?"

"If you hadn't already bought the damn ranch, I'd

advise apprenticing for a few months with one of the local sheep men.''

''John, the guy I bought the place from, already sold his flock. The fields are fallow. I have time to learn what I need to know. I'll have to start working on the house, too. Probably spend my nights doing repairs. I could apprentice with someone during the day. Any idea who I should approach?''

''Not for sure. Based on talk I hear at grange meetings, your best bet would be one of the older Basque ranchers. Some have diversified into apples and grapes over the last twenty years, but a fair number of families still run sheep exclusively.''

Stopped in the act of tipping up his own beer, Gabe couldn't contain a smile that soon spread across his face.

''Hey, wait a damn minute.'' Colt gripped Gabe's arm. ''Tell me this whole stupid scheme isn't so you can get close to Summer's friend Izzy.''

Sobering, Gabe stared straight into Coltrane's eyes. ''The thought never entered my mind,'' he lied through his teeth. ''Hey, speaking of your beautiful bride, ask her to give me a rain check on the chili, please.'' He pulled back his sleeve and checked his watch. ''After talking to you, I realize I can't go into sheep-raising cold. If I leave now, I should just make the library before it closes. You said to read up on sheep.'' Gabe pressed his half-drunk beer into Coltrane's free hand. ''Well, thanks for the advice. I'm gonna go do exactly that.''

CHAPTER FIVE

THE ONLY BANK IN TOWN opened its doors at 10:00 a.m. In spite of sitting up half the night scouring the books on sheep-raising that he'd checked out of the library, Gabe arrived ten minutes before the first bank employees showed up. By fifteen after the hour, he was convinced John Campos had changed his mind and stood him up. He was hunting for his cell phone when he saw John pull into the parking space off to his left, driving a pickup too disreputable for words. The thing coughed and wheezed, belching blue smoke into the pristine air as it stopped with one last shuddering hiccup.

The truck wore so little paint it was impossible to tell either the color or the make. No wonder. Someone had apparently pieced a scavenged grill, hood and fenders on a box that had seen better days.

Gabe stepped out and circled behind John's vehicle. He walked quickly because he wanted to help the older man climb down. John's work-worn hands were so palsied, he shouldn't even be driving.

"I'm late because old Maribeth here wouldn't start." John bestowed a loving pat on the mottled hood. Gabe saw that it'd been tied shut with a length of clothesline.

"If you'd said something yesterday, John, I'd have been more than happy to swing by and pick you up for this meeting."

"Well, that's decent of you, young fella. But Maribeth and me go back a long way. She ran like a top when my sons were here to tinker with her." His dark eyes swept the barely awakened main street. "It'll be good to see my boys again," he said. "But this land's in my blood. Not easy to walk away from the only home I've ever known." His rumbling voice grew gruff. "This is what Basque *immigrantes* must have felt. Most were young men who fled Spain in search of independence. My dear grandmama already carried my papa in her womb, so Grandpapa wouldn't leave her behind."

"Haven't you all made good lives here?"

"Yes. But before I die or go blind, I need to see the valley of Sierra del Aralar and the mountains beyond, where my grandfather tended sheep as a boy."

In his reminiscing, John had given Gabe the perfect opening to inquire about a possible teacher for himself.

At first the old man seemed surprised, and maybe reluctant. "Are you sure you want to raise the woollies? It's a hard life, son."

"I've lived a hard life, John. I'm tougher than you might think."

The old man didn't cave in at that news, but shortly after they'd both signed the contract, John offered to introduce Gabe to his neighbors. "I have a good friend who lives directly across the road. Most other farms aren't within walking distance."

Back at their vehicles, John paused. "I'm leaving in a week. Only taking my clothes and the family Bible," he said. "Any furniture you don't want, give to St. Bonaventure Church and mission. They always have someone in need."

Gabe felt another wave of compassion for the bent

old man. "There's no rush, John. I'll give you time to pack whatever you want to ship to your sons. I'll even help, since they aren't able to come for you."

"No, no." Campos shook his shaggy head. "I'm only telling you this because if you still want to make some apprenticeship deal with a sheep man before lambing, you'd better see to it soon."

"I can do that. No problem. Thanks," Gabe said, stepping aside rather than doing what his instincts clamored—boosting the old guy into the cab. He stood helplessly by, holding his breath, watching with dismay as John came very close to the Lexus while jockeying his decrepit pickup out of its parking slot.

"Did John hit your car?" Her familiar voice with its slight accent spoke from directly behind Gabe, causing him to whirl in surprise.

Isabella Navarro, dressed in a springlike dress and matching jacket, squinted past him at the departing pickup, which chugged slowly up the street.

"He came close, but he managed to miss my SUV." Gabe took a moment to appreciate the picture Isabella made. It was the first time he'd seen her with her raven hair down and blowing in the wind. She wore the sides pulled back from her ears. Those loosely looped strands were secured high on her head with an ornate silver clasp.

"He shouldn't be driving," she said, shading her eyes to watch John's progress. "I don't think that truck's been out of his barn in a year. Two, maybe. Generally someone from the village brings him into town. I wonder what was so urgent that he came out here on his own." She continued to frown, first at the bank and then at John's rapidly departing pickup.

Electing to let Campos release his own information

on the sale of his property, Gabe noticed belatedly that Isabella carried a money bag emblazoned with the bank's logo. He realized she was going in, not coming out.

She headed toward the building, ready to go on about her business.

"Wait a minute. I didn't expect to see you today. Do you have—"

She held up a hand, halting his rush of words, which was sure to carry an invitation of some kind. "I have...no time. Not for anything. I'm in the middle of a big project and I only left it to make a deposit Trini and I both forgot to do yesterday." Dispensing a weak wave, she scurried through the revolving bank door that another patron had recently exited.

If Gabe's cell phone hadn't rung, summoning him through the open window of his SUV, he'd have waited right where he was until she came out of the building.

His caller turned out to be Marley Jones. "Gabriel, glad I caught you. SOS is ready to make the payoff on Marc's Utah deal. How soon can you get down there and put a package together? Marc's afraid the old rancher's family might be having second thoughts about selling to us. It seems there are rumors floating around that a Park City developer is nosing around the valley in search of land accessible to a lakefront. Marc thinks if we show this fellow the color of our money, he'll take our offer rather than wait."

Gabe swore succinctly. He didn't need this right now, just when he planned to get started learning the sheep trade. Yesterday, though, he'd assured Marley he'd complete the project still in the works. It meant he'd have to drive out to Campos's place—er, *his* place, he revised with no small amount of pride—right away.

"Tell Marc I'll book a flight for tomorrow. And that I'll call later with a time for him to pick me up at the closest airport. Ordinarily I'd drive to the site, but I'd better fly since we're in a time crunch."

"Still planning on leaving the agency to settle in Oregon?"

"Yep. In fact, I just forked over a bundle of cash for that piece of property I mentioned yesterday. You caught me leaving the bank."

"Probably just as well," Marley lamented. "Contributions are drying up all across the beltway. My past sponsors are even holding tight to their liquid cash. Oh, well—my wife's been bugging me to retire…again." He snorted, more to himself than for Gabe's benefit. "So I will, and I'll do nothing for a while but administer the trusts and endowments already set up to maintain current ecological ventures. Be sure and tell Coltrane not to worry. The partnership we struck with Summer is funded well past Rory's old age."

"Barring any major crash in the U.S. economy?" Gabe threw out as an afterthought.

"Poston, don't even whisper such a thing. I'm only good for one crisis at a time."

Gabe laughed.

"Oh, you were joking. Should've known that if you'd so much as a hint of a banking collapse, you wouldn't be putting money into a farm, of all things. You'd be hunkering down to wait it out. Talk to you later, Gabe. Take care, okay?"

Gabe grinned. The only person, other than himself, more bent on seeing his investments multiply was Marley Jones.

Only because he happened to glance out his side window before driving down the street did Gabe see Isabella leave the bank. From the way she tracked his progress, he realized she must've been standing inside waiting for him to depart. The fact that she wanted to avoid him that badly dampened his high spirits. He could only imagine her reaction once she discovered he now owned a ranch in her precious community.

Rather than go straight out to see John, Gabe swung by his room at the Inn. He booked a flight to Utah, leaving the return date open. In the two-plus years he'd been closing deals for SOS, he'd learned that it was impossible to judge how long a transfer process would take. No two banks operated the same way. That, plus the fact that he hated being cooped up, he'd never had any desire to work for a financial institution, no matter how much he loved working with numbers.

He stayed in his room only long enough to pack for his trip. He also left a message with Marc's answering service, telling him when the flight would arrive.

At approximately one o'clock, he set out for what used to be the Campos ranch. Farm? Ranch? Gabe didn't know which of those terms more accurately described the property he'd bought. Maybe neither, as his place had no animals.

Turning from the main highway onto a two-lane road that led into the lush green valley where he was about to begin a new stage of his life, Gabe felt his spirits lift. His recent uncertainty about what he should do next was gone. Isabella or not, he'd committed himself to this project. Of course, the books he'd read hadn't made sheep sound all that exciting. But raising the critters did appear to be a simple matter of making sure they had grass, water and fences to keep them from ending up as roadkill.

From what he'd seen touring John's upper and lower pastures, they filled the bill. Plus, a nice creek brimming with icy water that ran out of the mountains formed the boundary between his property and that of one neighbor. A neighbor whose house was set too far back from the road to see.

Pulling up in front of the weathered clapboard home he now owned, Gabe mentally listed the obvious cosmetic repairs it needed.

He tucked that list away, got out and soon tripped over a loose board on the top step. He added replacement steps to his growing list.

The old man took his time answering Gabe's knock. *"Bienvenido,* Gabriel. *Como—"*

Interrupting John's welcome, and in anticipation of his asking what had happened to bring Gabe out here so fast, he explained his changed circumstances. "So, if possible," he finished, "I'd like to advance meeting your neighbors. Especially if you're planning to leave next week. I'm not sure if I'll be in Utah one week or two."

Campos opened the screen door and stepped out on the porch. "I believe Benito and two of his sons-in-law were sharpening shears when I came home. Shearing starts before spring lambing ends." He narrowed dark eyes on Gabe. "Come, you'd better arrange to observe Benito through shearing, also."

"Oh. Can't I hire someone to shear for me?" Gabe felt new doubts about the whole process crowding in. "The book I read on sheep-raising said there were professional sheep-shearers who hired out to farmers."

"A book on raising sheep? Bah!" He held up his

weather-beaten hands. "A man is born to work with sheep. Or not," he added after making Gabe uncomfortable with a long searching stare. "Better you find out which you are before you purchase a flock, I think." John shuffled off the porch and headed for the front gate.

Gabe followed more slowly, wondering for the first time if the book had made the process appear *too* simple.

As he tramped across the dusty gravel road that separated the Campos clapboard home from a much larger, two-story sprawling ranch house—the only other structure in sight, except for a variety of sheds and barns—Gabe sincerely wished he'd bought jeans and boots before they had this visit. Mud squished under the soles of his loafers. John set his feet down so hard, some splattered on Gabe's khaki pants.

The old man bypassed the house altogether. As they rounded the corner of what turned out to be a chicken coop, Campos kept on walking toward a grove of trees. He scattered squawking chickens as he went.

Two men in the grove glanced up at their approach. The third and eldest, who wore a dark-red beret, continued to operate a foot-grinder. Sparks flew from under the shears he was grinding. One of the younger men finally caught his attention and all activity stopped.

Wheezing badly, John halted a few feet short of the trio. It gave Gabe time to assess all three neighbors. When the one bent over the wheel straightened and removed a set of carpenter's goggles, Gabe saw that he was tall, iron-haired and broad-shouldered. Both younger men were shorter, but equally muscled in their upper bodies. All had piercing black eyes that skipped over John and took Gabe's city clothes apart inch by curious inch.

The four friends began to speak over top of one another in that melodious language Gabe couldn't decipher. But he repeatedly caught the word *maketo* and, judging by their sidelong glances, figured out that they'd called him an outsider.

The gray-haired man, whom he deduced was Benito, wiped his hands down his overalls before grasping Gabe's right hand with a crushing shake.

Managing to paste on a thin smile, Gabe returned the pressure with much less fervor. Hoping Benito spoke some English, Gabe introduced himself.

"So, my good friend tells me you bought his place, Mr. Poston. What, if you don't mind my asking, made you choose to settle in our out-of-the-way corner of Oregon?" Benito's English was better than fair, Gabe noted, although he spoke with a lilting accent that reminded Gabe of Isabella Navarro.

"One of my best buddies married Summer Marsh. I'm sure you're familiar with the Forked Lightning property that lies beyond those mountains in the next valley. I spent a month here last winter, and when I came back for their wedding, something about this place got under my skin."

The older man nodded as if he knew what Gabe was talking about.

"And you want to raise sheep? Louis there, who is married to my oldest daughter, he gave up sheep for vineyards." Benito motioned the stockier of the two younger men forward. "Angel. Angel Oneida, husband of my next-to-youngest girl, he keeps a few angora goats. Otherwise, he helps tend my flocks. My sons,

Rick and Manuel, they got rid of all their sheep and went to apple orchards.''

"I've been reading up on sheep," Gabe said, not wanting to sound as uninformed as he felt. "Coltrane Quinn suggested I apprentice with a local sheep man for a few months to find out what I'd be getting into before I buy a flock. John agreed. I believe he thinks you might be amenable to such a plan." Gabe decided to quit pussyfooting around and state his objective straight off.

Benito tucked his thumbs under his overall straps. While he pondered Gabe's proposal, the younger men circled around. The one called Louis stuck out his hand. "I'm Louis Achabal. Your name's familiar, but I don't think we've met." He pumped Gabe's hand.

"Were you at Colt and Summer's wedding?" Gabe asked. "I met a lot of area ranchers there."

"Nope. Angel's wife went, but he couldn't go because he coaches his son's ball team. Their first practice was that afternoon. I had grape vines to nip."

"I'm sure we haven't met." Gabe wished Benito would make up his mind one way or the other so he could let them get back to work and then leave.

Benito was no longer studying Gabe. He'd turned his attention on John Campos. "I'm sorry to be losing you, *mi amigo*," he said, blinking back what Gabe was pretty certain were tears. "Change of any kind is difficult and better absorbed in little bits. I suggest we adjourn to Louis's *sidrerias* where we can sit and talk."

The others agreed so quickly and enthusiastically, Gabe had no choice but to concur. He hung back, slowing his steps to John's slower pace. "My Spanish is rusty and I don't know Basque at all. What's a *sidrerias?*

"Basques were forbidden to speak Euskera, our language, for so long, it's easy to slip into Spanish, which we were forced to use. Benito has invited us to his son-in-law's cider house."

Gabe nodded. A beer would suit him better, but perhaps these men didn't drink it. He knew next to nothing about Basque history or culture. He'd have to pick up a book when he went back to the library.

Louis's cider house turned out to be a cozy enclosure off the vat room of Achabal's winery. It looked to Gabe as if this might be a common meeting area. Six or so straight-backed wooden chairs sat around a low, square table.

Louis had hollered to his wife as the group of men tromped past his single-story dwelling. Two border collies roused themselves and wagged their tails. A plump, brown-haired woman stepped out on the back porch, and Louis jogged over to confer with her while the others continued.

It wasn't long before he rejoined them in the room. "Ruby sent *tapas* to celebrate John's sale. She suggested inviting him and Mr. Poston to dinner at the main house tonight, Benito."

"Please, call me Gabe. Mr. Poston is far too formal. But I couldn't put your wife out on such short notice, Benito. Besides, I'm going out of town for a few days. I've got an early flight tomorrow."

"Nonsense. You still have to eat." Benito removed his beret and swiped a fat green olive and a piece of ham off the platter Louis had set on the low table. "At times, my first-born is a wise woman," he said, spitting the olive pit into his hand.

No one paid Gabe any heed. Louis disappeared again, this time into the vat room. He wasn't gone five minutes, and returned with a tray of water glasses, each brimming with frosty red wine. He served his father-in-law first, then John and Gabe. It was almost a ritual, Gabe mused, observing how the younger men waited for Benito to sample his wine before they relaxed or even took a sip from their tumblers.

"Ah. *Perfecto.*" Benito smacked his lips. Louis beamed. Amid much boisterous toasting of John and himself, Gabe noticed that the others found time to drink heartily. So he followed their example.

"Why is this called a cider house?" he asked after Louis had retrieved a tall wooden pitcher and topped off everyone's glass.

"In the old country, apple harvests were plentiful. Good cider could be bartered in town for many scarce food items. Men from surrounding villages used to gather to taste from each vat. It grew into a tradition, which later extended to wines."

Gabe bobbed his head, suddenly realizing he'd been doing a lot of that in conjunction with chuckling at the men's bawdy jokes. "I'm no expert on wines. But, I'd say you have a winner here, Louis." Lifting his glass in salute, Gabe drained it.

As the afternoon wore on, all the food on the plate got consumed. There had been much talk about John returning to Vizcaya, or what the men referred to as *Euskedi.* As near as Gabe could tell, it was a province in Spain where the majority of John's family had lived and died. Evening shadows fell, and still not one word had been said concerning Gabe's request to apprentice with Benito.

At one point, Louis's wife slipped in to hand her

husband two piping hot loaves of bread. Again the wineglasses were refilled. Gabe, thoroughly mellow by now, ceased to worry. Not about learning sheep. Not about his upcoming trip to Utah. He settled in to enjoy the simple camaraderie of men, something he sorely missed since he, Colt, Moss and Marc had scattered to the four winds.

After the men had consumed their fill of the home-baked bread, Angel cleared the table and brought out a deck of cards.

Liking poker, Gabe was disappointed to discover they intended to play a game called *mus.* ''I'm told it's like whist,'' Angel whispered to him.

Attentive and good at cards, Gabe soon caught on to the spirited game. He became the focus of a lot of good-natured ribbing, though, as he lost hand after hand. He swallowed all their guff with equanimity, saying, ''You guys have the advantage. You grew up playing this.''

Midway through the fifth hand, after Gabe had shelled out all the change in his pockets, Benito pounded him on the back.

''You're a good sport. I think you'll fit in to our village just fine.''

Pleasantly buzzed, Gabe almost missed what had happened in that subtle exchange. ''Oh. Oh! Then you'll let me tag along and learn how to raise sheep?''

The older man shared an unspoken sign of agreement with Louis and Angel. They all broke into huge grins, and one at a time rose to shake Gabe's hand. His fingers tingled for several minutes afterward.

Pleased, Gabe assumed that would bring an end to their caucus. Wrong. The deck of cards disappeared and dominoes came out instead.

Gabe, known for his ability to add and subtract rapidly, again found himself on the short end of this highly competitive game. He slapped a hand over his glass the next time Louis poured a round. And still his companions outplayed him. As well, they kept everyone's score in their heads.

It soon became a matter of pride for Gabe to win at least one game. The door opened as he made his private vow. Three burly newcomers trudged inside. They pretty much filled the room. Benito rose fluidly to greet the new arrivals. Gabe got up more slowly, awfully afraid he was blinking like a hoot owl as his new mentor introduced him.

"These are my sons," Benito said proudly. "Ricardo, Joseph and Manuel, in order of their ages."

"*Chicos*, this is Gabe. He's going to be a neighboring sheep man. He bought John's house and pastures."

These men weren't nearly so quick to welcome Gabe. As each crunched his hand in turn, it flitted through Gabe's mind that he'd seen them somewhere. Before he could formulate the question free-floating inside his throbbing skull, Benito moved on to tell his sons about John's upcoming departure. "Louis said Ruby is preparing a small fiesta tonight at my *caserío*."

"Can't come," Joseph lamented, speaking directly to John. "Julie has a night class, and I have to take the kids to catechism. Do you need her to help with packing?"

John shook his head. "The furniture stays with the house. Everything, really, except for a Bible that's been in the Campos family for many, many years."

Manuel dropped down on one knee beside the old man's chair. "Tell those sons of yours we all miss them. We'll miss you, too, John." Both Manny and his brother Joe hugged John and kissed him soundly on both cheeks.

Gabe looked on, thinking how different their open display of affection was from the standard slap on the back common among the men of his acquaintance.

Benito's youngest son rose. "I'm darned sorry, but I'll have to skip the fiesta, too. I can't remember what's on our calendar, but when I left this morning Christina asked me to be home early. She's trying to teach as long as she can because she wants to save her sick leave for when the baby's born. But her legs swell. At night she needs to get off her feet."

Ricardo boomed in a voice as big as himself. "Count us in. Mama's probably already phoned Maria. If our kids don't have after-school activities, they'll tag along. Right now, though, I have to go home and wash up. I sprayed the orchards today." He wrapped a large hand around the doorknob.

Benito chuckled. "You switched to growing apples because you hated dealing with sheep-dip and wet wool. Judging by how little we see of you anymore, I'd say orchards are more work than sheep." He turned to Gabe. "Let this be a lesson, *mi amigo.*"

Louis followed his brothers-in-law to the door. "At least let me get you guys some wine to try at home. This is the first time I've cracked open a barrel made from the grapes I had sent over from Bayona. I'm days from bottling this batch, so I'll be interested in your opinions."

Gabe studied the men's retreating backs. It struck him how much he'd missed growing up without family. This was the life he'd want for any children he might have. Yes, he'd be sure to tell Marley he'd made a good decision, settling in this valley.

Louis wandered back in, and the domino game was picked up where they'd left off. Gabe won by a thin margin because all the others had to draw and he was able to play everything left in his hand. Delighted for him, those who stayed toasted him again, after Louis had topped off their glasses.

Gabe stared into the burgundy liquid. "You guys amaze me. I thought I'd met some men in the Marines who could put away a lot of booze without showing any effects. But compared to you…" He grinned sloppily. "I've gotta tell you, I'm feeling light-headed."

"No wonder," Angel yelped, wagging his watch under Benito's nose. "We've dithered away the afternoon. If we don't want the wives coming down here and yanking us out by our ears, we'd better wash up and head for your *caserío.*"

They all agreed it was later than anyone had realized.

Because John, the most senior of the group, stumbled as they trudged through the deepening shadows, Angel and Louis made a chair for him of their sturdy arms. Someone started to sing. Gabe didn't know the song, which was in Euskera, but that didn't stop him from adding his lusty baritone to the chorus.

Later he would think they must have looked and sounded like drunken sailors as they tripped up the steps and into the kitchen of the two-story house he'd passed by hours before.

The shocked expression on Isabella Navarro's face as she spun toward the door drove home with sobering clarity exactly what kind of ass he must appear. His presence stopped her cold in the act of removing her jacket. Obviously she'd shown up only moments before the men made their grand entrance.

It took Gabe several minutes of suffering through

introductions to actually figure out that Benito, who up to this point had not given his last name, was in fact Isabella's father. Luisa, her mother, along with Ruby, her eldest sister, had pulled together this impromptu fiesta.

Now Gabe knew why the men who'd stopped in at the cider house seemed familiar. They were Isabella's brothers. The ones he'd seen carrying Summer and Colt's wedding cake from the white van.

"What are you doing here?" she demanded, trying not to speak loudly enough for the others to hear.

"Probably the same thing you are. I was invited to John's going-away party."

"But I live here!"

"No shit? Uh...no kidding?" he scrambled to say. "Well, whaddya know. I just bought the property across the road. Your dad's going to teach me everything I need to know about sheep."

"You did this on purpose. You found out where I lived and...and...and..."

"And I arm-wrestled an old man out of his property? Hardly. I paid John top dollar for his land. So, how far away from here do you live?"

"I *said* I live here." She lowered her voice even more, for by now their heated exchange had drawn the attention of others. Even Rick's teenagers muted the TV and strained an ear to hear what had upset their aunt.

Isabella swallowed. "I...uh...moved home after...after..."

"That's okay. I think you may have said that, actually. But I swear I didn't know you were a neighbor of John's when I made the deal. Listen, I'm beginning to get the message that you'd like me to stay out of your life. Fine. I'll do that. But for the sake of the others, shouldn't we make the best of it tonight? Your sister arranged this celebration for John. I'd hate our petty squabbles to ruin it for the old guy.''

"This morning, at the bank, you deliberately acted as if you didn't know John Campos. That was very sneaky and underhanded.''

"Sneaky how? You asked if he'd sideswiped my SUV, and I said he didn't.''

"It was obvious I knew him well. Did you tell me you'd bought his ranch? No. That's what I call sneaky.'' Her voice rose.

Gabe remembered he'd sidestepped her pointed query because he'd thought it best to let John reveal his own decision to sell. Gabe's guilt must have shown on his face. Isabella crossed her arms and arched a smug brow.

Luisa Navarro, a tall woman whose slightly graying hair was tightly braided and wrapped around her head, broke away from the others. "Bella, *caro?* Is something wrong?''

Now it was Isabella's turn to act guilty. "Everything's fine, Mama. I'm very tired tonight. It got so warm in the bakery kitchen today, I had to frost Estrella Aguirre's wedding cake in the cooler. The frosting kept hardening in the tube, so I had to dash in and out of the cold. So maybe I caught a cold. I ache all over. If you'll excuse me, I'll go on up to my room.''

"Oh, bella, what will John think if you run off? Or Gabe. Your papa is pleased to have someone new to train in sheep-raising. You know how he's been since Rick and Manuel went their own ways.''

"I hear him over there expounding to Joe. Apparently he's forgotten Joe and Angel both tend his flocks.''

"They grew up in the trade," her mother said matter-of-factly. "Papa likes to teach innovative philosophies."

Isabella smiled at that. "I'll stay downstairs for a while if you'd like, Mama. Can I help in the kitchen?"

"No. Maria, Ruby and I have everything on the table. Just point Gabe toward the food. Oh, and get him a plate, will you?"

Isabella glowered in Gabe's direction. "I'm sure Mr. Poston is smart enough to follow his nose to the food. So, where's Trini? She took the day off work to attend the quilt show in Sisters with a couple of her friends. I thought she'd be back by now."

"She phoned fifteen minutes ago. She had to drop off Petra." Luisa seemed baffled by her daughter's rude treatment of a guest. "Bella, explain to Gabe what's in some of our local dishes." This time, Luisa's tone brooked no excuse for not obeying cheerfully.

Gabe, on firmer footing thanks to Luisa's reception, gave the older woman a warm smile. "I've sampled *migas.* I'd appreciate being steered away from anything that might set fire to my tongue."

Luisa laughed a tinkling laugh. "Isabella does love spicy dishes. I think you'll find the food on my table mild by comparison."

"Come on," Isabella all but growled. "I'll get you a plate. But then you're on your own."

"At least introduce me to your other sister and to Rick's wife. I've met everyone else."

Isabella complied, albeit grumpily. She feared that thanks to the town gossips, Ruby and Maria had heard all about Gabe Poston. She dutifully carried out Luisa's wishes, then dished up two items on her plate and with-drew into a quiet corner.

Taking the hint to leave her alone, Gabe joined the men—until Trini Navarro swept in and made a point of flirting outrageously with him.

The more Trini fawned over Gabe, the more annoyed Isabella became. Although she couldn't name one valid reason. Her younger sister was free to throw herself at any man she chose. Which didn't mean Isabella had to watch.

She'd hardly touched a bite. Knowing her mother would scold her soundly if she saw, Isabella sneaked into the kitchen, where she scraped her plate into the trash. Pleading a worsening headache, she fled upstairs.

But she couldn't block out the laughter or the lively beat of fiddle music cranked up loud enough for John to hear and enjoy.

Isabella was oh-so-tempted to tiptoe to the railing to see if Trini and Gabe Poston were dancing cheek to cheek. Instead, she covered her ears with the pillow and gazed at the bedside photos of Toni and Ramon. She had to remain clearheaded for them. If that meant denying herself a few fleeting pleasures, so be it. Trini was more than welcome to occupy Gabe Poston's free time. *All* his free time.

CHAPTER SIX

AFTER AN EVENTFUL TRIP to Utah, Gabe landed at the Pendleton airport at 11:00 p.m. in the midst of what the pilot informed passengers was a freak spring hailstorm. Gabe collected his bags, turned up his collar and ran for the SUV. Sleet pounded him from all directions. The soles of his dress shoes slid back two steps for every one he took. Cursing, he told himself he should've worn the jeans and boots he'd bought at that western shop in Salt Lake.

Ice crystals obliterated the vehicles in the parking lot and left a slick coating on everything. Once he got his bearings in the rows of cars and found his, Gabe discovered that his wipers were frozen to the windshield.

"Great!" he muttered, rubbing his cold hands together in between pawing through his console to see if he had anything available to chip away the ice. Finding nothing, he sat back, turned his defrosters on high and waited for the blades to thaw. A slow, irritating process, it turned out. In addition to the messy weather, a crosswind began buffeting his SUV.

Damn. He just wanted to get home. At least, he assumed John Campos had moved out as planned and that now he could legitimately call the ranch house his. Or had something gone wrong with those arrangements, too? Nothing would surprise Gabe after the week he'd had. It'd been bad enough that SOS ended up losing its chance to save the Utah property—one of the agency's last environmental deals, a good one Marc had spent months putting together. At the last minute, the owner had held out for a lot more money. Eventually their only choice had been to walk away.

As well as the only failure in his career with SOS, he'd had to put up with Marc criticizing the personal decision Gabe had made in buying the Oregon ranch. This damn storm was the perfect end to his crappy week.

Well, he'd found a gift to bring back for Isabella. He'd bought it on impulse but he was pleased with his decision. Gabe slapped at his pocket to be sure the bag was still there.

Eventually his method to free the wipers worked. However his hope that the storm was confined north of Callanton was dashed; the closer he got to his destination, the worse it grew.

Sometime after midnight, he turned down the lane to his new home. Not so much as a glimmer of light greeted his late arrival. Well, what had he expected? A brass band and sixteen hundred candles?

As he stepped from his snug vehicle, an icy blast of wind slammed his shoulders and knocked him sideways. That was when he realized all the lights he was missing on his side of the road blazed in profusion around Benito Navarro's property. Gabe suspected that every light in the house and barn—including those at the corners of the sheep pens—was glowing eerily through the slanting hail.

Obviously something was going on at his neighbors'.

Fearing some disaster, he tossed his suitcase back in the Lexus. Shoulders hunched, he loped across the road, pausing midway up their drive, unable to decide if he should stop at the house or continue on to the barn. Then he heard the muffled shouts of masculine voices and the barking of dogs out by the pens, so he altered his course. First thing, he bumped right into Angel Oneida.

"Whoa! Hey, Gabe, is that you? Mother Nature's giving you some welcome back." Angel sheltered a shivering, bleating lamb in the warmth of his fleecy jacket.

"I just now got home. I was unloading my bags when I saw all of Benito's lights. What's happening over here?"

Angel's face sobered suddenly as he peered through the water pouring off his cowboy hat. "The storm caused our ewes to start dropping lambs. Benito says we should've known something was up because the flocks in our high pastures were banding on their own. None of us saw that as significant, so the storm caught us flat-footed."

"Can I help?"

"You'd freeze in ten minutes dressed like that."

"I'll change. I have more appropriate gear in the car. By the way, did John get moved okay, or was he delayed by the weather?"

"He took off on schedule." Angel turned as a disembodied voice in the distance called his name. Without warning, he pulled the lamb out from under his coat and shoved it at Gabe. "Look, Louis needs me. Take this little guy to the barn. Bella's in there drying off our orphans. She'll feed the strongest ones. The weak get passed to Mama Luisa and Trini up at the *caserío*. We're throwing so many lambs at Bella, I'm sure she'd welcome a hand."

Gabe almost dropped the animal, whose coat had

begun to grow stiff in the short time he'd been exposed to the elements. Shifting his hold, he tucked the little fellow under his jacket. He wanted—needed—to ask more questions, but Angel disappeared into the pelting hail as quickly as he'd arrived.

Aware of the animal shivering under his wet light-weight wool suit coat, Gabe made a dash for the barn.

Isabella didn't even glance up when the door opened and a blast of cold air rustled the straw she'd strewn about the cavernous interior. She sat cross-legged with her back to the door, surrounded by a mass of woolly lambs all trying to stand on unsteady legs. Several butted her hips; more butted each other. All were trying to get at something she held. It looked to Gabe like five of the newborn lambs were sucking on the fat, elongated fingers of a rubber glove.

"Not another one, Angel," Isabella said tiredly. "It's almost time to feed the first batch again, and you keep finding new ones. How many more, do you think? I've only got two hands." Gabe saw her shoulders lift, then sink with a heavy sigh.

"I'm here to offer another pair. But you'll have to teach me. The set-up you have looks interesting. Far from simple, though."

She whipped her head around. "Oh!" Her heart thudded wildly from the shock of hearing the man she'd been thinking about. Until this moment, she had steadfastly refused to admit she'd missed Gabe Poston during his week-long absence. "Gabe? I...ah...was expecting Angel."

"So I gathered. Please don't kill the messenger, but I've brought you another mouth to feed. I met Angel on the road. He was called back to the pens. Sorry." Gabe moved farther into the barn so he could shut the door and block the howling wind. Bending, he found an empty spot on her lap for the still shivering animal he'd cradled against his white shirt.

"Poor baby," she crooned, her free hand shooting out to gather the lamb close. "Goodness, what a runt." Looking back at Gabe, she said, "If you'll take over for me here, I'll start warming this little guy. He's almost blue, or else I'd have you take him straight on to the kitchen where Mama and Trini are bottle-feeding the weaker lambs."

Without a word, Gabe crouched beside her and attempted to scoop the five animals currently on her lap into his larger hands. "Let's see if we can make this a seamless transfer."

"Gabe! Your jacket and pants are soaking." She shied away from the water dripping from his hair onto her hands. "Wait. You aren't dressed for this job. The lambs may be tiny, but their hooves are sharp as knives. Inside five minutes they'd have your nice suit shredded."

For the first time, Gabe noticed the holes in Isabella's jeans. He didn't let the fact that there were traces of blood around some of them deter him. "Don't worry. I'm about to trade my suits in on Farmer Gabe outfits." Smiling at her with calm assurance, he cleared a place on the floor next to her by gently scooting lambs aside with the toe of his wet shoe. Quickly, he wedged himself into the opening and landed on the hay with a grunt. "Damn, it's hard under that stuff."

"Cement usually is." She frowned as she edged away from his imposing body.

"Sorry. I seem to be apologizing a lot. But I really didn't mean to get you wet."

That wasn't why Isabella was frowning. His nearness

felt far too comforting. The night before he'd left town, she'd set down some rules for herself. One of them had been to step aside and give Trini her blessing with regard to pursuing this man. Not that Trini needed her older sister's okay. She'd always done as she darned well pleased.

Intent on getting the glove-finger nipples into the mouths he was supposed to be feeding, Gabe didn't realize Isabella had left to get a warm towel to wrap around the lamb he'd brought in. Nor did he think it odd that she'd let their conversation lapse. He was content to be in her company, and he felt relieved that his feelings for her hadn't changed, considering the badgering he'd gotten from Marc. Reggie had even landed a few verbal punches the night he phoned. Prompted by Marc, Gabe didn't doubt. He knew his friends thought he'd lost his mind, as buying a ranch had never figured in his plans. In Coltrane's and Reggie's, yes, but not his. Yet here he was, happy as a pig in slop, miserably wet, feeding greedy lambs out of a rubber kitchen glove.

Unable to contain a sappy grin, Gabe glanced over at Isabella. ''These guys have polished off all the milk in my glove. Where do I fill it up again? Or do they get more? Their little bellies are so round I'm thinking they're gonna burst.''

Isabella seemed to be having problems getting the lamb she'd taken from Gabe to eat. She had a pile of other bleating creatures fighting to grab the glove finger she was making an effort to preserve for the listless baby. ''I should've told you to push them away and feed five more. These lambs are all premature. They'll eat often, but we shouldn't give them too much at once. The milk needs to be warm so we'll only fill two gloves at a time. You'll do that by milking the goats in the four stalls on your left at the back of the barn.''

"You milk goats?'' Gabe thought he might have heard her wrong.

"Goat's milk is richer than cow's milk. If you've never milked a goat before, you may think it's harder than milking a cow.''

Gabe hadn't milked anything before. Not ever. But he had a streak of stubborn pride that wouldn't allow him to admit it. After making sure the glove he held was bone-dry, he climbed slowly to his feet, determined to do this. Men had been performing the chore of milking since heaven knew how far back in time.

"Angel referred to these lambs as orphans,'' he said. "What happened to their mothers?''

"Hard to tell. When the weather gets this bad, panic runs through a flock. It's why so many lambs are born prematurely. Sheep are not the brightest creatures on earth. They tend to follow the leader, even if it means leaving their offspring.''

"I have a lot to learn,'' he said. "Oh, before I forget, I brought you something from Utah.'' He reached in his pocket and pulled out a small sack. "It's not much, but when I saw it in a store, it sort of said *buy me to watch over Isabella.*''

She accepted the sack awkwardly. She wasn't used to receiving gifts for no reason. Finally, she opened it. The small filigree angel pin she pulled out brought a soft gasp to her lips. "I…it's beautiful.'' She rubbed a thumb over the wings several times before tucking the pin in her pocket. "Thank you, Gabe. I'll wear it every day at the trial.''

Gabe knew she'd been touched by his gift. But the tender moment they shared was soon over; there was work to be done. He made his way around the tumble of lambs, headed for the goats Isabella had directed him to.

The deeper he went in the barn, the dimmer the light. Peering over the last stall door, he saw a pair of bright eyes staring back. "Uh, Isabella, do I need a bucket of some sort, or do I squirt milk right into the glove?"

"There's a bucket hanging on the back wall," she called. "You may prefer to use it. I don't like wasting milk, so I milk into the glove."

If she could do that, so could he. Nonchalantly waving so that she'd know he'd heard, Gabe used his free hand to unlatch the door. The next thing he knew, the door flew open and something hit him square in the knees. A rush of air left his lungs seconds before his butt hit the concrete floor. During Gabe's next view of the goat's eyes, his own were crossed and he stared directly into a curious black pair. The animal's wiry beard tickled Gabe's nose.

"Gabe, I said the stalls of the milking goats were on your left. You opened one on your right. That's Herman, Papa's oldest billy goat. Hurry and get him back in his stall before he comes out and tramples some of the lambs."

Right now the beast was trampling Gabe. His knees still felt numb, as did his butt and the back of his head. He slapped at the goat's head with the glove he still held. Herman hooked the glove with his horns, ripped it out of Gabe's hand and tossed it into the stall where Gabe should have gone.

He tried rolling to the side, but Herman's head rammed him hard in the shoulder and sent him sprawling again. "Dammit," Gabe muttered. "I've had about enough of being your punching bag." Clenching his teeth, Gabe called on his hand-to-hand combat training. Feinting left, he distracted Herman. When the goat fell for the fake, Gabe grabbed him around the neck and by one horn. There ensued a tug-of-war. At one point, Gabe took a kick to his ribs and feared he might lose the battle. Always a man of grit, he hung on, literally bulldogging Herman back into his stall.

"What's all the scuffling back there?" Isabella yelled. "Gabe? Do you need me to help put Herman away?"

Gabe had released the goat and they were back to a staring match, with Gabe now standing solidly between Herman and freedom. They both lunged for the opening. Luckily, Gabe came out the victor. Panting hard, he slammed the door shut and heard the crack as the goat butted the door. Even though Gabe's hand shook as he dropped the latch in place, a satisfied grin kicked up one side of his mouth. "Mess with me, will you," he warned in a low voice. "Herman's back in quarters," he reported to Isabella. "Now I'm going to get the bucket and enough milk to fill the glove."

Another feat that proved easier said than done.

Two smaller, hornless nannies resided in the opposite stall. Instead of coming at him as he expected and as the billy goat had done, the nannies split and circled behind Gabe the minute he bent to retrieve the glove Herman had tossed inside. He swung around fast on knees beginning to tingle with life again, then swore more loudly than he'd intended. Again the nannies pulled the same trick. Plus, one kicked the bucket out of his hand. He saved it before it hit the floor.

"Hold still, you she-devils," he ordered in a quieter tone than he would've used had Isabella not been in the outer room.

One nanny approached him, seeming to react favorably to the softer rumble of his voice. So he kept talking to her, and thought he had it made even though his knees creaked as he reached for a swinging teat. Quick as lightning, two sharp hooves hit Gabe smack in the chest. Once more he landed flat on his butt in the corner.

Sore, aching and growing damned tired of coming out on the short end, Gabe shrugged out of his coat, dropped it over the smallest goat's head and manhandled her crossways into a corner. There, he proceeded to fill his glove, although it took him several tries to get the hang of it and the rhythm of coaxing milk from the nanny's full udder.

Triumphant—and sore—Gabe practically strutted back to Isabella with his prize.

"Gabe, good. The other lambs have drained my glove dry. I can't get the one you brought in to eat much at all. Do you mind letting me have the glove you just filled and go fill mine for yourself?"

Battered and bruised he might be, but could Gabe refuse Isabella Navarro anything when she asked so sweetly? Not on your life. Gathering his resolve, he blithely handed over the glove he'd almost killed himself to fill. He took the empty one from her, knowing that to repeat the process again meant doing battle with nanny number two. She was bigger and had butted him out the stall door.

Isabella's thanks followed Gabe. He was damn glad his buddies weren't around to see this insanity. He'd never hear the end of their ribbing.

Tarrying outside the stall, Gabe wondered if anyone had ever been killed trying to milk a goat. Since his jacket already smelled, he chose to use the same method to subdue nanny number two.

She was older and wiser. She promptly threw off Gabe's suit coat, grabbed it up in her mouth and shook it wildly as she raced around and around the stall. Before Gabe was able to snatch back his jacket, she dropped it on the floor and stomped on it with both feet. When she tired of that exercise, she lowered her head and munched contentedly on one sleeve.

"Hey!" Gabe's protest was met with stony indifference. "Ah, what the hell?" His jacket was already ruined. Sidling up to the little witch, Gabe dropped down on one knee and, ignoring the bucket he'd brought in again, he felt around with one hand and eventually squirted milk straight into the opening at the top of the glove.

So, he became the conqueror again. Or maybe not, since it had cost him a chunk of machismo, and an Armani suit coat.

Still, he felt good about his victory when he walked back to where Isabella sat. At first he didn't notice that his arrival had made no impression on her.

On second glance, Gabe noticed that she not only sat as silent as if she'd been carved from stone but that she'd dropped her rubber glove. Lambs were tugging and pulling and fighting over it. Milk spread across the hay all around Isabella's knees. Her one pant leg was soaked.

Gabe had tied the top of his glove closed. He carefully propped it against a piece of farm equipment sitting off to the side.

"Isabella? Are you okay?" Gabe sank down in front of her, heedless of the sharp pains that reminded him of his encounter with Herman.

She opened her eyes and raised them ever so slightly. If Gabe thought he'd been stabbed through the heart when they'd first met, seeing the pain-filled expression in her dark eyes, this time was far worse. Her pain had risen to the surface and was stark and immediate.

Mere moments later, he realized her fingers were flexing almost madly in the woolly coat of the lamb she'd been trying to feed. *The limp body of a now-dead lamb.*

"Oh, Isabella," Gabe murmured, as he tried to remove the lifeless animal from her arms. "It's not your fault. You did your best to save him."

She snatched her hands back so fast, Gabe was left grasping air. Still without word, Isabella cradled the creature to her breast and began a distraught keening. It was a tortured, gut-wrenching sound. Gabe didn't know how in God's name to help her.

Instinct said that someone who hurt this badly needed holding. Considering the distance she always maintained between them, Gabe didn't know if he should be the one to offer comfort. But right now there was no one else.

When he managed to get his feet under him, Gabe reached out slowly, so as not to startle her. Curling his hands around her upper arms, he rose with her, little by little. His knees screamed, but something stronger drove him.

What struck him was how little meat she had on her bones, and how she weighed next to nothing for a woman of her height. Taking greater care once they were both standing, he wrapped her and the inert lamb in a gentle embrace. And he rocked her from side to side, crooning nonsensical words close to her ear, just loud enough for her to hear him over the sound of her distress.

She shivered violently, yet he knew it was warm enough in the barn to have dried his wet clothing. Clearly, Isabella's coldness came from deep inside her. From the very depths of her soul.

It crossed Gabe's mind that he should be relieving her of the lamb. But he didn't know what the procedure was on the Navarro ranch for disposing of dead sheep. In an operation the size of theirs, he thought it'd probably be fairly common to lose animals for any number of reasons. And he doubted Isabella's reaction was solely because of the lamb.

As her shivering lessened, Gabe discovered his inclination had been right. Over and over she moaned, "They're not moving. Not breathing. My children," she said pitifully. "Julian did this. He couldn't have me, so he took what I loved most. My babies!" The sounds wracking her body grew more desperate.

"Shh." Cupping her head in one hand, he tried to ease her agony.

Suddenly the barn door opened. Joseph Navarro, Isabella's second-oldest brother, swept in on a shower of icy sleet. "What's this? What's going on here?" he demanded sharply, charging toward Gabe.

"Back off," Gabe spat, sharper still. "A lamb your sister was feeding, a little bit of a thing, died on her."

Easing back, Gabe studied Isabella's face. She remained locked in pain from another time. From another place. He didn't think she knew Joe had arrived. "I'm no psychiatrist, Joe, but I think the death of the lamb triggered memories of when she found her kids. I only did what I thought was best. I don't know about you, but I've never been alone with anyone when something like this occurred. In the military, we had nurses and doctors to handle PTSD incidents. At least, I think what she's going through is sort of like that. Post traumatic stress disorder,'' he said when Joe looked blank. ''Flashbacks,'' Gabe tried again.

''Right. The doctor warned us she might have those. Jeez, Poston, you should've taken the lamb away from her,'' Joe hissed, his voice dropping nearly to a whisper.

''I tried. She's holding on for dear life.'' Gabe continued to rock her from side to side.

''How long do these type of episodes last? Shall I go get Papa?'' Joe was close enough now to hear the wounded-animal sounds his sister made.

Gabe shook his head. ''Maybe your mom. She's at the house, Angel said.''

''Yeah. Probably the doctor told her what to do. I'll go get her and be right back.'' Joe flew out the door.

Gabe tried again to pry the lamb out of Isabella's arms. This time her fingers went slack, and he succeeded.

He'd have to leave her long enough to take care of the poor creature. But because Isabella began shivering uncontrollably again, he quickly wrapped the lamb in the soft towel she'd used to dry the animal earlier. Then Gabe placed the bundle well away from the lambs that remained underfoot.

Not really caring what Mrs. Navarro might think about finding her daughter locked in a near-stranger's arms, he enfolded her again.

''I'm s-ooo c-c-cold.'' Her teeth chattered.

Gabe was afraid to squeeze her any tighter for fear of cracking her fragile bones. Nevertheless, he turned up the collar on her denim jacket and drew his own tattered coat over her shoulders.

She wasn't shaking quite so hard when Luisa barreled through the door followed by Trini.

"Gabe. I didn't realize you were back." Trini sounded pleased about the discovery.

"I blew in on this storm. Mrs. Navarro, has Isabella ever suffered a spell like this before?"

Nodding, Luisa snapped her fingers at Joe. She barked out orders in rapid Euskera.

It was only when he approached and stripped Gabe's jacket from around his sister that Gabe realized Joe intended to wrap her in a heavy wool blanket.

Joseph Navarro, a man with large hands, tenderly cocooned his sister from head to toe. He picked her up as if she weighed nothing and strode out the door, his mother hot on his heels. That left Gabe alone with Trini.

No longer responsible for Isabella's care, Gabe felt his own knees wobbling. "She'll be all right, won't she?"

Trini glanced first at the door, then back at Gabe. "You do know about her children?"

"Yes," he said slowly. "But Isabella. Will she be okay?"

"She found them, you know. Came home after work, hit the garage door opener and boom, there they all were."

Gabe felt his stomach heave. "God, Trini. How can you sound so matter-of-fact about something so awful? I can't begin to imagine what that was like for her."

"It was horrible. For the whole family. And it's going to get worse, I think, the closer it gets to Julian's trial."

"I'm surprised they're trying him. Anyone who'd do something like that is certifiably insane."

"Don't let Bella hear you say that. She's determined to see Julian get a hundred years in prison."

Gabe pondered Trini's explosive admission. "I don't blame her. For what he did, he should fry. But we don't fry crazies. And won't he be as safely put away in an asylum?"

"To you and me, yes. Not to Bella."

"I don't understand." Gabe rubbed the back of his neck.

"But you'd like to. You care a lot about my sister, don't you?"

Gabe's fingers stilled. "Angel asked me to help Isabella feed orphaned lambs—he said I wasn't dressed to work outside. He gave me a lamb to bring in. Isabella was feeding it when it died. I'll bury him, if you tell me where."

"Tonight?"

Gabe inclined his head.

Trini crossed her arms in a speculative manner. "Angel's right. You aren't dressed for working outside. Which includes digging a hole in half-frozen ground at 2:00 a.m."

"I'll go home first and put on jeans and boots, and a fleece-lined jacket."

Trini tilted her head. A small dimple winked in one cheek. "Stubborn," she announced. "You're a lot like Bella, I think." She bent over and picked up the glove her sister had been using to feed the lambs—the one whose milk had spilled. "Go on, Gabe. Bury the lamb. I'll carry on here."

"I'm coming back," he said, donning his pathetic excuse for a jacket. "When I do, will you go check on

Isabella for me? I won't rest until I know she's doing better.''

"Mama has medicine to give her. It makes her sleep. I recommend you go grab some, too. Sleep, I mean. Although John probably left the house a mess. Maybe you won't want to sleep there until after your housekeeper cleans the place.''

Gabe halted in his tracks. "Housekeeper? I haven't hired one.''

"How much would you pay?" Trini assessed him as if seeing him in a new light.

Gabe hesitated. Was she offering to clean his house? Nah. Surely her family wouldn't approve. He supposed Trini could be inquiring for a friend. "I'll pay the going rate for the area. Do you know someone?''

"Me. I'll start tomorrow. I have a shortened class schedule on Tuesday and Thursday mornings. And I'm free all day on Saturday unless Bella caters a party or a wedding. I wanted her to give me extra hours, but she can't afford to at the moment.''

"Uh, Trini. I thought you asked what I'd pay because maybe you knew someone who does housework for a living.''

"Oh, don't look so terrified. I'll do a good job, and I promise not to chase you around the bed.'' She grinned cheekily.

"Somehow I doubt your parents would approve under any circumstances.''

"I'm twenty-five, Gabe. I live at home to save money while I'm getting my Master's. I'm behind schedule because I took a hiatus from school and bummed around California for a while. But I know what's bugging you. You're worried what Bella will think.''

"No. And no to your offer." Gabe turned away and walked over to where he'd left the lamb. "I recall John had some wood crates on his back porch. The ground under that big old fir tree out in the back yard should be fairly dry, don't you think? If anyone asks, that's where I'm burying this little guy."

Trini Navarro's amused chuckle followed Gabe out the door. He was glad to escape. He'd met his share of women like Isabella's sister. She wasn't interested in him personally, probably even considered him too old for her, which he was. But she was born to flirt and make mischief.

Bracing for the elements, Gabe was happy to see the storm abating. The wind was still cold as sin. Even at that, he decided to bury the lamb before he changed clothes.

Floodlights ringed the perimeter of his house and provided all the light he needed. He'd been right about the old tree; the ground under the branches was dry. Gabe knew the animal had been largely a symbol to Isabella. Yet he felt she'd want him to take special pains with this particular lamb. It seemed fitting to him, too.

Gabe's fingers froze, but he got the job done. Only then did he go inside the warm house to shower and change.

He gave silent thanks to John Campos for leaving the furnace on low. Once he was warm and dry and comfortable again, Gabe trekked back across the road. He decided against making Trini his go-between and veered off to knock on the Navarros' back door.

Luisa answered, and waited while Gabe removed his hat. "Gabe. I almost didn't recognize you. You changed your clothes, and now you look like my men-folk.''

''I'm headed out to help with the sheep. But first, I'd like to know how Isabella's doing.''

''She'll be fine. One of us should've anticipated that this could happen. She loves the lambs so. We all do, but they were always more precious to Bella. We shouldn't have left her alone.''

''She wasn't alone, Mrs. Navarro. I was there. I…I didn't know what to do except hold her and rock her. So that's what I did.''

''You did right, Gabe.'' The woman seemed to take a keen interest in watching him.

''We…ll.'' Gabe fumbled for words. ''I'd better go,'' he said abruptly, jamming his new Stetson back on his head. ''I've apparently got a whole lot to learn about raising sheep, so if you'll excuse me, there's no time like the present.''

Gabe was halfway to the pens before he heard the door shut. And he knew, that like Trini, Luisa Navarro was standing there, weighing his interest in Isabella.

CHAPTER SEVEN

WITH THE ADVENT of dawn, the men working to save the flock began to see their first real break in the weather. Though ice crusted every blade of grass and each twig on newly budded trees, the merciless sleet that had battered them through the night had finally ceased. Clouds, which had hung up on the mountain peaks, moved on to cause problems in Idaho and points east.

Gabe stood with the other men, surveying the milling animals they and the dogs had spent all night herding into pens. "How many sheep did you lose, Benito?"

"It's hard to get an accurate count," the older man said. "Thanks to all of you, less than I would've if it'd only been me and the women. Thirty to forty ewes, I'd guess. No rams. We saved two who'd somehow landed on their backs in ravines. Sheep can't roll over, you know, once they end up on their backs."

"Wow. Thirty sounds like a lot to lose." Gabe stripped off his gloves and inspected a deep scratch he'd gotten somehow.

"Not so many," Angel answered him. "When that freak storm hit, I figured the toll would be high. It wouldn't be the first time. Our lamb loss was relatively low this time."

"God has blessed us. We must give thanks by lighting an extra candle at Mass," Benito said, glancing up as Ricardo, the oldest of his children, drove in unexpectedly to inquire about how his family survived the storm. Rick and Manny ran beef cattle, and together owned apple and peach orchards. "How did your stock and your fruit trees fare?" his father asked.

Rick shook his head. "We won't know for maybe two weeks. Manny and I distributed and tended smudge pots all night. Louis, what about your grapes?"

"If the ground didn't freeze too deep, and if we don't have another storm on the horizon, I think they'll pull through. My vines are the hardy kind grown on the higher elevations in France. I more or less left them alone so I could lend a hand over here."

"We all worked our butts off," exclaimed Joe. "Including Gabe. He said he wanted to learn sheep-raising. This was his baptism by fire."

"More like baptism by ice," Gabe shot back, in hopes of keeping them from knowing his butt was dragging. He'd considered himself in good shape, since he worked out a lot. He'd definitely used a different set of muscles throughout the night. Muscles he was discovering for the first time... Suddenly he didn't know what made him think he had what it took to be a sheep man. This was not the life he'd imagined.

Benito settled a heavy hand on Gabe's shoulder. "Gabe pulled his weight last night when it counted. He's one of us now. Luisa and the others will have prepared a meal. Let's go eat—we can talk at the table."

Rick acted as if he'd like to say something—maybe rebut his father's statement, Gabe thought. However, the men who'd worked shoulder to shoulder to save the Navarro flock closed ranks around their new neighbor.

"I should probably go on home. I have no idea what I need to take care of there." Gabe started to split off from the larger group at the crossroads.

"Eat first," Benito said. It sounded like an order.

Gabe took a quick look at the other men's faces. Apparently, when Benito Navarro gave an order it was followed to the letter.

Ricardo, who looked most like his dad, possessing a big, stocky build and swarthy skin, let his smoldering dark eyes speak his mind on the subject. He'd have been perfectly happy if Gabe got lost.

His attitude, more than Benito's edict, decided Gabe. He hadn't done anything to Isabella's oldest brother and was stubborn enough to force the other man's hand. He'd see how long it took for Rick to voice his objections.

The Navarros' big, old kitchen was filled with activity. Warm air and spicy cooking aromas enveloped the bone-weary men as they trooped in from the cold. Children, ranging from approximately eight to fifteen, were bottle-feeding lambs. A makeshift pen sat between the stove and a huge refrigerator.

He and the others had stopped in an anteroom of sorts, set adjacent to the kitchen. There they all shed coats, boots, gloves and hats. On sweaty, stockinged feet, they fanned out across the highly polished linoleum floor.

Gabe searched for Isabella among the roomful of gaily chattering women and noisy children. The cold, hard knot in his stomach dissolved the minute he caught sight of her—and saw that she seemed unaffected by the lambs or the children. She stood at a center island next to her sister, Sylvia, and she seemed relaxed. The women were cutting up fragrant cantaloupe and honeydew melons. Isabella's skin was paler than normal and dark circles ringed her eyes, but to Gabe she looked more like her old self. Even her hair was done in the same intricate braid as it had been the first time he laid eyes on her. His heart gave a happy skip.

As nonchalantly as possible, he worked his way over to her. Her thick lashes lifted when his shadow fell across her cutting board. "Hi." Gabe tucked his fingers in the front pockets of his jeans. "I'm glad to see you up and about this morning." He heard Sylvia suck in a sharp breath, and wondered if no one in the family ever inquired about Isabella's well-being following one of her flashback incidents.

"I'm doing better, thanks." Her cheeks grew slightly pink, as though she was embarrassed. Her next words confirmed that she was. "I'm sorry if I created a scene last night and alarmed you."

"Not at all. My main concern was not to blunder and do anything to make it worse for you."

Both sisters stared at him without speaking for such a long time, Gabe became flustered. Eventually they went back to cutting fruit and he drifted away. He soon got caught up in meeting the Navarro grandchildren. They were all older than Isabella's children would have been, but Gabe still wondered if being around her brothers' and sisters' broods exacerbated the terrible aching loss she had to be feeling all the time.

And Manny's wife, Christina, was pregnant with their first child. How would Isabella make it through that?

Despite his concerns about Isabella, Gabe enjoyed the boisterousness of the extended Navarro clan. Once they were seated, great platters of *huevos al plato* were passed around the banquet-sized, U-shaped table. Gabe declined the salsa that everyone else generously ladled over the ham and eggs. He scarfed down too many of the piping-hot apple fritters they called *buñuelos*. And *empanadas*, a flaky pastry filled with finely chopped meat and cheese. Already full up to his ears, Gabe still found room, as did the others, to sample the array of fresh fruit. No wonder all the men in the family were so burly if they ate like this every day.

The women left their seats and began to clear plates from the table. Gabe rose and started to help.

Angel pulled him down with a glower. "It's our coffee time," he said.

Gabe sank back without comment, although his gaze tracked Isabella's progress back and forth from the table to the sink.

The coffee turned out to be hot and strong, just the way Gabe liked it. He leaned back in his chair and enjoyed it and the conversation. A small furor in another part of the kitchen drew his attention. But it was only Maria and Julie rounding up all the kids. Apparently their job was to take the younger children to school while the other women dispensed with dishes.

The men downed a huge pot of coffee and divvied up the daily chores. Or at least those working with Benito; Rick and Manuel would be heading over to their own farms.

As they scraped back their chairs and went out to reclaim their jackets and boots, Luisa handed each man a good-sized brown paper sack. "It's your lunch," Benito informed Gabe, who'd started to unroll the top to look in his bag. "Sheepherders rarely eat a hot meal midday. Ordinarily we wash our sandwiches down with water from one of our springs. Today, we'll each carry a thermos of hot mulled cider. Maria will bring them out and she'll feed the dogs before she goes home.''

Gabe guessed that meant he was continuing his training. "I figured on spending either mornings or afternoons learning what I need to know before I buy any sheep. The rest of the time I intended to make my house livable. Considering what I saw last night, I probably ought to check pens and fences, too. I have no idea how sturdy they are.''

"We'll help you check fences when you're ready to purchase your flock. As far as making the house habitable—Louis, run back and have Ruby assemble a women's brigade for however many days it takes to fix up Gabe's house. It may take a few, tell her. John Campos didn't have much heart for taking care of things after his sons left.'' Benito acted as though it was totally natural for him to be handing out orders regarding Gabe's house.

"I can't ask your wives to take time from their own homes to fix up mine.''

"You aren't asking,'' Angel pointed out.

There was little Gabe could say to counter that logic. Presumably the crew of women would sweep, dust and maybe straighten a few cupboards. He'd simply pay them for their time.

Considering this arrangement, Gabe supposed he could've hired Trini Navarro two mornings a week and Saturdays, and been done with it. The flirtatious way she'd acted last night had made Gabe suspect her motives. Perhaps it was common in this large family to do chores in order to earn money. What did he know about families, especially families of this size, since he'd never been involved with one? He could have misread her. Maybe he'd imagined there was more to her offer than she'd intended.

He doubted it...

Putting the whole matter out of his mind, Gabe fell in step with Benito. He spent the entire morning after his sleepless night trying to match orphaned lambs with ewes who'd given birth during the storm. He learned that getting sheep to do *anything* was all-consuming, backbreaking work.

Some ewes picked through the mess of babies and staked their claims. A few didn't want anything to do with the pushing, bleating throng. And Gabe lost count of the number of times he'd been kicked and kicked hard for trying to force a ewe to take responsibility for one of the lambs.

He barely noticed the hours that passed. Joe had to holler at him three times in order to let Gabe know they were breaking for lunch.

"Hurry up," Joe urged, motioning with his hand. "The faster we eat, the more time we'll have for a game of *cesta punta.* Angel called Manny and Rick. They're calling some of their neighbors. Our makeshift court's a little muddy, but that's to be expected in a barnyard."

"Okay. What's *cesta punta,* or whatever you called it?" Gabe rolled his shoulders five or six times to work out the kinks. He stopped with his shoulders still hunched, letting Joe shut the heavy barn door. Damn, but his arms felt as if they might fall off. Carrying fat ewes around did that to a man.

Joe seemed eager to explain. "*Cesta punta* is the style of *pelota* we happen to play. It's like racquetball. You could say it's a Basque national pastime."

"I've never heard of it. Maybe I'll just watch you guys."

"Chicken." Joe made clucking sounds and poked Gabe in the ribs. "I guarantee you'll like it. And you'll learn faster if you jump right in."

Gabe's mouth felt cottony, and his eyes were gritty from lack of sleep. He found it astonishing that when they joined Benito, Louis and Angel, not one of the men seemed any the worse for wear. In fact, excitement about the proposed game had obviously revved these guys up.

Manny and Rick showed up in a panel truck. Several big guys Gabe had never seen before crawled out of the back.

Angel nudged Gabe. "See the tall skinny guy? The one rolling up the sleeves on his shirt? That's Julio Baroja. You wanna be careful around him. Julio's fast on his feet."

"The morning I ate at Isabella's bakery, a woman by that last name came in. Any relation to Julio?"

"Probably. There are Barojas all over the valley. Julio's *amachu* sticks her nose in everybody's business."

"*Amachu?*"

"Sorry, that's Euskera for mother. Anyway, Gabe, you don't want to badmouth a Baroja. There's a good chance the person you're talking to is some kind of cousin."

Gabe had finished his sandwich and was watching the men, who'd strapped elongated net baskets to their hands and had begun batting balls around. They were a little larger than a tennis ball. One went wild. Angel ducked. The ball hit the side of Gabe's face. Working his jaw back and forth, he bent to pick up the errant ball and discovered it was hard rubber. "I get it," he muttered to Angel. "If Julio stomps me into the court, I can't go around town bellyaching or I might get my clock cleaned by some distant cousin."

Angel raised an eyebrow.

"Never mind," Gabe said, shaking his head. "*Clean my clock* is old-fashioned slang for kick ass."

Angel grinned. "Come on. Drink your cider and I'll show you a few moves so you won't make a complete fool of yourself."

Gabe poured his thermos cap full of cider. He took a huge swallow. The air whooshed out of his lungs, and bright, starry spots rendered him virtually blind. Talk about kick ass. The fermented drink packed a wallop.

Louis, who'd joined them, pounded Gabe between the shoulder blades. "Jeez, Angel, didn't you warn him to take it easy on Mama Navarro's cider?"

Gabe's eyes were still watering, but he'd managed to catch his breath. "Thanks," he croaked to Louis.

Angel, who looked anything but angelic, did his best to appear contrite. "Since you're such good friends with Bella and Trini, I figured they'd mention the cider recipe that's been passed down through at least five generations."

Gabe saw right through Angel's faux innocence. Dumping the remainder of the cider from his cup, he recapped the thermos, then flung back his head and laughed.

Louis and Angel were pleased by Gabe's reaction. All began guffawing.

Rick jogged up, panting a bit from his short, vigorous exchange with Julio on the court. "So, let us all in on the joke."

Still grinning, Angel admitted wanting to see how

Gabe handled a practical joke. "Mama's mulled cider isn't anything like what's in your thermos. Gabe. We switched yours to the high-octane stuff Louis made last year for the *Tamborrada*."

"That's one of our Basque festivals," Louis quickly interjected. "I won't bore you with details, but it includes bands and floats. The day ends with a potluck plus a surprise stage play a group works on secretly all year, and ripe cider. Old custom, but cool."

"You'll see next January," Angel put in.

Rick stopped with a bottle of water halfway to his lips. "Why will he?"

"Because he's our neighbor," Louis explained patiently.

"He's not Basque. Five bucks says he doesn't last a year."

Gabe eyed Rick narrowly. "There's nothing wrong with my hearing, Navarro. Perhaps you should be placing that wager with me."

"Rick, what's gotten into you?" Standing, Joe clapped his older sibling on the shoulder. "You've carried a chip around all day. Come on, warm-up's over. Let's go take the edge off in a game."

Angel, too, inserted his stocky body between Rick and Gabe.

When Rick had turned and loped back to the muddy clay court, Angel detained Gabe. "Rick's got a heart of gold. He's just worried about his orchards. His oldest kid starts college next year, and he has two coming along right after. He's counting heavily on that crop."

Gabe doubted Rick's posturing had to do with crops or tuition. He'd bet it had to do with the interest he'd shown in Isabella. But then...if he had a sister who'd been badly hurt by a man, he'd probably throw up a protective shield if some stranger came sniffing around her, too. Except that Isabella's husband hadn't stumbled in off the street. Arana was Basque—one of them.

Gabe would much rather have gone back to thinking about Isabella than get wiped in the mud by her brothers. And *pelota* turned out to be a major cardiovascular workout. Midway through the game, his lungs screamed for mercy.

"I'm getting too old for this type of punishment," he muttered, not intending for anyone to hear.

He didn't know Joe had crept up behind him.

"Hey." Joe snapped the ball to Gabe. "You're holding up okay for an old geezer. How old are you, anyway?"

"Thirty-eight." Gabe spun the ball away.

"Shoot, Rick's older than you. He's over the hill—forty," Manny taunted, obviously to needle his brother. "Gabe, you're doing great. Most newcomers don't last this long, so we'll understand if you sit out the second half."

"I play handball and racquetball," Gabe grunted. He didn't say so, but he was determined to last through to the end, if for no other reason than to show Rick Navarro he wasn't a quitter.

His pride cost him dearly, but he managed to hide his heaving chest and walk off the court without limping when the game finally wound down.

However, Gabe wasn't at all sure he'd last to the end of the day. The sheep were no more tractable after lunch. No one was happier to see the sun set and hear Benito call it a day than Gabe.

"Coming up to the *caserío* for supper?" Joe asked, slowing to walk with Gabe while the others dispersed.

"Thanks, but no." He squinted into the evening

gloom at Benito striding out ahead. "Your dad amazes me. He's worked side by side all day with young guys, and he's still walking tall."

"He's aged this past year. Took what happened to Bella really hard. He doesn't know how to help her through this ordeal. All he knows how to do is to work harder. She'd never ask for money, so for him it comes down to putting more food on the table."

"Is your sister strapped for cash?"

"The judge moved Julian's trial to Bend. She'll have to stay there or commute. Either way, her bakery suffers."

"Bend, huh? I guess the judge felt a jury out of this jurisdiction would be more impartial. For good reason, I'd think. Keep someone from lynching the bastard."

"That's what the prosecutor said. Hey, are you a lawyer? Trini heard you were."

"I have a law degree, but my expertise is in financial law. The state's prosecuting this case, right?"

"Yes, but Bella wants to learn as much as she can so there're no slipups."

"She'll wear herself out trying to second-guess the defense."

"That's the way Bella is. Sure you won't come in for supper?"

"Thanks, but no. I've got some phone calls to make. What time shall I be here in the morning?"

"We start before sunup."

Gabe threw him a backhanded wave. He hoped he could get out of bed, period, let alone before the sun came up.

He'd traveled partway down his driveway, then realized there were lights on in his house. Hadn't he shut them off after he'd changed into jeans? Maybe not.

He'd been kind of rattled, and worried sick about Isabella.

Not wanting to muddy the hardwood floors, Gabe removed his boots. He'd no sooner set foot inside the house than he heard feminine voices coming from the kitchen. He'd totally forgotten that Benito had arranged to have Ruby organize a cleaning party until he walked into the kitchen and saw her and Isabella scrubbing his stove. He noticed the improvement immediately. Where there'd been a pervasive odor of stale onions and garlic, he now smelled a fresh, apple-cinnamon scent. "What a difference you ladies have made to this place in only one day."

Isabella dropped her sponge. "Gabe! We didn't hear you come in. Is something wrong? Why are you home already?"

"We've finished for the day. It's getting dark."

"So late?" Ruby exclaimed. "Goodness, Mama will wonder why I haven't come to help with supper. I thought she'd send Teresa to fetch us." She stripped off her rubber gloves and dropped them in a basket before dashing out the back door.

"How long have you been here?" Gabe casually inspected the changes.

"Ruby and Sylvia cleaned the living and dining rooms this morning. Then Sylvia had a meeting at church. I closed the bakery at four and came straight over here. The two of them had already started on the kitchen."

"Well, you've worked miracles. How much do I owe you for your time and for cleaning materials?" Gabe reached for his wallet.

"We can't charge you," Sylvia and Isabella protested in unison. "If John had been quicker to pack, we'd have had this done before you got back from Utah," Sylvia added.

"I don't feel right about letting you work without pay."

"You pitched in at our place last night. Neighbors help neighbors." Sylvia headed for the back door as if the issue had been settled. "Let those drip pans soak overnight, Bella. Ruby and I can finish in the morning. Oh, maybe you'd leave us a note as to what needs done in the bedrooms, Gabe. Tag any furniture you don't want. The church thrift shop will send over a crew to pick it up."

Isabella read the indecisiveness on Gabe's face. "Syl, I'm going to stick around and tidy up what we started. Tell Mama I'll be along in a bit. But don't let her hold up supper. I'm really not hungry."

"When are you?" Sylvia eyed her sister with a perplexed expression. "Are you sure, Bella?" She hovered near the door, finally asking outright, although in a low voice, "Aren't you worried what people like Dolores Santiago or Nona Baroja will say if they learn you spent time alone with Gabe?"

Isabella rolled her eyes. "Honestly, Sylvia. Those two and Aunt Carmen need to get a life."

"It's you I'm worried about, *caro*."

"I'll be fine. After all, my whole family is within shouting distance," she said wryly.

Still frowning unhappily, Sylvia went out, but she left the door ajar.

For several seconds after Gabe had shut it, the only noise in the kitchen was Isabella's scrubbing, which vied with the loudly ticking wall clock.

"I'd hate to cause you problems in the community.

That's the big reason I refused Trini's offer to keep house for me.''

"And the small reason is?''

Gabe propped a hip against the counter next to the stove. "Tell me why you sent Sylvia home.''

Markedly flustered, Isabella swung around and plunged her hands in the soapy water again. "Call me compulsive. I don't like leaving chores half-done.''

"Fair enough. I could be wrong about Trini having an ulterior motive for her offer. If I've misjudged her, I'm sorry.''

Isabella's spine stiffened, then slowly relaxed. "I should take exception just because she's my sister. But Trini's young, and flirtatious. The rest of us believe it's because Papa let her spend a year in California with his cousins.''

"And?''

She turned to gaze at him curiously. "And nothing.''

"And her older siblings envy her? Or is it just you?''

"No!'' With jerky motions, Isabella scooped out the drip pans. She dried all four and popped them beneath the burners. "Trini told me, ah…how you handled the lamb last night,'' she blurted. "Thank you.''

"You're welcome.'' Gabe watched her peel off her gloves. He knew if he didn't think of something to stop her, she'd run away in a minute or two. "Stay and join me for a cup of coffee, will you? I noticed someone cleaned the coffee-maker. That day I was at your bakery, I drove on over to Burns.'' He smiled as charmingly as he could. "All I bought was a coffee grinder and a variety pack of beans.'' He fell silent, well aware that—as a caterer—her indecision warred with her curiosity to learn what kinds of beans he'd bought.

Curiosity won, as Gabe had hoped.

"If you have Amaretto, I can't possibly bring myself to turn down your invitation."

"What do you know? You're in luck. If you'll give me a minute, I have to get the package. It's still in my SUV."

Isabella caught him as he limped toward the door. "Gabe, wait. Forgive me for not realizing how badly you must want to shower. I should take off and let you get at it."

"I'll do a quick once-over with a washcloth, if you'll dig out the coffee and grinder."

There was a wistfulness to his words which Isabella found compelling. "Okay, give me your key. I'll even brew the coffee…. That ought to allow you time to shower."

"Okay—thanks. I won't be long."

"You're not used to physical labor, are you?" Seeing how fast Gabe glanced away, Isabella sighed. "You'd drop in your tracks before you'd admit it. Am I right?"

"On the walk home tonight, I got to thinking how great a hot tub would feel about now. Tomorrow I'll see about ordering one. Can't you picture it in the breezeway between the house and the garage?"

"A hot tub? I've only ever seen them in home decorating magazines. Buy one of those, and you'll have to post no-trespassing signs."

"Why? Oh, you mean the neighbors will sneak over and use it?"

"More like they'll figure a way to add a chute and fill it with sheep-dip."

Gabe tipped back his head and broke into laughter. The image her words brought to mind suddenly struck him as hilarious.

Isabella snatched the keys from his hand and rushed out to find the coffee and grinder. When she returned, she heard the shower. As the coffee perked, she compiled a list of what he needed to fill his cupboards. She decided he lacked just about everything. Dragging out a wastebasket, Isabella began pitching opened boxes and cartons right and left.

Gabe walked back in to see her standing on a kitchen chair, stretched up on tiptoe, her entire upper body leaning sideways as she reached inside one of his cabinets. Some three inches of pale skin showed in the gap between her sweater and slacks. It was a fine view. He all but swallowed his tongue and must've made some noise—enough to startle her. She yelped and lost her footing, and knocked her head on the frame. Her arms flailed as she started to go over backward.

Despite the protests of every bone in his body, Gabe dashed across the kitchen in record time. He caught Isabella as she tumbled. Even then, her foot knocked over the chair. It smacked down hard on Gabe's bare foot, striking him across the big toe and rendering his whole foot numb.

Isabella struggled to be set free. "Put me down! Let me go this instant."

He set her on the kitchen counter. "Goddamn," he exclaimed, hopping around on one foot as he tried to inspect his bruised toe.

A trill of laughter brought Gabe's attention back to the woman he'd unceremoniously dumped. A woman he'd thought couldn't laugh. All Gabe managed in the throes of pain was to gape at her classically beautiful face, made more beautiful by genuine mirth. So what that it came at his expense?

"We'd pass for walk-ons in a 'Three Stooges' skit,"

she said. "I hope you didn't hit the counter? Trini broke her toe once kicking Manny. She missed him and struck the wall instead. You wouldn't believe how long she limped around." Isabella's smile began to fade, replaced by concern. Jumping off the counter, she knelt to inspect Gabe's foot.

"It's okay. I'm okay." He stumbled back two steps, fighting the effect of her warm breath.

"Oh, that's good." She rose, rubbing nervously along her arms. "But...your toe's going to be badly bruised."

"It's nothing."

"I'm sorry I was hysterical, yelling at you like that. When Julian got angry with me, he liked to catch me off guard, grab me from behind and shake me until my teeth rattled." She turned away—but not before Gabe saw that the life had been snuffed from her eyes again.

"Julian's a sick bastard. I'd never raise a hand toward you or any woman, Isabella," he said softly. "Ever."

She looked at him and nodded, yet her teeth worried her bottom lip.

"Hey, let's test that coffee. I figure we've got about ten minutes before someone from your family shows up to escort you home."

"They wouldn't dare. I may be living at home again, but they respect that I'm a grown woman."

"Okay. Then have a seat. I'll do the honors and pour." Gabe picked up the pot, Then he whirled back, wearing a sheepish expression. "Uh...do I have cups?"

Isabella pointed to a cabinet directly behind him. She could have gone and retrieved them for him. Except...she recalled how it'd felt to have the hands now holding the coffeepot wrapped around her waist. Her mother said Gabe had held her and rocked her last night during her flashback, too. Luckily the episode was shorter than normal. Did that indicate her subconscious was forgetting Julian's horrible deed? She couldn't let that happen. Not until he was imprisoned for the rest of his natural life.

Feeling guilty, she remembered the true reason she'd stayed behind after Sylvia left. Isabella had some legal questions she hoped Gabe would answer. She needed his professional advice; she couldn't allow herself to become too aware of him as a man.

Gabe noticed a pensive expression on her face as he handed her a cup, then took his seat across from her. "Is the coffee that bad?"

"No. It's tasty." Isabella wished the Amaretto was more than flavoring so it would anesthetize her jumpy stomach. "I heard you're a lawyer. Is that true?"

"I'm a CPA, but I have a law degree, as I told Joe earlier."

"Do you have access to a law library?"

"No, but I did a bit of work with Summer Quinn's attorney in Callanton. Larkin Crosley has an extensive library. I imagine he'd make it available to me. Is there something in particular you need?"

Isabella opened her mouth to ask if Gabe would help her track cases similar to hers, but someone pounded heavily on the kitchen door.

Gabe yelled, "It's unlocked."

Isabella was the only one who was shocked to see Rick Navarro's scowling face thrust through a narrow crack in the door. "Papa sent me to walk you home, Bella."

"Are you psychic?" she mouthed to Gabe. "We just

sat down to have coffee, Rick. Thank Papa for his concern, but I'll stay to finish my cup.''

Rick flung open the door and stepped inside.

Gabe half expected the burly man to sling his sister over his shoulder and march off with her. He didn't. Rick pulled out one of the chairs and wedged himself between Isabella and Gabe. ''The coffee smells good. Think I'll join you in a cup. That way you won't have to walk home alone, Bella.''

Hiding a smile, Gabe rose to fill another cup. The ball was back in Isabella's court. Gabe didn't envy her; he'd observed Rick's calculated moves in *pelota* today. The man wouldn't be out-maneuvered easily.

And Isabella didn't try. She appeared completely impassive.

It wasn't until he and Rick were both yawning over their coffee that Gabe realized Isabella was sipping hers so slowly she'd actually orchestrated the final move to suit herself in dragging out her visit.

Rick knew it, too. Gabe was careful to not crack a smile until after he'd finally seen them out and made his way to the bedroom. If all families were such a pain in the ass, maybe he hadn't missed anything by growing up without one.

The hell of it was, he *had* missed out. And for so many years he'd carried around a load of hatred for Russ Poston. He thought he'd let go of the anger, but in spending these several days with the Navarros, he was again reminded of everything Russ had stolen from him.

Aching and bleary-eyed, he stood gazing discontentedly at a room that was impossible to sleep in. Given his lack of even a couch, he elected to go back to the Inn until he was able to make this place livable.

CHAPTER EIGHT

ISABELLA RAN OUT of the house to nab Gabe the next morning. Out of breath from her dash down the steps and across the yard, she thrust a lunch sack and bottle of water into his hands without any greeting.

"Good morning to you, too," he teased, recognizing the sack as similar to yesterday's lunchtime offering.

She rubbed at the goose bumps peppering her arms. "You probably think I should've stood up to my brother last night."

"I think Rick got your point." Gabe slipped off his jacket and draped it around her shoulders. "I'm on my way to the house. You shouldn't have run out without a coat."

Pulling the jacket warmed by his body heat around her, Isabella averted her eyes. "I wanted to follow up on something we started to discuss last night. And I'd rather the others didn't overhear. Barely knowing you and all, I hate to impose—but I'll trade cleaning your house for a chance to spend time in a law library with you, reading up on cases similar to mine. I'd ask Summer to introduce me to her lawyer, only she's got her hands full between the ranch and morning sickness."

"Morning sickness? Summer and Coltrane are going to have a baby?"

Isabella clapped a hand over her mouth. "Your friend didn't tell you? My gosh, maybe no one's supposed to know. She's playing it low-key, but I can tell she's walking on air. Anyway, that's why I'd rather not bother her at the moment.''

"What will you gain from plowing through old cases?"

"I'm only interested in cases the state won. Reading the transcripts, I may come across necessary information this prosecutor hasn't asked me to provide.''

"You don't think he's competent?"

"He's swamped.'' She linked her hands tight as they walked slowly toward her parents' house. "Trini says he doesn't care about my case. I wouldn't go that far, but any way I can help him is better for me.''

Gabe considered her request. Could reading cases help? Or would they cause her flashbacks? That was definitely a concern. However, he wasn't stupid enough to let an opportunity to spend more time with her get away from him. "Tell you what. I won't have you killing yourself adding house-cleaning to your job. If Larkin Crosley okays our doing research at his office, I'll help you in exchange for you advising me on the furniture I need to buy. I've decided to continue leasing my condo to skiers, so I can't take any of my furniture.'' He grinned. "Is it a deal?''

"Deal.'' She had reached the first step leading up to the house, turned and poked her hand out through Gabe's jacket. When their hands met, Isabella experienced an odd thrill. She pulled back fast, not wanting to believe it might be more than excitement over finally getting to study other cases like her own. She even shrugged off his jacket and hurriedly returned it to him.

"I told your dad I'd need my afternoons free to take care of loose ends involved with the move. I'll try to connect with Larkin sometime today. How about meeting me in Callanton at the Green Willow around six? We'll grab a bite to eat and work out a schedule I can take back for his approval.''

Isabella's mind ground to a halt at the part about meeting him for dinner. ''Why dinner?'' she blurted. ''Can't you swing past the bakery with his answer?''

Gabe recognized the panic behind her reluctance to eat with him. ''Eating's part of the deal, Isabella. I can't run on empty the way you apparently do.''

''Oh. Is that why you're following me into the house? For breakfast?''

''I'm meeting the guys here.''

''They've been out with the sheep for an hour. Mama and Trini are the only ones still inside.''

''Holy cow! I thought I got here early.'' Gabe immediately clattered back down the stairs.

''Don't let Joe and Angel call you a slacker. And don't tell them I kept you up last night. They probably got to sleep at least an hour before you did. I hope you zonked out the minute Rick and I left.''

''Are you kidding? I couldn't find the bed for all the junk John Campos left stacked around. I ended up staying at the Inn last night.''

''Gabe, you didn't! We have extra beds. Why on earth didn't you say something?''

''To be honest, I thought it was a matter of shoving a few boxes aside. Frankly, all the mattresses in that house are disgusting. Hauling them to the dump is another item on my day's agenda.''

''I should've guessed, based on the condition of the rest of the house. Ruby, Sylvia and I thought we shouldn't poke around your bedrooms without your okay. I'm doubly sorry now for keeping you up—all because I was annoyed with Rick. We can put off contacting Mr. Crosley for a few days.''

Gabe heard her disappointment. ''It only takes a minute to make a phone call, or drop in and see if he's amenable. But I repeat—skipping dinner is not an option.''

''Six o'clock, you said?''

''Yes, at the Green Willow.'' Clutching the lunch sack between his teeth, Gabe waved her inside while he shrugged into his jacket. He didn't give her time to reconsider and refuse, but literally ran out to the sheep pens.

Isabella turned away, commanding the flutters in her stomach to cease and desist. She reached for the doorknob, but the door flew open, almost knocking her off the top step.

Trini craned her neck, trying to see around her sister. ''Did I hear you talking to Gabe? Why didn't you invite him in for coffee? And what are you doing outside without a coat? Mama said that according to the thermometer by the kitchen window, it's barely twenty degrees this morning.''

Isabella brushed by her. ''Mama and I were upstairs making beds. She saw Gabe coming across the road and asked me to run out and give him his lunch. So I did. And you're right. It's chilly. Come in and close the door.''

''What did he say? Did he ask about me? I mean, did he ask why I hadn't helped Ruby and Sylvia clean his house?''

''Why would he?''

''Because I asked Ruby to recommend me for the job. Gabe said he's going to hire someone to clean a couple of days a week. Since Papa cut back on my spending money, I need to find a way to earn some more.''

''I offered you extra hours at the bakery.''

''You didn't tell Gabe that, did you? If you did, you probably ruined my chances,'' Trini wailed. ''Darn it, Bella! He's the best-looking guy to show up around here in I don't know how long. Everyone except you is drooling over him. After my advanced accounting class, a group of us stopped for a beer at White's. Megan Ward bragged to everyone that Gabe likes her. She got positively snotty when I said he'd moved in across the road from us and is apprenticing under Papa. If I cleaned his house, I'd have the inside track. And Megan would be livid.''

Isabella knew Megan Ward by sight only. She was nearer Trini's age. Megan was, however, a waitress at the Green Willow Café. And Isabella had already agreed to meet Gabe there at six tonight.

''Well, aren't you going to say anything, Bella?'' Trini followed her into the kitchen. ''You have that look. You did screw it up for me, didn't you?''

Luisa Navarro turned from where she was slicing cabbage at the sink. ''Goodness, what are you girls fighting about? Bella, did you catch Gabe and give him his lunch?''

''Yes, Mama. Will you tell Sylvia and Ruby they'll have to finish his house without me? I'll be, uh…working late tonight. Oh, and tell them Gabe mentioned he'll be replacing all the mattresses. So there's no need for them to waste time airing out the ones John left.''

Trini inserted herself in front of her older sister. ''You went to Gabe's with Ruby and Syl?'' Her jaw dropped. ''You're awfully well informed about our neighbor's future plans for someone who merely took him his lunch.''

"Oh, good grief! Ruby had errands to run. And I went over because things were dead at the bakery, so I closed early.''

"Things were dead yesterday, yet you're working late tonight?'' Trini crossed her arms and tapped her toe in irritation.

Isabella was tired of this sparring. She deliberately skirted Trini. Over her shoulder, she flung out casually, "I'm meeting Gabe in town tonight.''

"Ma...ma, I want a chance with Gabe and Bella—''

Luisa's head whipped from one daughter to the other. "For heaven's sake, Trini, you're acting like a girl in junior high school.'' Gentling her voice, she interrupted Isabella's exit. "Bella, I sense this man has developed some kind of an interest in you. It's not like you to lead anyone on. Nor is it your nature to deliberately hurt your sister. Ricardo is quite sure you're playing with fire. Should I be worried?''

Isabella gripped the stair railing. She still had her back to Trini and her mother, since she'd started upstairs to her room. She wanted to deny that there was any type of personal relationship between her and Gabe Poston. She tried, but couldn't squeeze the words past a stricture in her throat. "No, Mama, you shouldn't worry.''

Once she'd forced out those words, Isabella found it easier to face her mother and sister. "I don't know if Trini told you, but Gabe's an attorney. I haven't made any secret of the fact that I'd like to get my hands on transcripts from cases like Julian's. Gabe has access to a law library. He's going to see if he can get me in to read old transcripts.''

''Well, why didn't you say so?'' Trini said, walking to the foot of the stairs. ''Don't I feel foolish now? But you made it sound so...so clandestine.''

''Did I? Or is that your immaturity showing, Trini? I said before and I'll say it again. Gabe is too old for you.''

''Christina's six years younger than Manny. Plus, she's three years younger than me. No one jumped all over *him* when he asked Christina to marry him.''

Luisa calmly went back to chopping her cabbage. ''I rarely take the side of one of my children over another,'' she said in Euskera. ''But Bella's absolutely correct this time, Trinidad Lucinda. There's at least twice the difference between you and Gabe as there is between Manuel and Christina.''

''Twice?'' Trini yelped. ''No way. That would make him almost as old as Ricardo.''

Luisa and Isabella both paused, each of them slowly arching an eyebrow.

''Get outta here,'' Trini scoffed. ''Before I go to class today, I'm walking right out to the sheep pens and I'm going to ask how old he is.''

Doubting her sister had the nerve, Isabella ran lightly upstairs, where she gathered her jacket and purse before heading off to the bakery. As she passed the bathroom, she took a last peek at her pale face in the mirror. Grimacing at the strained image that appeared before her, she pledged to take steps to get closer to her old self.

What that entailed she wasn't quite sure. Step one

was probably to eat more. So it was just as well that Gabe had badgered her into meeting him for a meal.

THAT AFTERNOON, Trini breezed into the bakery half an hour late. Isabella didn't even realize she was late until she happened to glance up at the clock. So much for her vow to eat more regularly. She'd just worked through lunch again.

Tossing her backpack on a chair in the corner of the kitchen, Trini swiped a finger around the cake bowl Isabella was trying to pour from.

"Stop that." Isabella smacked her sister's fingers with the flat side of a rubber scraper. "Did you even wash after you handled all those textbooks?"

"Nag, nag, nag. You aren't my *amachu,*" she said.

Isabella's eyes lost all trace of light. She'd relished her role as mother to Antonia and Ramon. And she'd been good at it.

Trini knew at once she'd committed a grievous error. "God, Bella. I didn't mean to remind you." She snatched the heavy crockery bowl out of her sister's shaking hands, and finished pouring the cake batter into the four tins. "I'm miffed because you and Mama were right this morning and I was wrong."

"Wh-a-at?" Isabella shook away lingering thoughts of her children.

"About Gabe Poston being too old for me. You and Mama came closer to the mark than I did. He's thirty-eight. Thirteen years older than me. Ugh."

"You actually went out and asked him his age? Trini, for heaven's sake! That's rude."

"Relax. He and Papa had gone out to test the various pastures for sweet grass. Joe's the one who told me. He said he asked Gabe the same thing. So why is it rude for me but not for Joe?"

"It's equally rude of Joe. Surely you aspire to better manners than our brothers."

"You're right. They can be gross. They'd lick this bowl clean." Trini grinned as Isabella grabbed the bowl out of her hand and stuck it under a stream of water.

"Kidding aside," Trini said, watching Isabella check the heat in the oven before she popped in the four tins. "The guy's five years older than you, Bella. I don't understand how he can still look so hot."

The oven door slipped out of Isabella's hand and slammed, making both women wince. "I guess that reveals your opinion of me."

"I can't even open my mouth but I stick my foot in it," Trini complained. She threw up her hands, then spontaneously hugged her sister. "You had good reason to age in the last ten months. Get Julian's trial behind you, and then we'll worry about finding you new makeup and stuff."

Isabella patted Trini awkwardly. It was still far from a compliment, and yet she knew the statement carried more than a grain of truth. In the months since she'd innocently walked in on a worse tragedy than she could ever have comprehended, she hadn't given a damn about her appearance. Until now. Today, Trini's careless remarks grated on her like nails screeching across a chalkboard.

Isabella tried not to think about her business meeting with Gabe Poston as anything other than that. Business. How she looked was irrelevant, she told herself staunchly.

Fortunately, she was quickly distracted from any thoughts of Gabe when Trini changed the subject with lightning speed.

"Elena Sancho's papa bought her a new car," she

said. "A blue Camaro with wire rims. Can you believe she's mad because it's not a convertible? Oh, and Orella Valdez broke up with Fernando. Again! For good, she says, like we don't all know there isn't anyone else who'd put up with all the crap she throws at him."

Customers came in and Trini went out to help them. Ten minutes later, she returned and picked up where she'd left off. "Fernando always cries on my shoulder. I don't know why, when I never sympathize. We all know he's too good for Orella. Guess what? I saw Ramona hanging with a really cute guy this week." Their cousin Ramona was a year younger than Trini. "No way is he Basque. If Aunt Carmen gets wind of it, she'll shit a brick."

"Trini!"

"Well, she will and you know it. Aunt Carmen is such a cultural snob."

Isabella closed her eyes momentarily, feeling the niggle of a beginning headache. "The sun's out again. Why don't you make today's bank deposit, and then deliver Soledad Capel's cake? Whatever you do, while you're at the Capels', don't mention seeing Ramona with that guy."

Trini smirked. "Bella, Bella. Always the family peacemaker. Okay, I'll be good. But I must admit it's tempting. That day Gabe rode with you to the cemetery, Aunt Carmen was on the phone to Mama before we even knew who he was. She's such a busybody. Papa's always so fair about things. It's hard to believe they had the same parents."

"Aunt Carmen's not alone in her thinking. And we don't really know how fair Papa would be if one of his children decided to marry a non-Basque. So far, his beliefs have never been put to the test."

"Hmm. Do you suppose he'd spring for a trip to

Bilbao or San Sebastian for me? We haven't seen a new Basque family here in five years. I'll never marry anyone from our village."

"You could become a nun," Isabella said with a remarkably straight face.

"Yeah, right. Just for that, I'm going straight home when I finish deliveries. I'll see you at supper. And I'll never speak to you again if you so much as hint that horrible idea to Papa."

"I'm not coming home for supper," Isabella called as Trini slammed into the office to tally the day's receipts. "Remind Mama that I'm staying in town to meet Gabe."

"Hmm. There's a thought. Maybe you'll be the first to marry outside the clan."

Isabella threw a pot holder at her sister. "I said it's not *that* kind of meeting."

"Really, Bella? Be honest. Don't you ever want to get married again? I can't believe you want to spend the rest of your life alone."

She was right; it was a prospect that didn't hold any appeal for Isabella. Neither did the possibility of repeating a marriage like the one she'd suffered through with Julian. "Huh, with six brothers and sisters and all their families showing up at the house on a daily basis, you and I have a different concept of living alone."

"You know what I mean. What about sex? Can you live a celibate life forever?"

Isabella took several minutes to answer. And when she finally did, her words were stiff, unemotional. "I can barely remember back to a time when Julian didn't use sex as a method of punishment. Only the first year of our marriage was anywhere near normal. But then we had the children. They were my only bright spot."

Trini looked stricken. "Bella! None of us even suspected."

"I've never told anyone that. Promise me you'll keep it to yourself."

"I won't breathe a word." Subdued, Trini bent to the task of logging in receipts, and Isabella withdrew to the kitchen where she pulled the cakes out of the oven and set them to cool.

A short time later, she heard the back door open and close, and the delivery van start up. She almost wished she hadn't sent Trini off for the remainder of the afternoon. Not after her sister had stoked fires better left to die along with her failed marriage.

Isabella smoothed the creamy frosting between the cooled cake layers. It was a simple task that allowed her mind to drift. To the act of sex. To memories of the few times her body had reacted in a warm and positive way. To thoughts of Gabe Poston's gentle hands, which were at odds with his wicked smile.

Right in the middle of her lonely kitchen, Isabella's body grew warm. She was struck by yearnings of what might have been. Yearnings for a man other than the one with whom she'd spoken vows.

The spatula slipped from her weak fingers, fell and spattered pale-yellow frosting across the tile floor.

The familiar motions of cleaning it up and finding a clean spatula diverted her attention. Thankfully, she'd no sooner finished decorating the cake that had been commissioned for a local rancher's upcoming birthday than the bell over her front door jingled. A mother and daughter Isabella didn't recognize wanted to discuss catering a wedding scheduled for early fall.

"September tenth, you said?" Isabella flipped the pages in her weekly planner. "The day looks clear. Are you planning a church reception, or one in your home?''

''I haven't decided,'' announced the eager, fresh-faced girl. ''Could I hold the date with a deposit for now?''

''Certainly. Depending on the size of your party, you've allowed plenty of time to fine-tune decorations, choose a menu and decide on all the trimmings that'll make your day special.'' Isabella mentioned a nominal deposit fee. ''Just fill out this form with your name and address. The reception will be held locally, won't it?'' She noticed a Portland address on the woman's check.

''My fiancé's found a house on the outskirts of Callanton. He's determined to buy it. Mother and I drove up to give it our okay. It's beautiful. Fully furnished. I can't believe the owner walked away and left it. Actually, the real estate agent didn't give us much information.''

Isabella felt an iciness steal over her.

''He seemed so reluctant I wondered if he had authorization to sell it,'' the mother was saying. ''I inquired at the bank, and the manager said the property *is* for sale. Cindy, give her the address.''

Cindy wrote it with a flourish, but Isabella didn't need the girl to finish. The chill that enveloped her had served as premonition.

Closing her book, Isabella tried not to show the revulsion she felt. *Her house.* This nice young woman was planning a celebration in the house beset by tragedy.

''I'm afraid I can't handle your reception, after all,'' Isabella said, hearing the words leave her lips as she handed back the mother's check.

"No?" Cindy looked bewildered. "I thought you said that day was okay?"

Even as she fought to stave off the darkness threatening to close in on her, Isabella tried to stay calm. Maybe Cindy could be happy there. And Lord knew, the money from the house sale would make it easier to take time off for the trial. Of course, Julian's half of the proceeds would buy him more people to work on his defense....

She had to make up something believable and get these people out of her shop. She grabbed at the first thought that came to mind. "I...I...may be planning my own wedding in September." The lie seemed to roll off her tongue. "In fact, I'm meeting my boyfriend later today. I'm fairly sure he's going to give me a ring. All my life I've dreamed of a fall wedding." Isabella reached for a card file and avoided making eye contact with the pair while she shuffled through the cards. "Here are the names of two other caterers in the area. Either one will do a fine job. I...ah...hate to rush you, but I've got pastry due out of the oven."

They acted more than a little shocked at being hustled out. Isabella hurried across the room the minute the door closed, and turned the dead bolt. Her hands and knees shook. She managed to make it all the way to the kitchen before she sank down on the floor, huddled in misery.

She rocked back and forth, wishing for cleansing tears. As usual, her eyes remained parched and dry.

Trini had taken the van, but she'd left the keys to the family car. With no purpose or destination in mind, Isabella left the bakery and drove aimlessly. Somehow it didn't surprise her when she pulled into the empty parking lot of St. Bonaventure church.

Confession was good for the soul. She felt guilty over hiding the truth from Cindy, felt she'd been unfair to this friendly, pleasant girl.

It was dark and comforting inside the church. And claustrophobic inside the confessional. Isabella almost fled at that point; then she heard one of the priests slide open the opposite door. "Father, forgive me for I have sinned—in word if not in deed," she began, hands clasped so tight in her lap she felt the pain. *Good. She needed to feel something.* Speaking of feeling… While she was here, she ought to confess the feelings she'd had for Gabe Poston, too.

NOT WANTING TO BE LATE for his meeting with Isabella, Gabe rushed into the Green Willow Café at five minutes before the hour. A quick perusal of the seated customers told him he'd beaten her to the restaurant.

Megan Ward saw him standing next to the sign asking that patrons wait to be seated. She patted her blond hair into place and greeted him with a wide smile. "Gabe. I couldn't believe my ears the other night when Trini Navarro said you'd bought a ranch in the area. I guess it's true."

"It is," Gabe acknowledged, purposely not elaborating.

"Well, that's nice." Her smile turned up a few watts. "Are you eating at the counter? Or if you'd like company, I'll seat you in a booth and join you in…oh, ten minutes. I'm due for a break then."

"I would like a booth. I'm meeting a woman," he added quickly so Megan wouldn't get the wrong impression. "She should be along shortly."

"Who?" Megan demanded as if it was her right to know.

"I'll sit facing the door so I can see her when she comes in," Gabe said. "But if I could trouble you for coffee now? Otherwise, I'll wait to order."

"Uh…sure." Megan sped off in front of him, apparently getting the message.

Gabe downed the first cup of coffee in short order. He'd worked hard to grab a shower after leaving Benito's, and still accomplish all his errands before seeing Isabella.

The old lawyer, Larkin Crosley, had talked his ear off. He'd twisted Gabe's arm every way from Sunday, trying to sell him his law practice. Larkin said a town the size of Callanton needed a CPA and an all-purpose lawyer. He further noted that it wouldn't take much for Gabe to broaden his scope into corporate and civil law.

Recalling the bruises he'd discovered on his arms and legs while showering—the result, Gabe assumed, of wrestling sheep—made Larkin's offer worth considering. He poured himself a second cup of coffee, musing about sheep men. Were they born that way, as John Campos had implied? Was it work that you grasped instinctively, rather than a skill to be learned?

Gabe checked his watch and the door for the umpteenth time. Isabella was late. Fifteen minutes late. She didn't strike him as the type to keep a man waiting on purpose. Unless she intended to stand him up altogether…

Megan, who'd had her eye on him and likewise on the entrance to the café, approached his booth with a saucy switch to her backside.

"If your date was due here at six, you guys must've got your wires crossed. You've had a chance to look at the menu, so if you'll tell me what you'd like, I'll give your order to the cook before I take my break."

Gabe considered admitting this evening was business rather than a real date. He knew Isabella would prefer he not give the wrong impression. On the other hand, Megan wasn't anyone he wanted to encourage. "My…friend could've gotten tied up at work. Bring me a bottle of merlot and two glasses, please." He named a specific winery. "That'll give us a chance to unwind. We'll order when you return. Or…is that Helen coming to relieve you? She can handle our table if my date's too hungry to wait."

Megan flounced off and returned to plunk down a bottle of red wine and two glasses.

Gabe read the label. "Hey—this isn't what I ordered." Holding his temper, he handed the bottle back to Megan, who'd brought a wine Gabe thought tasted like kerosene. He accepted the new bottle with equanimity.

He'd about given up on Isabella when the door slid silently open and she slipped in. She was balanced on the balls of her feet, as though she could turn and leave at any moment. He'd seen her wan and nervous before. But never this bad.

Jumping up, Gabe moved to take her arm. "Hello, there. I hope you like red wine. I took the liberty of ordering that and coffee. Helen," he called to the older waitress working the counter. "Do you mind bringing us a warm-up?"

The waitress met them at his booth. "Isabella," she exclaimed. "This is a rare treat. Well, I don't blame you for letting this handsome devil bring you out of hiding. Say, I hear from Summer that your catering business has really taken off."

Clearing her throat, Isabella mumbled something that passed for agreement.

Gabe wanted to put her at ease. Helen and Megan were both outgoing, jovial women. Either one of them could overwhelm Isabella without trying. "We'll talk a while and enjoy our wine and be ready to order in fifteen minutes or so."

Helen knew when to leave her customers alone. She nodded and withdrew.

"Busy day?" Gabe inquired, after pouring them each a half glass of wine.

Isabella spun her glass around and around. "Trying, certainly."

Nothing followed that response. Gabe felt himself growing edgy. "I have good news for you."

"You do?"

"Larkin Crosley has agreed to let us use his library any evening we want." Gabe patted his pocket. "He gave me a key."

"Fine. Very good. Shall we set a time? How about tomorrow at six?" Pushing the wine aside, she collected the purse she'd dropped on the seat beside her.

"That's it? You're going?"

She opened her mouth to say something, but one of two women who bustled past the booth, being led by Helen, suddenly stopped. The younger of the two, a freckled redhead, squeezed Isabella's arm. "It *is* you," she said, bending to study Isabella's left hand. "Darn. He hasn't given you the ring yet?" Just as quickly, the young woman dropped Isabella's hand and turned flashing green eyes on Gabe. "You don't *look* bashful," she announced. Then, because the woman she was with called, "Cindy, come sit down," the girl wafted a sparkling diamond under Gabe's nose and sashayed on past. Or she did after whispering something to Isabella that Gabe didn't catch.

He wasn't at all sure what had happened, but Isabella had turned white and red, then white again.

"What was all that about?" he murmured.

"Nothing. Er…she must have me confused with someone else. Look, Gabe, this has really been a horrible day for me. And I wouldn't be good company." She slid out of the booth.

Confused, Gabe rose, too. He shelled out what he hoped would cover the coffee and wine and enough for a tip, then ran after his rapidly departing date.

Helping her silently into her car, he saw by a clock tower down the street that it was going on seven. "I didn't eat, and neither did you. I did pick up brochures on living- and dining-room furniture. We made a bargain, remember? I'd arrange for access to the law library, and you'd advise me on furniture. Meet me at my house in half an hour, okay? I'll pick up a pizza on my way out of town."

Isabella thought about the lengthy lecture she'd received from Father Espinosa about the dangers of lustful thoughts. She also recalled the twist of joy her stomach had given when Gabe came forward to greet her at the restaurant. Still, she intended to decline his invitation.

"All right. I'll be there," she said, shocking herself.

Gabe didn't rush right over to his own SUV but stood gaping after Isabella's retreating car. Damn, the woman tied him in knots. Maybe he should forget about raising sheep and furthering a relationship with Isabella Navarro. *Maybe.* But he hadn't done anything reckless in many long years. It was about time he shook up his life.

CHAPTER NINE

WHEN GABE REACHED the only pizza parlor in town, he realized he'd forgotten to ask Isabella's preference in toppings. As he didn't want to leave her with too much time to change her mind, he ordered medium pizzas in three varieties. Plain cheese, sausage and mushroom, and one all-veggie. So what if he had a ton left over? He'd been known to eat cold pizza for breakfast.

The aroma tantalized him throughout the drive home.

He halfway didn't expect Isabella to be at his house. His fear seemed warranted when he saw her car—or rather her sister's car—parked alongside the catering van in the Navarro driveway. Gabe got out of the SUV, feeling downright discouraged.

"Boy, something smells delicious." Isabella emerged from the shadows that ringed Gabe's porch.

A stab of pure pleasure made him fumble the boxes. "And I've been thinking I'd have to bribe you to eat once I got here."

"I wasn't hungry until you opened your car door and the smell of the pizza hit me. By the way, I stopped for soda and beer. I was pretty sure your fridge was still empty. And I brought a spare microwave from my bakery. Use it until you get settled."

He'd finally managed to collect the stacked pizza

cartons and close the door with his hip—still bruised from where several rams had butted him. "Ow, dang!"

"What'd you do?" She moved into the moonlight. "Gosh, are you planning a party? Tell me you didn't buy all that for the two of us."

"I brought several choices because I never thought to ask what toppings you liked. Don't worry, it'll keep. Any guy who spent time in the military considers pizza a staple."

"The military? Oh, now it makes sense why Summer's husband has such an odd assortment of friends." Isabella opened the front door and stepped aside to let Gabe pass. In this neck of the woods, people didn't lock their doors.

Gabe flipped on lights as he walked through the house. "Odd? That's not very flattering."

"I didn't mean funny-odd. Eclectic, maybe. I could see a horse-trainer and a vet being pals. But Trini, Sylvia and I couldn't figure out Colt's close association with a lawyer and a car salesman. I mean, you guys seem as close as my brothers are."

"I'm a CPA with a backup degree in law. Marc? Someone with his gift for blarney could sell anything. So happens he's had a lifelong love affair with fancy cars. He could probably build one if he set his mind to it. In the beginning, in boot camp, we were four cocky kids who all had a lot of growing up to do. Say, the pizza does need reheating. Pick what you want. I'll plug in the microwave. And thanks. I'll return yours after I buy my own. I don't know how John managed without one."

"Here, let me do that." Isabella attempted to relieve him of the plates he'd pulled from the cupboard.

He retained a firm grip. "You're the one who had the bad day. Sit. Tonight you get to be the guest."

She blinked at him. "I can't let you wait on me."

Gabe laughed. "Why not? There's no law against it, is there?"

Sitting, she laced her fingers together. "Here in the valley, our families are pretty traditional. Women's domain is house, food, garden, kids. Men take care of flocks, orchards and income."

"Which pizza?" Gabe asked again.

Isabella frowned as she selected a narrow slice of cheese and one of the veggie pizza.

Gabe slid her plate into the oven, set out two glasses and asked whether she wanted soda or beer.

"Beer. Save the glass."

He opened two bottles, adding those plus utensils and napkins to the items already on the table. "You run a business, Isabella. Yet, along with most of the women in your family, you worked night after night saving lambs. Seems to me that was in addition to what you normally do."

"So, there are a few exceptions," she said, accepting the plate he set in front of her. "Historically speaking, though, the exchange of tasks doesn't go both ways. Isn't that the case with your family, too?"

He removed his piping hot plate and took a seat opposite her. "My family?" He cut off a bite of pizza and chewed as long as he dared. Once he'd swallowed, he dodged her question. "My family was nothing like yours. For one thing, my folks were never home. I guess you could say the Marines ended up being my family." He could've told her the family he'd been born into made dysfunctional appear normal, but something held him back.

During the time it took each of them to finish what was on their plates, Gabe admitted to having had a skewed view of life when he'd landed in the military at eighteen.

"One of the tough guys, huh?"

"I was pretty much a bad-ass kid," he said, shrugging off the fact that he'd had a choice of three-to-five in prison for getting caught making book on horse races or four years in the service of his country.

"A lot of teen boys are filled with rage. Perhaps rage is what made you a survivor," she half-mused. "It does keep a person going."

"No." Gabe shook his head. "Rage in any form is a mind-numbing emotion, Isabella. That's not good. It's debilitating. People have to move beyond rage or hate or whatever you want to call it, or they lose out on the important things in life."

"You're wrong. I'll never stop hating Julian. I'm consumed by rage. It's what gets me out of bed every morning, Gabe. It's what keeps my heart from breaking into a million bits. Without anger, I'm afraid I'd feel nothing at all."

She'd lashed out automatically. And fast. So, what was the best way to respond to the vehemence he felt in her every word? After a moment's silence, Gabe lazily lifted his beer. "I didn't say I recovered overnight, Isabella."

Her eyes never strayed from his throat as he swallowed. The broad hand holding his beer remained rock-steady. Hers jerked spasmodically. The mere mention of her ex-husband made it hurt to breathe. "We're talking apples and oranges. I'm quite sure any sins you committed as a teen can't hold a candle to Julian's."

Gabe lowered his bottle and rolled it between his

hands. "There's no crime worse than his. I'm not arguing that point. In fact, I'm not arguing any point."

"It sounded like you were."

He reached across the table and captured one of her fluttering hands. "I'm in your corner, Isabella."

She snatched her hand away and sipped from her beer. Setting her beer down hard, she licked her lower lip. "I want Julian to rot in hell. Furthermore, I intend to see that he does. I'm hoping to learn a lot from the summaries of similar cases."

"I doubt we'll find any the prosecutor hasn't already pulled up for review."

"I'll be looking at them from a different perspective. James Hayden is…so dispassionate about everything."

"In first-year law, they stress objectivity. To reach this stage in his career, Hayden's probably handled hundreds of cases as bad as yours." Gabe helped himself to another piece of pizza and slowly ate it cold.

"That's just it. To Hayden this is simply another case among many he's prosecuted. Well, to me it's more. Much, much more."

Gabe wiped his fingers on his napkin and tossed it aside. "There's such a thing as getting too close to a case, Isabella. Effective lawyers have learned to separate their feelings toward the person on trial from whatever heinous act he's committed. Otherwise, they'd go off the deep end themselves. Which brings me to another question. Are you going to hold up okay, poring over abstract after abstract of cases that bear a resemblance to yours?"

"I will."

She said it with such cold sincerity, Gabe believed her. At least he believed she'd give it her best shot. He sensed that she was hanging on by a worn thread, however. Because of that, because of his sympathy, his compassion, he was moved to touch her face. Just a feather-light skimming of his fingers along her jaw.

Closing her eyes, Isabella savored the human touch, the warmth emanating from his very masculine hand. She leaned into his palm, even as some shadowy fear warned her to pull away.

Drawn by her fragility as well as her unexpected compliance, Gabe was shaken by how badly he longed to kiss her lips. Lips that were full, slightly parted and naked of lipstick. *His naked lips covering hers...*

He rose out of his chair and braced his free hand on the table. He didn't want to frighten Isabella into bolting, so he spoke quietly before she could react. "I'm going to kiss you, Isabella." Gabe knew her eyes flew wide open. He closed the narrow gap, not giving her time to think or draw back.

He kept it light when he would've liked to deepen the kiss. His hand slid from her jaw to the back of her head, and he curled his fingers around her nape. What he *wanted* to do was thrust them under the silky knot of her thick braid.

The connection lasted longer than he'd thought she would allow. But not nearly long enough to put out the fire deep within his belly. Despite his reluctance, Gabe released her the moment he felt the slightest pressure of her head against his hand.

He stared directly into her eyes, trying to gauge her mood as he eased away. She made no move to slap him. That was good. And her breath was unsteady, and that, too, he took as a positive sign.

"It's been half a lifetime since I've shared a kiss as sweet as that," she whispered in a voice as strained as her breathing.

Sweet? Gabe sank heavily into the chair, forgetting all about the bruises he'd sustained from herding stubborn sheep. But something loomed larger than his pain—the belief that there wasn't a man alive who'd want the word *sweet* attached to the first kiss he gave a woman he'd been lusting after in his dreams. Fantastic, maybe. Sexy, definitely. But...*sweet?* Not on your life.

"You groaned. Was I that rusty?"

Gabe, who'd shut his eyes and flopped against the back of his chair, muttered, "I sat down too hard. I forgot my behind's black and blue thanks to your father's cantankerous sheep."

"Did you do something to provoke the rams?"

"They take exception to my cutting out the ewes I'm trying to match with the newborn lambs."

"Gabe, I think you're supposed to pen the rams first. A ram's role is to protect his ewes. Didn't whoever assigned you the task warn how the rams might act? Surely it wasn't Papa."

"No. He and Louis are working one pasture. Joe and Angel are with the dogs in another. Rick!" Gabe shot bolt upright. "Why, that sneaky, low-down, no good bast—" He bit off the expletive the moment Isabella's eyebrows shot up.

"I swear it's not my imagination. Rick volunteered. He promised Benito he and Manny would give me a lift to the upper pasture and show me what I needed to know to cut out the proper ewes. Boy, I've been had."

"Papa will skin Rick alive."

"Don't tell him. Rick's waiting for me to bitch. Why else would he leave his orchard and drop by when we broke for lunch? I'll bet he's laughing his head off."

"I don't understand why he'd pick on you."

"A guess?" Gabe drawled. "I'd say he sees it as protecting his flock."

"His flo...? Oh? Me? Or Trini do you think?"

Gabe closed the pizza boxes and got up to store them in the fridge. "I haven't kissed Trini. Haven't shown any signs of wanting to, either." His declaration came out muffled because his head was in the fridge.

"You only kissed me tonight. Rick can't know that."

"Right. But it's been on my mind for a while. Guys sense these things in one another."

Isabella stood up and put their beer bottles on the counter near the sink. "Rick's not my keeper." She stalked toward the back door.

"Wait a minute. It's pitch dark out. I'll walk you home." Gabe grabbed a jacket off a hook nailed inside the laundry room.

"It's barely a thousand yards. And it was dark when I brought myself over here."

"Humor me."

"Gabe," she said in an unmistakably cautious tone. "I hope I'm not being presumptuous saying this—but don't waste your time pursuing me. If you are, I mean. If that's what your invitations and your kiss were all about, you need to give it up."

"Mind telling me why?" he inquired mildly.

Isabella buried her hands deep in the pockets of the jacket she'd never removed while in Gabe's house. "I should think that's evident. I've got nothing to offer. Not to friends or family. I've got nothing to give to anyone. I'm empty. In here." She placed a hand over her heart.

"You're young," Gabe reminded her. "You have two-thirds of your life ahead of you." He took her elbow and steered her around a pothole in the gravel road.

"Listen to me, Gabe. I'm trying to do you a favor. You're wasting your time on something that can never be. I'm dead inside."

As she said this, they reached the steps leading to the porch that surrounded the Navarros' rambling farmhouse. A border collie trotted out to bark but soon returned to the sheep pen.

Gabe wasn't in the habit of kissing any woman without warning. But he folded his arms around Isabella and leaned against the huge old mountain laurel that shaded the front steps. He felt the crunch of bark between his shoulder blades and noted Isabella's gasp with satisfaction as her body touched his. While he had her off guard, Gabe kissed her in a way that could by no means be described as *sweet*. He devoured her lips until she grasped his face between her hands and kissed him back with equal passion.

They were both panting when they finally broke apart. In the light from the porch that filtered through the leaves, Gabe could see he'd left her lips rosy and damp. Isabella's eyes, partially hidden by half-closed lids were less revealing. But he caught enough of a glimpse to know he'd evoked at least a glimmer of desire.

Tracing her bottom lip with the work-roughened pad of his thumb, Gabe waited until Isabella met his eyes. "No. You're definitely not dead inside." Dropping his hand, he turned and walked away and was soon swallowed in darkness.

Isabella wavered. She fought against the hunger welling inside her. She shivered from the cold wind, which had suddenly sprung up, rattling the branches above her head.

Behind her, the door opened. Trini stepped onto the porch. "Bella, so you're home. Mama thought she heard noises out here. It must've been you driving in. If my brakes are squeaking again, I'll have Joe take a look at them this weekend."

Steadying herself, Isabella clutched the railing. "Your brakes are fine. A wind's come up. Someone needs to cut a few branches away from the house before they rub the paint off." She walked up the steps and hurried past her sister, determined not to show any reaction to Gabe's kiss that could be questioned by her family. He'd been mistaken. He might have aroused a physical longing in her, but her heart remained as lifeless as ever. It'd be best if she forgot about the idea of looking at old court cases with him. Yes, that would definitely be best.

Trini followed Isabella inside and before they reached the stairs, leaned over to murmur conspiratorially, "Did you have a good time with Gabe tonight? Is he a good kisser?"

"What?" Isabella tripped over the sleeve of the jacket she'd just removed.

Trini poked her. "Only kidding, Bella. I wanted to shake you up. You seem so…distracted tonight. Wasn't he able to get permission for you to see those court cases?"

"He did, but—"

"Good," Trini said, talking right over her sister. "Hayden phoned an hour ago. They've assigned a trial date. Jury selection starts Tuesday of next week. You need to phone him back. He'd like to get together with you on Monday for a last look at your deposition and his notes. So if you and Gabe find anything new, I guess you'll want to show him then.''

Isabella sagged against the wall. ''It's really going to happen. I've waited so long.''

''Yeah, well since Hayden phoned, the family's been arguing over what to do.''

''Arguing? Why? Aren't they pleased it'll finally be decided?''

''It's the timing, Bella. But go on into the living room, they'll tell you.''

She did go inside, unsure what problems awaited her. ''Mama. Papa. Rick. Ruby. Joe.'' One by one Isabella named them. Only the sisters-in-law and brothers-in-law were missing. ''Trini tells me this meeting concerns Julian's trial. I don't understand. We've all been waiting…praying for this call.''

Benito got up and dragged a chair in front of the fireplace. ''We all want to be there for you, *caro*. But we prayed…since they waited this long, they'd hold off till summer.'' Gathering Isabella's hand in his gnarled one, he sat her gently in the chair.

''Yeah,'' Joe grumbled. He paused in his whittling to scowl. Whittling was Joe's way of calming an attack of nerves. ''Their timing couldn't be worse, Bella. For any of us. We're smack in the middle of a bumper lamb crop. Within two weeks, there'll be more dropping all across the hills. Rick's leased equipment to fertilize all his orchards, otherwise his apples won't be worth marketing. And if Manny and Louis want a grape crop, they've gotta do whatever it is they do to the vines this time of year.''

''Cluster thinning,'' Manny supplied from the corner.

Isabella fought a surge of panic. She'd counted on

the support of her family during a time that was sure to be the roughest ordeal she'd faced since the funerals. Her turbulent eyes sought those of her mother and her three sisters.

Trini glanced guiltily away. "I have tests in all my classes coming up, and no break until Easter."

Ruby wrung work-worn hands. "Either Sylvia or I should stick close to home in case Christina goes into labor. We promised Manny. Not only that, I'm drowning in berries I have to turn into jam before they rot. I picked everything at once after the storm. So, Sylvia, I'll stay home for Christina. You and Mama go with Isabella."

Benito roused himself. "I need your mama to help with the sick or premature lambs. Trying to run back and forth to Bend every day is out of the question."

"I thought I'd book a motel, Papa. I'm not sure I'm up to driving that route every day, either." Isabella twisted a button on her blouse.

Sylvia went to hug her. "Bella, Angel won't want me staying in Bend for...how long will the trial run? Our kids have games and band practice after school. I'm in a car pool. I can try and trade one or two days, but... Oh, why did they move the trial anyway?"

"There's no guessing how long it'll be," Luisa said. "I asked that when Mr. Hayden phoned. He said jury selection alone could take a week or more."

Isabella rubbed her hands along her skirt. "Look, I don't want any of you making sacrifices. I can handle the jury selection process on my own. After the trial starts, maybe some of you will be able to spare a day here and there."

"We should all be lined up with you," Benito insisted. "Did the prosecutor tell the judge it'd cause a hardship on you to move the trial, Bella?"

"He did, Papa. He filed three different motions. They all failed."

"Why?" Manny demanded.

"A number of reasons," Isabella said bitterly. "Too much local media coverage. Overwhelming sentiment in the valley. Hayden said a change of venue isn't uncommon in high-profile cases—they think it's easier to select jurors that way. Fair jurors."

"As if anyone who sees the facts won't think Julian's nuts," Rick snapped.

Isabella jumped up. "Take care where you say that, Rick. Half of Julian's defense hinges on his copping an insanity plea. I want him convicted of murder."

Joe closed his knife and pocketed the whistle he was carving. "What else does he have as a defense?"

"Read the papers, Joe. The creep Julian's folks hired to defend him leaked suggestions to the press that Julian's been maligned. He's saying Bella drove Julian to commit what they're terming a *crime of passion*." Manny's dark eyes flashed malevolently.

"Ah, to hell with the flock," Benito exclaimed. "I won't allow Bella to sit in that courtroom alone if that's how they're going to treat her."

"Papa, the trial itself will be civilized. Those are just words Julian's lawyer will throw around. Compared to what I've already faced, what can mere words do to hurt me?"

"I don't like it," Benito insisted. His scowl cowed everyone in the room. All at once he snapped his fingers. "What about Gabe? Joe, can he learn enough in a week to take my place? That'll free me up to go with Bella."

Joe snorted. "Three months maybe, Papa. No way could he be ready in one week. Especially during the most frantic lambing season yet."

Luisa Navarro clasped her husband's arm. "Benito, perhaps a better solution would be to ask Gabe to attend the trial instead of me."

Rick catapulted from his chair, knocking it over with a bang. "What kind of damn fool idea is that, Mama? The man's a *maketo*," he spat. An outsider.

"No, Papa." Isabella picked up her brother's chair. "Much as it pains me to agree with Rick when he's acting like a billy goat, I have to say he's right. Gabe has no stake in this."

Manny stood. "It's getting late. I've gotta go home."

"Me, too." Joe retrieved a pile of jackets. As he handed them around, he said, "I recall a conversation with Gabe where he mentioned that Summer Marsh…er…Quinn had clued him in on Bella's situation. I think he's sympathetic."

Trini straightened from where she bent to stoke the fire. "Gabe knows as much as anyone who isn't family. Not only did he accompany Bella to the cemetery, he's wangled access to Larkin Crosley's law library for her to read about similar cases. And he knows his way around a courthouse."

That information slowly seeped through to the family members still pondering Isabella's fate.

"I said I'll handle this on my own," Isabella snapped, even though she felt a niggle of guilt. After all, she'd asked Gabe to do her a favor; she'd agreed to help him choose furniture in return. And tonight, she'd run off without even looking at his brochures.

Still, that deal was between her and Gabe. It had nothing to do with tonight's family summit.

To stave off another clan discussion, Isabella made a point of kissing everyone and pointedly saying goodnight. As fast as her feet would carry her, she ran up to her room. Her family might not approve of her taking matters into her own hands, but in the past they'd abided by her wishes. She had no reason to doubt the same would be true in this instance.

THE NEXT EVENING, when she met Gabe outside Larkin Crosley's office, she discovered how wrong she'd been.

He greeted her, saying, "Why didn't you tell me last night that they're going to begin jury selection? No wonder you had a rotten day. That news alone would jangle your nerves, let alone finding out most of your family can't be there for you."

Unlocking the main building door, Gabe moved aside to let Isabella precede him into a foyer lit only by the exit sign.

"My day fell apart before any of that. I didn't learn the trial updates until after I arrived home last night."

"I'm glad, because I hope you know I'd never have waited for your dad to ask me to go with you. I'd have volunteered on my own."

Gabe had trailed her up one flight of warped oak steps. She stopped on the landing. "Why? Why would Papa ask, and why would you agree? Curiosity? You can read about it in the newspaper or watch highlights on TV. We're the best sideshow in the valley," she said bitterly, letting her frustration from last night emerge. Her lack of sleep didn't help, either.

Ignoring her anger, Gabe calmly sorted through the keys on the ring. When he found the one he wanted, he fit it in the door emblazoned with Crosley's name. "You could've slapped me last night. Then your irritation over my kissing you would all be out of your system by now."

Pausing inside the office, which smelled of musty books and lemon furniture polish, Isabella flinched when Gabe turned on the bright overhead lights. "This isn't about a kiss."

"No?" He slid home the dead bolt and tucked the keys back in his pocket.

"It's about my father's arrogance. And yours."

"Your father's anything but arrogant, Isabella. He approached me with hat in hand because he loves you. I agreed out of respect for him, and because I've been in lonely spots myself. I know what a difference it makes to have a friend standing by your side."

The low murmur of Gabe's voice, coupled with his sincerity, pierced the armor she thought she had solidly in place. "You humble me, Gabe."

He shrugged offhandedly, suddenly embarrassed. "Forget it. Let's get to work. Larkin gave me the general layout of his library, and showed me how to use his card catalogue. I wish he had his index computerized. But he doesn't, so we'll have to work around that. Why don't you have a seat at that long table? I'll start pulling books."

"I brought some yellow tablets to take notes." She pulled them out of a straw handbag.

"I'd like to say there's no way we'll find that many of these awful cases. I know better. Unfortunately there are a lot of sick people in this world."

"Julian's not sick. He's perfectly healthy. And he was fine the morning he came and got Antonia and Ramon for their visitation."

"I know that's what you believe, Isabella. But something must have snapped after you saw him. Spite doesn't seem enough of a motive for murder-suicide."

She pressed her lips in a thin line and clapped her hands over her ears, spinning away from Gabe.

He dropped his chin to his chest and massaged the back of his neck. He noticed her shoulders shaking and moved in behind her, looping his arms around her. "The last thing I'd ever do is hurt you, Isabella," he declared. "Either way, the state is going to put Julian away for a long, long time, whether they incarcerate or institutionalize him. Won't you be better served devoting your time and energy to healing yourself?"

"I'll never heal. Never, never, never," she chanted in a raspy voice.

Pressing a soft kiss to her ear, Gabe felt her stiffen, and he ended up patting her awkwardly. "I'll start digging out books." There was a raw bleakness in his voice.

She'd managed to pull herself together by the time he came back carrying two fat volumes of text.

He took a minute and showed her how to scan the cases he'd marked. "The first part of a court document is fairly standard posturing on the part of both law teams. You'll want to skip the opening arguments and read the closing summation."

When Gabe deposited the sixth book on the table, he noticed that Isabella sat staring into space. All she'd written was maybe three pages of notes.

"Need a break?" he asked, sliding into a chair across from her. "Larkin said he got rid of his coffee-maker. He's here so few hours a day that if he wants coffee, he runs down to the Green Willow. They're probably still open. I'd be glad to go grab a couple of take-out cups.''

Isabella lowered her head. She began rubbing her forehead with the tips of her fingers. "I know you warned me," she said. "Reading these graphic descriptions is more difficult than I ever dreamed."

Rising, Gabe circled the table. Standing behind her, he rested his hands on her fragile shoulder bones and walked his thumbs up her tense spine.

"That feels good."

"Are you finding anything worthwhile?"

She sighed. "I don't know. I want so badly to cry. But…I can't."

Gabe tugged her up, out of her chair. He took her in his arms, wanting to cry for her. With her. Odd. And unnerving, as he'd never been a man who showed emotion easily. For much of his life, he'd been cast in the role of protector. He'd just never felt such *intensity* about keeping anyone safe. More, even, than the times he'd sent men under his command to face an enemy.

Isabella burrowed into the snug hollow in the middle of his chest. She ran her hands up under his collar, smoothing her palms back and forth over the crispness of his shirt.

After several minutes, he shifted. The slow friction of her hands, along with the sweet scent of her perfume, stirred a portion of his body he didn't think she wanted to stir.

"So, do we buckle down and between the two of us get through this nasty chore? Or shall we call it a night, return the books to the shelves and I'll see you home?"

Lifting her head, Isabella gazed at him from cloudy eyes. "I need to buckle down and get the job done," she said with resolve. "But first, I have to thank you.

You're the only man I know who seems to understand the value of a simple hug. My sisters hug me often. Or Mama. A man's hug is…well, different. I can't tell you how badly I needed what you just did. A plain old hug with no sexual strings attached.''

''Uh…any time,'' he offered magnanimously. Although the promise had no more than slipped past his lips when Gabe realized it'd be next to impossible to keep. He *wanted* sexual strings. But, Gabe knew he had to be patient. This wounded woman didn't need a lover now. Until she figured out she did, he'd wait. He'd be her protector, her friend, her guardian.

By God, he'd be her fortress through this whole messy trial.

CHAPTER TEN

GABE SAT beside Isabella, interpreting the legal jargon, while she took notes. Their arms brushed on occasion. His doggedly pragmatic dissection of each transcript helped her stay focused so that her mind didn't drift off on other tangents.

"You're good at legalese," she said when they had two cases left to go. "I mean, you instinctively zero in on the facts that make each argument unique. What on earth made you decide to change occupations? And to raise sheep, of all things?"

"Now you sound like Marc and Reggie. They ganged up on me during my last visit to Utah. They're both convinced I'm certifiable." Rocking back in his chair, Gabe rubbed a hand over the bristle of his five o'clock shadow.

She closed the book they'd finished and set it aside before dusting off the next one. "Must be a male mid-life thing." Isabella found Gabe's marker and let the pages fall open.

He stifled a yawn. "It's funny, but I dreamed up the idea of owning a farm at Coltrane and Summer's wedding reception. Believe it or not, what you just suggested crossed my mind. So, let me pose a question to you. Is it so difficult to imagine me spending the rest of my days herding sheep?"

Isabella analyzed him, much as she'd done that day

at the Quinns' reception. Only then he'd been oblivious to her stares. She saw things now that weren't evident then. His strong but lean hands were capable of incredible tenderness. A fine sensitivity ran true and deep within his striking blue eyes.

He gave a nervous laugh. "You're having to work too hard at that assignment, Isabella. I think I get the picture."

"Actually, I was thinking you're a bit of a mystery. Undoubtedly a man of many talents who could do whatever he set his mind to."

"You're a diplomat."

She uncapped and recapped her pen. "I don't want to be. I want to be a woman who forms opinions and speaks her mind."

Gabe stilled her busy fingers, wishing he could rid them of their tremor. "If you ask me, the world needs more diplomats. Shall we finish up the cases we have out, refile the books, then decide if we need to meet again tomorrow night?"

"Yes. Let's." Isabella was vaguely disappointed that Gabe had chosen to change the subject. She wanted him to understand what she'd endured living with Julian—the subtle oppression he'd hidden from her until after the children were born and she was trapped. But why would Gabe understand? And if he did begin to put the pieces together, might he blame her for not leaving Julian sooner?

Flipping to a clean page on her pad, Isabella chanced to see her watch. "Goodness, we've been at this nearly three hours."

"Tedious process. It's the stuff lawyers don't have time for once they accept a new case on top of a hundred ongoing ones. Most hire second- and third-year law students for the type of work you're wading through.''

"I knew nothing about lawyers until Summer decided to divorce Frank Marsh. I...I followed her example.'' Isabella choked up. "You have no idea how I regret taking that first step. Toni and Ramon paid for my mistake.''

"Not your fault, Isabella. Maybe the divorce made Julian crazy. And maybe he would've gone berserk anyway.''

"The divorce certainly provoked him, but Julian wasn't crazy,'' she said so loudly that her words echoed back from the cavernous racks of law books.

Gabe berated himself for opening his mouth. Isabella's mind was closed to the slightest suggestion that her ex suffered from mental problems. "Can you dissect the last two cases alone? If so, I'll start putting these books away.'' He pushed out of his chair and picked up four volumes.

Isabella turned to watch his retreating back. Good as he was to look at, it was a crying shame he was so pigheaded. Avoidance of truth—that was how the counselor she'd gone to for a short time would have labeled the way Gabe abruptly changed the subject whenever something came up that he didn't care to discuss. But from the sound of it, his childhood hadn't been rosy. And who was she to judge anyone? She hadn't liked what the counselor had to say, so she'd quit her sessions. She'd told her family time and money were the main reason she'd stopped going. They all thought she was coping admirably.

Rolling her shoulders, Isabella pulled the book closer. The visits to the psychologist began too soon after she'd opened the garage door on a scene that would live forever in her mind. How could anyone who hadn't walked in her shoes presume to know what she needed?

She rubbed idly at her stomach, at the almost constant pain there. She'd only copied two items out of the book. Yet when Gabe returned for the second batch, she slammed it shut and added it to his stack. Resolutely, she drew the last one toward her.

"Did you decide whether or not to come back tomorrow?" Gabe asked, sliding into the empty chair next to her again.

"Can I let you know later? Tomorrow afternoon I meet with James Hayden to go over my deposition. I'll show him what we've gathered and see if he thinks any of it's relevant. How many more cases in this state haven't we looked at?"

"We've covered about half."

"There are that many?" She traced the gold lettering on the outside of the book as she closed it. "One day my life history will be laid bare just like these. Other people, complete strangers, will read it, and maybe cite us as an example."

The pupils of her eyes had become black holes of despair. Gabe thought this exercise was taking too great a toll on her already brittle constitution. "Answer me truthfully, Isabella. Did you eat anything at all before you came here tonight?"

"If I had, I probably would've embarrassed both of us by losing it all over Larkin Crosley's law books."

Gabe pried the last book out of her hand. "I'm taking you out for a decent meal. And none of this two little pieces of pizza crap."

"This late, there's nothing open."

"We'll drive to Burns. They have several restaurants

open until at least eleven. And a pancake house that's twenty-four hours a day."

"Breakfast might be palatable. I can't believe I've agreed to drive fifteen minutes for something I could whip up in ten." She stood rather clumsily and gathered her notes.

"You're not driving. I am. Bacon and eggs will hit the spot, provided the cook doesn't toss in a handful of chiles." He winked.

"I'll never live down those *migas*. You think I haven't noticed how thoroughly you inspect any morsel that comes out of our kitchen?"

He shut out the lights in Larkin's office, locked the door and guided Isabella to the stairs. "I guess you heard how your brothers-in-law scalded my lungs with that battery acid they call hard cider?"

"The fact that you laughed made a big hit with them." She gazed on him favorably, too, as he opened the passenger door and handed her into the SUV. "For a man who describes himself as having been a bad-ass kid, you have impeccable manners."

"The Corps taught me, ma'am. You've heard of that book, *All I Really Need to Know I Learned in Kindergarten?* Well, the Marine Corps was my kindergarten. And when they signed me on, they taught me a bunch of new rules. For starters, I disliked taking orders. The Corps is built around giving—and taking—them." He paused for a moment. "When push comes to shove, I owe Coltrane, Moss and Marc for recognizing I wasn't as tough inside as I tried to let on. I owe those three a lot. Maybe everything I am."

"The fact that you let them influence you is a testament to your adaptability, Gabe. I've read that guys who grow up in big families like mine do best in the military. If you're an only child, you probably never had to share with a soul.''

"I grew up fast, that's for sure. But maybe it forced me to interact with a broad range of people.''

Isabella pulled her sweater more tightly around her and stared at the moonlit scenery as it flew past. "I had a wonderful childhood. Happy. Loving. Supportive. As a result, I came away with false expectations that my life would always be that way.''

Gabe glanced over and realized she was twisting a nonexistent ring around the third finger of her left hand. Not for the first time in their brief history, he floundered, having no idea what to say to her. He decided to stick to something neutral.

"There are CDs in the center console. See if there's one you like. I'm warning you, though, I don't have highbrow tastes in music.''

"Do men and women ever agree on music or movies?'' She opened the console and rummaged through the stored discs. "I take that back. You have a lot of stuff I enjoy.'' Selecting an early Beach Boys CD, she popped it in the player. "California Girls'' blared out. Adjusting the volume, she settled back, wearing an actual smile.

Gabe wasn't about to confess that it wasn't his CD, but one of three Mossberger had left in the SUV the weekend of Coltrane's wedding.

"What did you and your husband do for fun?''

She rolled her head in his direction, never lifting it from the headrest. "Together?'' She had to think hard. "Well, we have a week-long celebration on *Jueves Gordo.* Fat Thursday. There's a carnival, and street dances. The men do a lot of drinking and we all gorge ourselves. Everyone parties so much that on *Viernes Flaco* we all flake out. Nobody goes to work.''

''Thin Friday?'' Gabe laughed.

''Very good. You're picking up Euskera.''

''So what else?''

''There's a group in the community dedicated to preserving Basque dances and costumes. My daughter, Antonia, attended a class at the Basque Center Saturday mornings. She loved dancing. And flowers. And butterflies.''

A mantle of gloom at once descended on Isabella.

Gabe kicked himself. Wasn't there *any* topic that didn't risk reminding her of her loss? The upbeat music filling the vehicle seemed all wrong.

Isabella must have thought so, too. She reached over and punched the eject button. Soberly, she returned the disc to its case.

He was fairly sure that the military psychologist he'd seen—the man who'd helped him forgive his parents' transgressions in order to get on with his life—would say Isabella needed to talk about her good memories. Gabe was in no way inclined to test his theory, however. Eventually, her silence got to him. He was relieved when they reached their destination.

''We can't not talk for the entire meal,'' he said after they'd parked, walked into the chain restaurant and been seated and given menus by the hostess. In all that time they hadn't exchanged a word.

''I'm sorry.''

''For…?'' He raised his eyes from the open menu.

''I'm not good company.''

''Your company's just fine, Isabella. I'd like to find some common ground. Subjects we can discuss in order to learn more about each other—preferably without causing you grief.''

"I am grieving, Gabe. Always. You don't seem to understand that I'll live in a state of grief forever.''

Gabe tore his gaze away from her unhappy face, but he couldn't concentrate on his menu. If he really believed she'd never stop grieving, he might as well pack it in and forget all about her. But he couldn't see himself abandoning her. Time. She needed time. Also patience and unwavering support. Those worked; he knew that from experience.

Closing the menu, Gabe pushed it to the edge of the table. "Darn. No *migas*." A mischievous smile replaced his frown. "I'm going to settle for plain, boring number four. Does anything here appeal to you? Me, maybe?" He wagged his eyebrows.

"A waffle," she said, ignoring his attempts at humor. "Papa used to take us kids to this restaurant after the Sheepherder's Ball. I always got a waffle with strawberries and whipped cream. They have it under seasonal items."

Gabe signaled the waitress. "Is it possible to get a strawberry waffle tonight?"

"Yeah. Got some nice California berries this week.'' The waitress cracked her gum. "Would you be wantin' that waffle with cream, sir?"

"Whipped. And it's for the lady. I'll take your number four. Eggs scrambled. And coffee black, please.'' He indicated that Isabella should order her own beverage.

"Hot tea, I think.'' She listened to the waitress name ten or so varieties. "I'll try cinnamon spice.''

They both watched the waitress rip their order sheet off her pad and clip it on the cook's carousel.

"Tell me what ideas you have for renovating John's house." Isabella introduced a new subject out of the blue.

Gabe drummed his fingers on the table as the waitress delivered their drinks. "Summer gave me the name of a builder who's done work for her," he said after the waitress had gone. "He'll swing by tomorrow and give me an estimate. I gather he's a fair architect. He knows my house and says it's well built. We agreed that most of what I need is cosmetic, but I'd like the master bedroom enlarged, a screened porch added all the way across the back of the house, and skylights installed in the two bathrooms."

"That sounds more than cosmetic to me. Will you remove a wall between the large bedroom and one of the smaller ones?"

"No, I'll leave the three smaller bedrooms as they are."

"What does a bachelor need with four bedrooms?"

Gabe hesitated. They were chatting genially and he didn't want her to clam up again. But she was waiting expectantly. "I'm not getting any younger," he mumbled. "Lately I've been thinking about starting a family. Not until the house is spruced up, and I settle on a direction for my future," he hurriedly added.

That was enough to make Isabella close down again. It was fortunate for both of them that the waitress brought their order. She set the strawberry confection in front of Isabella, then plopped a sizzling plate of pancakes, bacon and eggs in front of Gabe. With a flourish, she produced catsup, Tabasco and the bill from a deep apron pocket before warming Gabe's coffee. "More hot water?" she asked Isabella.

"Uh, no thanks. This…ah…waffle seems much bigger than I remember it as a kid."

The waitress cracked her gum. "Same size. Kids gobble them up. Adults rarely finish one. I've yet to bring one to an adult who didn't gasp. It's sad that the stuff we loved as kids never quite measures up to our memories. If you'd rather order something else, I'll take that back to the kitchen." She pulled out her order pad.

"No. It's fine." Isabella picked up her fork, so the waitress flitted off to greet another customer.

Gabe peppered his eggs and doused his pancakes in syrup. He'd taken a few bites when he realized Isabella hadn't moved a muscle. "Are you sure you wouldn't rather choose a different dish?" he asked after swallowing.

Guiltily, she cut through her waffle. "Sorry. I…it's…uh, great. Thank you for letting me order it."

She carried the fork to her lips, but as Gabe went back to his meal, he noticed that Isabella secreted the portion she'd cut in the folds of her paper napkin.

"Isabella," he said softly. "Don't apologize every time I ask a personal question. I sure as hell don't want you eating something you can barely manage to look at."

"I'm sorry." She dropped her fork. A shadow of fear replaced the routinely dead expression in her eyes.

"Dammit, Isabella! Did Benito force you to clean your plate when you were little or something?" He closed his eyes, shocked by her sudden pallor. "Trade plates with me." Opening his eyes, he made the switch. "My mission tonight is to see you put something in your stomach. Anything. Dammit, woman, you'll keel over if you keep losing weight."

Wordlessly, she accepted his plate and at once popped a bite of egg into her mouth. Her hand quivered, but her color seeped back little by little as Gabe dug into the frothy strawberries and cream.

Finally, after several seconds, she again attempted to take the blame. "I don't recall strawberry waffles being so sweet. My stomach balked. Here, please, this is what *you* wanted. Take some bacon. Honestly, it's too much for me."

"Okay, but only if you promise to eat one piece and all the eggs." Gabe stabbed the remaining slices of bacon. He couldn't possibly know how Julian had made mealtimes an ordeal, how he'd harangued her and the kids. It was all about control, the shrink had told her, and that she did agree with.

She didn't quite clean up all the scrambled eggs. "I'm full," she announced. "Gabe, really, I have no appetite," she said when he looked skeptical.

"You don't want to faint during the trial." He decided to try a new tack and appeal to the one thing that seemed to drive her very existence.

"Absolutely not. Okay. I'll try to eat a little every day."

Pushing the half-demolished waffle aside, Gabe folded his napkin and drained his coffee cup. As he dug out his wallet, he broached a topic that had been on his mind. "I skied some in Bend this past winter before I closed the SOS books on Summer's ranch, so I got to know the place. How about if I book our rooms for the trial?"

He'd said rooms—plural—so Isabella had no reason to believe he had anything inappropriate in mind. "Would you do that? I'm not familiar with Bend at all. I'd be grateful. But…arrange it so that we split the bill.''

An objection rose to the tip of his tongue, but Gabe bit it back. ''No problem. Now if you're finished and ready to leave, I wouldn't mind running by the furniture store I told you about last night. They're open until ten.''

''Sure. I meant to apologize for dashing off before we had a chance to look at your brochures.''

''You were not happy with me, if I recall. Isabella, do you ever raise your voice when you get mad?'' he asked. ''Even a little?'' He opened the restaurant's outer door and they emerged into the cooler night air.

Making a show of buttoning her sweater, Isabella acted as if she didn't hear his question.

Gabe wasn't buying it. ''I thought as much,'' he said, unlocking the passenger door. He waited until she'd slipped in, which in the SUV put her level with his eyes. ''Try it next time someone irritates you. I'll bet they think twice about intimidating you again.'' He shut her door with a soft click.

He hadn't expected her to respond. In fact, he just wanted to plant the seed. Under all her pain and grief, a vital, fiery woman lay dormant. Flashes of passion she didn't even know she possessed were what had first attracted Gabe. That passion still attracted him and made him more determined than ever to hang around for the long haul.

The furniture store they drove to was indeed open; they walked in with twenty minutes to spare.

''Oh, will you look at that luscious leather sofa and chair.'' Isabella homed in on the very set Gabe liked best. More satisfied than he had any right to be, he followed her over and showed her a palette of available colors.

"Definitely this shade of nut-brown. Not the one with reddish hues. I can see this set arranged in front of a blazing fireplace." She stroked the sample, and Gabe quite frankly found himself wishing she'd touch him instead. Her fingers were delicate but strong. He'd seen how compassionately they'd ministered to a sick lamb. And also their strength when she kneaded bread dough.

"I've always coveted leather," she murmured. "Julian said it was too expensive. And that I'd let the kids ruin it. Which wasn't true. He never allowed them in the living room with food, drinks or toys, anyway."

"Didn't he know leather lasts a lifetime? The salesman said they put a finish on it now that makes it easier to clean. One of the reasons this group appealed to me is because the stuff's…I don't know…bounceable? I mean, I walked in and could instantly visualize a bunch of kids dressed in pj's playing on these fat cushions."

"Are you saying this is the set you're considering?"

"Yep. And you picked the color I favored, too. I just didn't know if it'd be too dark for that oak-paneled room."

"I don't think so. Did you know there are fantastic hardwood floors under that ratty rug of John's? If it were me, I'd buy an area rug in blacks and reds and rusts. The Paiutes weave some beautiful ones. Of course they're expensive. But if you drove out to the reservation, you'd get a better deal, and maybe they'd make you matching sofa pillows."

"I like that idea. I knew you'd have an eye for what I needed to give the house character."

She blushed. "Oh, you probably shouldn't listen to

me. I do have ideas but not one iota of training. Julian hired a design expert to do our house. After all, what do I know?''

He eyed her speculatively. ''You have a house?''

''Not…not really. Technically it's half mine. Julian's parents plan to use his half of the money to help pay for his defense. They demanded I sell. Recently I relisted it, and already there's a sale pending. I can't bear to drive past—even drive down the street.''

Isabella shut her eyes and rubbed her forehead. ''Gabe, do you remember the woman who stopped at the Green Willow and spoke to me the other night? Her fiancé made an offer on the house. I've gotta tell you why I bolted from the restaurant. She came to the bakery wanting me to do her wedding reception…there…at the house.'' Her voice cracked. Taking a deep breath, Isabella sank down on the sofa. ''I know the Realtor didn't tell her…what ha-app-ened there. I'm not blaming the agency, but I can't cater her reception. So I made up the first excuse that came into my head. I said I was meeting my boyfriend later, and that I expected him to give me a ring. I implied I'd be planning my own wedding for September. I'm so sorry, Gabe. Who would've dreamed she'd turn up at the Green Willow and assume you were my fictitious boyfriend?''

Gabe knelt in front of her. ''If the circumstances weren't so tragic, the incident itself would be humorous. Chances of that happening have got to be one in a million. So that's why you ran out like a bat out of hell. Jeez, why didn't you say something? I'd have played along.''

''Lies always catch up to a person. I want you to know I went to confession and was given penance.''

"Penance? Hmm. Will they take it back and give you brownie points if I put a ring on your finger?" he teased.

"Gabe! Don't make fun of something I take seriously. I've always been scrupulously honest. And like I told Trini, Julian's defense team would love to dig up some dirt on me. I shouldn't even be out with you this late. If someone in his family should see us, they'd blow it way out of proportion."

"Why? You and Julian were divorced before he went nuts."

"You don't understand."

"No?"

"It doesn't matter. Could you take me back to Callanton?"

"Sure," he said, helping her up from the soft couch. "But since we're here, could you spare me ten more minutes? I see that the salesman I spoke with last week has finished with his other customer. I may as well buy this while I'm here. Otherwise I risk having it sold out from under me."

"You're buying it tonight? The entire set?"

He chuckled. "Yes. I just needed your opinion. You agreed with me, so why drag my feet? You haven't suddenly changed your mind, have you?"

"No. But, Gabe, what if you take my word, and spend an indecent amount of money only to discover everyone else hates how it looks in your house?"

"Everyone who? It's my house."

"Everyone like…whatever woman you marry. You said you've decided it's time to settle down and start a family. That process usually begins with marriage."

Gabe shook his head. She really didn't have a clue that he'd fallen for her. He'd turned his life upside down to be near her, and she didn't have a God-damned clue.

It was probably a good thing the salesman rushed up right then, or Gabe might have blown any chance he had with Isabella by blurting the truth. Instead, he filled out the forms, signed the credit slip and gave directions for delivery. He'd obviously put too much store in that last kiss he'd given her. Man, was he arrogant, assuming she'd get the message on the basis of a couple of kisses.

He didn't doubt that the guys would rib him unmercifully about losing his touch. They used to call him Cool Hand Gabe for the phenomenal luck he had with women. That was probably all it had been, too. Luck. Obviously he needed to revise his methods to make any headway with Isabella.

Damn. She was the only woman who counted. The only one he wanted to impress.

Gabe unlocked her door and boosted her up into the Lexus. As he stuck his copy of the receipt between his teeth in order to steady her with both hands, she said, "This is probably tacky, but I've never met anyone who visited a furniture store twice, then—just like that—bought a whole living room full of top-of-the-line stuff. The people I know comparison shop."

"Really? Don't forget to buckle up." He whistled an off-key tune as he walked around the hood. He felt as if he'd accomplished something tonight. When he climbed in, before he fired the engine, he conferred with Isabella over trying another CD. They eventually agreed on a U2 album recorded the year the group came out of retirement.

"Has Papa talked to you about how much time and money it takes to build an income-producing flock of sheep? I thought I'd ask, as you seem bent on throwing your money around.''

"We discussed the prices wool and mohair topped out at this past shearing season. Benito said domestic demand for wool is up. I got the impression Angel and Louis would like to double the goat herd and add dairy goats, but Joe's adamantly opposed.'' Gabe turned down the music as they left the city lights behind. He wanted to hear what a knowledgeable bystander had to say on the subject.

"Mountain lions in these parts consider goat a delicacy. That's one reason Joe's against expanding the herd.''

"Yeah, but red fox prey on lambs. So that's one reason. What's another?''

Isabella lowered the music even more. "I'm sure if you asked Joe, he'd tell you. Our range, as well as Angel and Louis's, currently run the maximum stock advisable to maintain healthy animals. Papa wants to buy more pastureland. To do that, he'd have to second-mortgage the house. Joe's afraid Papa's age makes such a big loan inadvisable.'' She held up a hand when Gabe started to interrupt. "I already know what you're going to ask. What about leasing more government-held space?''

"It is logical, given how long it takes to build high-peak production.''

"Yes, but ranchers have quotas for leased lands. I don't know the formula, but they're calculated in part on acres owned. Without expanding their current holdings, none of them can bump up their leased portions.''

"So, the only ways this operation can increase profits is to run more efficiently, gain higher output of wool and mohair from existing flocks, or add land.''

She nodded. "And the market fluctuates wildly from year to year."

"Your family's been honest with me about the volatility of the industry. The extent of their knowledge is amazing. Me, I think I've learned to tell the difference between the Romanovs and the Rambouillets. And that's about all."

"Yet you still come back day after day. I couldn't believe it when Joe said you'd quit your job with SOS."

"Talk about volatility. That agency depends entirely on the largesse of benefactors. Today, those creatures are scarcer than the rarest breed of sheep and goats."

"Gabe, where are we?" Isabella leaned forward to peer out the front windshield.

"Nearly home, why?"

"I left my van in Callanton. It's parked in front of Mr. Crosley's office."

"Damn, I forgot. Well, it's too late to turn back. I'll collect you in the morning and give you a lift to town."

"We could go back now."

"Doesn't make much sense. We're two minutes from home."

"So we are." She sighed. "Stop here. I'll hike to the house." Unfastening her seat belt, she gathered her purse and her pads of notes.

Gabe dealt her a look Isabella was beginning to recognize. "I've never thrown a date out in the middle of the road," he said. "And I don't intend to start now."

"This wasn't a date." She felt heat stinging her cheeks. "Oh—did I forget to thank you for feeding me earlier?"

He turned into her drive, stopping well away from the light that spilled from the porch lamp. "Thanks aren't necessary, but I won't turn down a good-night kiss.''

Before she was able to find a comeback, Gabe bounded out and around the SUV. Yanking open the passenger door, he tumbled her into his waiting arms.

If possible, this kiss took more starch out of her legs than the previous one. There was a roaring in her ears, and Isabella completely lost her grip on her purse. Her notepads slipped from her hands, as well. Something struck her foot, but she couldn't identify what because her legs and feet had gone numb. With her hands freed, she grabbed Gabe's shirtfront, and hung on for dear life.

The noise inside her head and the storm in her chest didn't abate until Isabella realized their lips had disconnected.

Gabe studied her with a smile that could only be described as immensely satisfied. ''Someone's stepped out on your porch, Isabella. I'll collect the stuff you dropped if you'll turn loose of my shirt.''

''Oh. Oh, of course.'' More embarrassed than she ever remembered being, she released Gabe at once. The last time she'd experienced this kind of disorientation, she'd sampled too much of her brother-in-law's new batch of wine.

Gabe carefully pressed her possessions into her hands.

Thankfully a gusty wind sprang up then, cooling the fever that fired through her veins.

''Hi, Luisa.'' Gabe's voice came at Isabella through a fog. She forced herself to listen, to pay attention.

''It was late when we finished going through Crosley's records,'' Gabe was saying. ''We drove to Burns for a bite to eat. Considering the late hour, we left

Isabella's van in town. I'll take her to get it tomorrow morning.''

"I'm glad you ate." The older woman tightened the sash on her robe and bent to pat the dog who'd bounded up the steps. "The others have gone to bed. Bella, I stayed up to tell you James Hayden has to switch your meeting from afternoon to morning. Will that put you in a bind at the bakery?"

"No, Mama. I cleared my calendar of outside jobs because of the trial starting next week. Today I sold all perishable items to Phil Eubanks at the Mercantile. As of now, I'm free."

"Not the rest of us, unfortunately," her mother said. "Dawn comes early, as you know. You'd better let Gabe get home to bed now."

Dropping out of the clouds after she'd finally shaken off the lingering effects of his kiss, it was all Isabella could do to glance over at Gabe.

If he suffered any of the same consequences, she detected no sign of it as he slid a hand around her waist and guided her to the steps leading up to the porch, where her mother waited. His touch evoked an involuntary shiver.

"You're cold," he murmured. "I'll say good-night, ladies."

Isabella's brain registered the sound of his SUV starting and backing down the drive. Her mother chattered away as they entered the house, but Isabella didn't assimilate a single thing she said. Gabe's kiss had utterly destroyed her ability to think.

CHAPTER ELEVEN

SLEEP ELUDED ISABELLA for another night. She told herself it was nerves caused by the long-awaited start of Julian's trial. In reality, her mind kept jumping back to the times Gabe Poston had kissed her—and to her own reaction, which had gone from surprise, to excitement, to participation in at least two instances.

Toward morning, she came to the same conclusion she'd reached before. She had no right to the happiness Gabe's kisses brought her. She had even less right to long for the intimate physical aspects of a relationship with him. Her purpose over the next few weeks was to see that justice was done for her children. Gabe Poston was a distraction she couldn't afford.

Having decided that, Isabella showered and dressed for the day. She made her way downstairs early for the express purpose of asking someone in her family to spare the time to run her into town.

Seeing Gabe seated at the breakfast table, laughing with her father and brother, blew Isabella's newfound resolve straight to hell.

As if radar had kicked in, he glanced up and saw her. A slow, sexy smile spread across his face. Sheesh, he didn't even have to *try* to look sexy; it came naturally.

The impact of that smile slammed into Isabella's midriff with the force of a stampede. A rush of emotions, none strengthening her resolve to cut him out of her life, tore at her heart. A heart boarded up and chained to keep feelings out. Especially those that might leave her open to falling in love again. Because love only led to pain and sorrow.

Then why did that very same heart turn handsprings starting the instant she set eyes on Gabriel Poston?

"Ah, I see you're finally up." Rising, Gabe grabbed a clean mug and filled it with coffee from the pot before he crossed over to Isabella. She hadn't budged from the stairs.

Benito, Luisa, Joe and Angel all broke off eating long enough to greet Isabella.

As Gabe pressed the pottery mug into her cold hands, he took note of the dark circles ringing her perpetually haunted eyes. "Maybe I should ask if you even went to bed last night. Caffeine probably isn't what you need most, but maybe it'll jump-start your system. Has this appointment with Hayden got you rattled?"

She took a sip of the hot coffee, grateful for the chance to calm her nerves. "I shouldn't be nervous. It's the waiting that's been hell. That's winding down."

"I can hardly imagine what any of this ordeal's been like for you."

"That's a jury's job, isn't it? Twelve people who've never experienced what I've had to go through will try to put themselves in my shoes."

The pessimism overriding her statement told Gabe she wanted reassurances from him that nobody could give. "I believe juries do their best, Isabella. But they're only human, after all."

"What if their best isn't good enough?"

Luisa called out from the table. "Come have breakfast while it's warm. I made *tortilla de cebolla y anchoas,* Bella.''

Isabella's tense body relaxed. ''Mama, I can always count on you for comfort food. It's lucky home is always there to catch you when you fall,'' she said to Gabe.

''I wouldn't know about that,'' he murmured. ''I like tortillas. Shall I increase my life insurance policy before I sample the dish she's fixed?''

''Scrambled eggs, wild mushrooms, garlic and anchovies.''

Gabe clapped a hand over his heart. ''Things were looking up until you mentioned anchovies.''

''Hmm, this family loves them. Don't we?'' she asked at large as she slipped past Gabe and led the way to the table.

Benito gestured with his fork. ''Wanna keep those rams at a distance? Load up on Luisa's garlic and anchovy paste. The boys and I pile it on our morning toast.''

''Maybe I'll pass,'' Gabe said, not sure whether or not these practical jokers were having him on again. ''I'll just do sprints every morning to insure my ability to outrun the rams and billy goats.''

''Where's Trini?'' Isabella asked after the laughter died down.

Luisa rolled her eyes. ''She claimed to be studying late last night with friends. When I knocked on her door to wake her, she yelled, 'Go away and don't bother me until ten.'''

''I thought if I rode into town with her, Gabe could go on out and work with Papa. But Hayden moved our meeting up to seven-fifteen.''

Benito stopped spooning a second helping of the egg

mixture onto his plate. "We've already decided Gabe should sit in on your meeting."

"Who decided?" Isabella crushed her crisp napkin under a restless hand.

"I did." Benito spoke with finality.

Gabe squeezed her knee. "Would you have your father and brothers let their businesses slide so one of them could go in my place? They will, you know. In a heartbeat. If you fire me from the job as your escort."

Isabella didn't need Gabe's hand on her knee this morning. Not when his good-night kiss had been to blame for her bleary eyes. She hadn't wanted to ride into town with him at all today. But neither did she want to cause hardship for anyone in her family.

She deliberately got up so that Gabe's hand fell. Leaning down, she dropped a kiss on her father's leathery cheek. "Don't worry, Papa. I ought to consider myself fortunate to have Gabe tag along, given his background in law."

Scooting his chair back, Gabe climbed awkwardly to his feet. He wondered what would happen when they got out to his SUV. Isabella barely managed to keep her smoldering anger in check. He couldn't believe the others at the table all nodded, happily accepting her at her word.

Today, the silence vibrating around her inside the vehicle was even harder to accept than her stillness had been last night.

"Yell and throw things before we get to the highway," he said, once he'd backed from the lane onto the gravel county road.

She presented him with her back and persisted in staring out the window.

"You know next to nothing about me." She finally

turned. "If I felt like making a point, that would be it. We've known each other a matter of weeks. We're practically strangers. Why are you trying to make it seem as if we're more?"

"Phew!" Lifting a hand from the steering wheel, Gabe scrubbed his face. "I see you can fight with the gloves off when it suits you."

"Some honesty from you in return would be refreshing."

His eyes flashed. "I'm *always* honest. I...just maybe...didn't go far enough in a previous explanation. I told the truth about changing careers because SOS is losing its funding. I neglected to say it was something I decided after I set eyes on you at Coltrane and Summer's reception—before I explored any other options."

Isabella's jaw flopped like a landed fish. "But...but why? Why me? Why not someone like Megan Ward, Dawn Cunningham or Maggie Fitzgerald? Or even Trini. She's interested in you. So is Megan. A lot, I hear."

"I'm not interested in them."

"You're not?" Isabella said in a small voice.

Gabe shook his head. "Don't look at me like that. You asked for honesty."

Isabella knew she was clinging to her purse, holding it like a shield. "I can't deal with what you're implying, Gabe. It frightens me."

"You're not alone," he said, his blue eyes deepening. "My friends think I've taken leave of my senses."

"So, you're saying you don't make a habit of..." Isabella took one hand off her purse and waved it airily.

"Nope. I always err on the side of caution, in business and in my private life."

"Then...?"

"Why did I buy a sheep ranch when I don't know squat about sheep? You tell me."

Isabella scowled. "How would I know? I've *said* we're practically strangers."

He dragged his eyes from the road and stared at her for a long moment. "Tell you what, Isabella. When you figure it out, we'll have this conversation again. Until that point, let's try and be friends. Before you say anything else, I'm going on record with a promise. Believe me when I tell you I'd sell out and walk away before I'd cause you or your family any harm."

She sawed her top lip between her teeth, clearly thinking hard about what Gabe had said. Her response didn't come until they'd arrived at the parking lot across the street from the county courthouse, where James Hayden had his office.

Gabe took a ticket from the attendant, parked and had come around to help her out. Before he could, she stayed him with a glance. "I value my friends, Gabe. I can't afford to turn one away. As long as you understand there's no point in hoping for more, I'll accept your offer of friendship."

Gabe did want more. He wasn't sure how much more, but he knew he spent a lot of time at night thinking about having her in his bed. However, today she looked more fragile than she had yesterday and the day before. Plus, her eyes, which never failed to cause turbulence in his stomach, appeared more hollow, sunken and bruised in the struggling morning sunlight.

"Friends it is, Isabella." Taking her hand, Gabe helped her out and then tucked her ice-cold fingers under his arm. "Stop worrying. Concentrate on what's taking place in a few minutes. Take your time answering each of Hayden's questions. His goal today is to test your memory to see what kind of witness you'll make in the event he needs to put you on the stand at some point."

"You think he will? Have me testify? Julian's parents told Papa a wife can't testify against her husband."

"You were divorced, Isabella. You won't need to adhere to that statute."

"Good. I'd like a chance to talk to jurors."

"You may think that now. Actually, being a witness is hard. Defense attorneys can be brutal. They'll twist your words and try to undermine your credibility."

"They've tried to do that already. Through the media."

Gabe opened the courthouse door. "Reporters are a whole other side of a high-profile trial. I don't know how Hayden's advised you, but I'd suggest hustling past them without saying a word."

As they reached the crowd waiting for the elevators, Isabella yanked Gabe's sleeve. "If I say nothing, won't they print whatever lies Julian's lawyers feed them?"

"The day's transcripts are open to the public. What reporters will try and wrest from you is private stuff. If defense lawyers are bad, newshounds are worse. The more intelligent they are, the more gifted with words, the more clever the slant they put on a story." Gabe spoke from experience. Even though it seemed a lifetime ago, he remembered how reporters in his hometown had assassinated his mother's character. She had her faults, but it wasn't until years later that he understood most of them were addictive habits succored by poverty, scant education and an absent husband whose family treated her like trash.

"I'll keep that in mind," Isabella muttered before falling silent during the brief elevator ride. She was nervous, she realized, as they faced the door listed on her message slip.

Gabe seemed instinctively to know how she felt. He slid a bolstering arm around her shoulders. "You'll do fine," he promised, smiling down on her upturned face.

His staunch belief in her gave her the burst of courage she needed. Isabella walked out from under his arm, squared her shoulders and stepped up to the harried secretary's desk. "We're here to see Mr. Hayden. I'm Isabella Navarro."

The secretary wasn't fast enough to hide the pitying expression that flashed across her face. Obviously, having dealt with many such cases, she soon recovered and donned a more professional mask. "Will you have a seat, please? Mr. Hayden is finishing some dictation. Ah...you said, *we?* My schedule lists only Ms. Navarro."

Isabella telegraphed Gabe a silent, frustrated plea.

He approached the secretary with a smile. "I'm a family friend. Gabriel Poston. Ms. Navarro's father had a situation at the ranch, and I'm filling in for him." He neglected to mention that he had a degree in law, as he preferred to sit and observe Hayden at work. Gabe deftly extracted a business card from a gold case he removed from an inside pocket. "This shows I'm a CPA and gives an address on the beltway in D.C. Tell Mr. Hayden not to worry about his taxes though—the agency I represent isn't part of the IRS."

The woman behind the desk laughed and tucked Gabe's card under a clip on the file. Isabella hadn't tumbled to the fact before now, but Gabe again wore a dark suit that demanded respect. Had she been so nervous earlier that she'd missed his upscale suit, his white shirt and the geometric print tie with splashes of color that matched his eyes? *Obviously she had.*

As they sat in the waiting area, she brought up his appearance. "I must say, you look at home in a suit."

"I don't mind them. Reggie and Coltrane hate to dress up. It's why they gravitated toward Special Forces," he said with a grin. "They preferred battle gear."

"I don't know much about the military. Special Forces. Are those equivalent to the Green Berets?"

"Yes. Except we were Marines."

"Did you all retire?"

"We mustered out. They would've stayed in, but I met a couple of guys who'd pay big bucks in the private sector for doing pretty much what we did in the Corps. Only without the ritual and regimentation. Outside, we were our own bosses."

"Summer told me what happened to Coltrane. Were you involved in that mess?"

Gabe shifted in the chair and plucked at the crease in his suit pants. "Sometimes things go wrong. It doesn't matter how careful you are."

"How well I know." Cynicism threaded Isabella's words.

"Hey, you aren't blaming yourself for what Julian did, are you?"

She paid an inordinate amount of attention to her carefully tented fingers.

The secretary rose and called for Isabella before Gabe could arrange his thoughts. He reminded himself to return to this conversation after Hayden's meeting. If Isabella had somehow taken part of Julian's guilt upon herself, no wonder she couldn't get on with her life.

Colt had tried to crawl into booze once he was rescued from the rebel prison. It was months before Gabe and company worked through Colt's problems and got down deep enough to learn he blamed himself for screwing up the operation, which had resulted in a loss of life. Gabe supposed that was similar in a way to the fact that Isabella had been the one to find Julian and her kids. Gabe understood her feelings a little better now, understood her sense of guilt.

James Hayden had a so-so handshake. Gabe didn't have a lot of experience with state prosecutors, except to know that many of them aspired to eventually end up in politics. He hoped this guy was tougher than he looked, hoped he could argue and argue well. Too early to say. He'd reserve judgment for the moment.

They were seated at a round table. Hayden—as he quickly discovered—knew more about him than Gabe had told the secretary, which indicated the prosecutor had done at least a brief background check. Hayden went up a notch in Gabe's estimation.

"Okay, Isabella. Let's get down to brass tacks. I apologize for not getting to this sooner. I've been up to my eyeballs in a case we just wrapped up." Hayden opened her file and turned the page on a legal tablet. He removed three pens from his shirt pocket and lined them up in front of him. "There's one area we haven't covered. I wanted to wait until we were closer to jury selection. Give me a rundown on Julian's weaknesses. All of them."

Isabella had been digging through her purse. She'd pulled out the notes she'd taken at Larkin Crosley's law library. Glancing up with a start, she fumbled and dropped the whole packet. Papers slid every which way.

Gabe knelt to retrieve the pages. He heard her groping for words to respond.

"Take your time," Hayden instructed.

"Is this necessary?" she asked, grinding her teeth. "I've worked hard to put that man out of my mind."

"I know. But if I know specific flaws in his character, I can salt carefully worded questions in with a general list we ask potential jurors. The more people we can seat who are biased against his flaws, the better jurors they'll make for us."

"Well, that shouldn't be difficult. His flaws are too numerous to count."

Hayden rolled his eyes, appealing to Gabe for help.

Gabe set the stack of notes aside and took Isabella's hand. She gripped his tightly. He noticed her palm was wet and that her fingers trembled. He hoped Hayden wouldn't have to put her on the stand; she was already a mass of nerves and the trial hadn't begun.

"James needs you to be less vague, Isabella. Start with easy stuff. For instance, did Julian have a temper?"

"That depends on who you ask."

"I'm asking you." Hayden gnashed his teeth.

"Friends, coworkers and acquaintances saw a different face than the one Julian showed me."

James snapped forward in his chair. "So, this guy's a chameleon?"

"That's putting it nicely, but…yes. He had a vicious temper. Only at home, and only after the kids were in bed asleep."

Hayden scribbled on his pad. "No guy can be that controlled all the time. I'll put a team out in the community. We'll trace all the way to his preschool years if we have to. What other endearing habits should we investigate?''

''Gabe helped me extract precedent-setting cases out of old transcripts. Unless Oregon law has changed, some of these winning arguments may be useful to you.'' She handed him the notes.

He read them over, clipped them to her folder, then returned to his former line of questioning. All in all, Hayden grilled Isabella for an hour. Toward the end, her responses were only a few words, and those he had to pry out of her. She nearly wrung Gabe's hand from his wrist. At times her body shook so hard he worried she'd break.

James flipped to a clean sheet on his tablet and picked up the last of his pens. Gabe removed his glasses, stood and tugged her to her feet. ''Enough, James. I know you have a job to do. But if you don't let up, she's not going to make it to the trial.''

The attorney had been intent on his work. He blinked red-rimmed eyes and let his shoulders sag as if seeing the result of his probing for the first time. ''I'm trying to get a profile on this guy.''

''What have you been doing for ten months?'' Gabe snapped. And there went his plan not to interfere, to quietly observe.

''Juggling two hundred open cases with two assistants, five investigators and me to accomplish what law firms like the one Arana hired assign to twenty associates. So don't waltz into my office and give me flak.''

Gabe shook his head. ''Sorry. But you can see that Isabella needs a break.''

She'd been staring wide-eyed at the two men. ''Gabe, thanks, but I'm okay. I've pledged to help convict Julian. I'm just worried about how the answers I gave will play to a jury. In effect, I said Julian has a split personality." She clutched Gabe's hand. "God, I can't let jurors think he's crazy. He's not."

Hayden and Gabe exchanged a glance. Gabe knew then that they both thought Julian Arana was as crazy as a loon. But for Isabella's sake, Gabe hoped James could get a Murder One conviction.

James assumed his prosecutorial smile. "Right off the bat, I'll attempt to seat more women than men." Faced with Isabella's puzzled expression, James explained, "I'm reviewing the sequence this trial will take. In phase one, the jury we seat will determine if Julian's mentally competent to stand for capital charges. This may take a while. Both teams will unload their big guns. If the jury finds Julian able, we'll proceed to determining his guilt or innocence. Almost all the evidence will already be out. Often that part goes fast."

"If he's not found competent," Gabe said, "a judge will determine how many years he spends in a mental institution."

"No," Isabella cried, at the same time James bobbed his head. She grabbed his arm. "He killed my babies to punish me for leaving him. You can't let him get away with murder. You *can't*." Her voice rose.

Hayden wrested free of her. "Take her out the back way, Poston. Get a grip, Isabella. An outburst like this in court and I won't bet two cents on our chances of winning. If there's any hint of a replay of this scene, I'll bar you from proceedings."

Her face turned ashen. "I promise I'll keep it together," she whispered.

Gabe moved her to the door. Seconds before they

exited, he turned back to James. "Is there a number we can reach you at if Isabella changes her mind about sitting in?"

"I won't," she quickly interjected. "I'll be there. Tomorrow, in Bend, at ten o'clock, correct?"

"Cecilia has a folder with all the information you'll need. Oh, do you know where you'll be staying?"

Isabella deferred to Gabe. He patted his pockets and eventually pulled out a scrap of paper with an address and phone number. "I booked a cottage in a gated resort. It's roomy enough to accommodate Isabella's family if they're able to get away. Plus, security there is tight enough to discourage reporters."

"Good." James straightened his rumpled tie while studying Gabe from a new angle. "I'm afraid I didn't catch what you're doing now, Poston. Those transcripts you identified are impressive. I don't suppose I could entice you into interviewing for one of the openings on our staff?"

Gabe laughed. "I'm not licensed to practice law in Oregon. At the moment I'm considering raising sheep."

"Sheep? Isn't that a waste of your talent?"

"Maybe. Maybe not. If I should decide differently, I'll more than likely buy out Larkin Crosley's general practice. He's in Callanton."

"I know Crosley. He's hung on ten years past his prime. It's probably a smart move. But if you change your mind, let me know."

Isabella arrived back, having picked up the information from Cecilia. She listened intently to the men's conversation. Once they'd cleared the hall and had started down the back stairs, she frowned at Gabe. "I can't afford to stay at a resort."

"Sure you can. It's off-season." He named a figure well below what he'd put on his credit card.

"I suppose I can swing that. Gabe, Papa will be disappointed to learn you're giving up running sheep so soon. Are you really thinking about buying Mr. Crosley's practice? Or were you feeding James a line, too?"

"What do you mean, *too?* I haven't fed anyone a line. This morning your father didn't seem too disappointed when I offered to lease my pastures to him for the purpose of expanding his angora goat herd."

"You talked to Papa?"

"While you were getting in your beauty sleep."

She blushed profusely. "That would take more hours than there are in any given day, I'm afraid. Everyone knows I'm the least pretty of the Navarro sisters."

"Then everyone is blind," Gabe said flatly. "Wait here while I go around and get the car. James seemed to think that with the trial getting under way, there might be newshounds hanging around out front."

"Won't they know the trial's been moved to Bend?"

"My guess is they'll stake out your bakery, Hayden's office, your house and the grocery store where you shop."

What little color she had drained from her face. "I'm catering Estrella Aguirre's wedding this evening. Surely they won't disrupt that."

"Can you let Trini, Sylvia and Ruby handle it?"

"No. It's my responsibility. Our families have been friends for years. She's their youngest daughter. It takes weeks to prepare a Basque wedding."

"They're different from other weddings?"

"Your education is deficient. They last for three days or more. The party moves from the church to the bride's home, to the groom's home to the homes of friends. Why don't you come with me and see first-hand?''

''Uh, I'll think about it. I have a tendency to get claustrophobic at weddings. Gotta go get the car. Be right back.''

Her eyebrows spiked upward. But he'd disappeared out the door before she had an opportunity to tease him about his phobia. Maybe he'd been dumped at the altar. Frankly, she found that hard to comprehend. However, she didn't know a lot about his background; she didn't even know if he'd ever been married.

The question bothered her so much, it was the first thing she asked after he'd pulled up and she'd hopped in the SUV.

''Where did that question come from?'' He seemed amused. ''I haven't been married. Why would you think I had?''

''Usually a person who systematically avoids family events has a psychological dread of them, based on experience. You know, events like weddings, holidays…funerals.'' She whispered the last.

Boy, howdy, had she nailed him square. Gabe wasn't ready to bare his soul to her. Mostly because he made a habit of keeping his quirks to himself. Always, in the back of his mind, Gabe worried that if a woman he liked knew all about his family background, she'd be scared right off. An addict mother, a loser father…

''No big deal,'' he said suddenly. ''Hell, I'll go. You've intrigued me now. It's too bad we can't stay for the whole thing. Really? A three-day wedding? Hey, does that mean no honeymoon?''

Color rushed up Isabella's neck again as she suddenly pictured what it'd be like to spend a magical first night in bed with Gabe Poston.

"Well," he drawled, his Texas boyhood accent coming to the fore. "It's a logical question if I'm to be educated in your traditions."

"We…uh…call it *luna de miel.*"

"Ah, a night of honey. I like the sound of a one-night special. American honeymoons are so commercial they're like…vacations."

"I agree," she blurted, then thought about what she'd said and quickly covered her mouth with her hand.

Gabe only grinned. "Now don't be saying you're sorry for speaking your mind. By the way, changing the subject, Trini's wrong about Hayden. The guy's overworked, but he has a fire in the belly for his job."

"I'm glad. I thought so, too. Honestly, I've never heard him speak with the passion he showed today."

"Maybe I should rile him every day." Gabe's smile spread.

"Are you really planning to sit in on the trial?"

"Guaranteed. I wish your family could all be there for you. Since they can't, I've appointed myself their surrogate."

"How can I thank you? I've been counting on them being in my corner. I was sick when the storm brought lambing on early."

"Relax. Use this wedding tonight to unwind. Sample some of Louis's wine and just kick back."

"And have Julian's parents report to his lawyers? I don't think so, Gabe. Besides, I'm going as the caterer, not as a family friend."

"You have to deal with his parents the night before they start picking a jury? Who in God's name would invite them, knowing you were catering the reception?"

"Ours is a small intimate community. Javier and Elena Arana grew up with Estrella's parents, the same as mine. I'll have to avoid them if at all possible."

"Point them out and I'll run interference."

"I need you to stay out of this, Gabe. The Aranas are doing their damnedest to ruin my name in the valley. If it weren't for the fact that I'm the only Basque caterer on this side of the Idaho border, I think Estrella's parents would've canceled their order. I know you and I are just friends. I also know Elena's propensity for—how do you say it—making mountains out of mole holes."

"Molehills. All right, I'll try and abide by your wishes, Isabella. But I'm not making promises. I won't stand idly by and let someone attack your character."

Isabella's heart sped up, and she felt an odd warmth she hadn't experienced in such a long time. Had she *ever* had a man, other than her brothers, so unquestionably behind her? Certainly back when they were dating, Julian had warned his friends to watch their mouths around her. Who knew what else he'd said to them in private? In light of what she knew about him now, his warnings probably had been more about staking his territory than about her.

"If I begged you not to engage the Aranas in any confrontation, Gabe, would you respect my request?"

He stopped outside her bakery. Judging by the tension filling the SUV, Gabe felt the question had more significance than any of the others she'd asked him. Needing to touch her, he bent and brushed his lips over hers.

Feeling no response, he slowly withdrew until he sat

upright, facing her again. "If something means that much to you, Isabella, of course I give you my word. It's not my wish to make your life harder. In fact, what I had in mind is the opposite."

For the first time in their brief relationship, she voluntarily touched him. Isabella laid a hand alongside Gabe's cheek, and she actually smiled at him.

He basked in the brilliance of that smile for hours after she'd left his vehicle.

CHAPTER TWELVE

ONE HOUR INTO the two-and-a-half-hour drive from Callanton to Bend, Gabe glanced over at Isabella, who'd been asleep since he'd picked her up. He stifled a yawn, envying her. She hadn't exaggerated one bit about the partying fools who'd attended Estrella's wedding. For himself, he'd called a halt at 3:00 a.m., but he had no idea how long Isabella had stuck around. The long tables set up at each end of the Basque Center had never lacked for food, which was her doing.

Every time Gabe thought the musicians were winding down, a new group showed up with drums, horns and stringed instruments, and the crowds surged into the center of the hall again.

Gabe hadn't danced so much in years. But he never circled the floor with Isabella. She wouldn't dance with anyone except her brothers, one dance each. Gabe whirled around the floor with her sisters, her mother and her sisters-in-law, including Christina, who couldn't see her toes due to her advanced pregnancy. Gabe met a lot of nice people at the wedding, and a few who studied him suspiciously.

Heading that list were Mr. and Mrs. Arana. They'd greeted him politely enough. But after listening to the whispers that trailed in the couple's wake, Gabe realized that had he not known Isabella, the Aranas' allegations might have raised doubts about her.

He managed to keep his promise and not confront them because everyone at the wedding strove so hard to be neutral.

The scenery flying past his window couldn't compare to the lush valley they'd left behind. Right before they'd driven off from the Navarros' *caserío,* Luisa had pressed a sack of food into Gabe's hands. Amid tears of regret about the family's not going to Bend, she asked him to stop at a little town called Brothers. There was a roadside picnic area nearby, according to Luisa. He should get Isabella to eat something. According to signs, they were nearing the spot. Gabe shook Isabella gently.

She opened one eyelid. "Are we there?" Bolting awake, she straightened her suit and shined the angel pin Gabe had given her, which adorned her lapel.

He was pleased but didn't say anything about it. "This isn't Bend, but it's our last chance to stretch our legs. We don't want to go into court looking like we just climbed out of bed."

"I've been so nervous, I can't believe I actually slept."

"Jury selection is boring. You won't want to sit through it after today."

"I will. If prospective jurors have to look at me every day, maybe they'll think about what I've lost. Everything," she said woodenly. "I've lost everything."

Patting her arm, Gabe pulled into the lay-by. Theirs was the only vehicle on the high windswept plateau. Dark clouds had hung up on a distant mountain peak, and he thought it might rain. "When you went upstairs to get your suitcase, your mom gave me a sack of *talos,* jam and sausages."

"I see a thermos. I only want coffee."

"Too much caffeine on an empty stomach will make you jittery. At least eat part of a *talos*. It'll be something to soak up the caffeine."

"Mama wanted to come. I wish she could have. Although I'd rather have them all at the trial."

"I know, sweetheart." As they stepped from the SUV, Gabe tugged Isabella into an embrace.

She burrowed close, accepting his solid warmth. Even then she shivered.

He briskly rubbed her back. "I hope it's warmer in Bend." The city, which had begun as a ranch community like Callanton, had grown steadily, thanks to tourists headed for Sun River and Mount Bachelor. "If you'd rather eat while we travel, I think we'll have time to check into the cottage, and freshen up before we need to be in court."

"Really? I'd like that." She ducked out of his arms so fast, Gabe cursed himself for making the suggestion.

Traffic remained light, and the rain held off. They reached the resort with an hour to spare. Gabe showed his ID at the main gate. A security guard called the front desk to confirm that they were registered, then provided Gabe with a sticker for his windshield and an electronic gate card. "The receptionist said you're involved in the big court case that's starting today. This card frees you up from checking with us each time. The gate arm swings shut fast, and ought to keep reporters from following you."

"Thanks. Yeah, media will be a problem if the case goes to trial." Gabe propped the tag where it could be readily seen and pocketed the card.

"Why did you say *if* the case goes to trial?" Isabella asked after they'd passed the gatehouse.

"Because it'd take too much time to explain the difference between phase one and phase two. Media coverage will triple if Julian's found competent to be charged with murder."

"He *has* been charged, hasn't he?"

"Yes and no. The charge goes into effect if he's medically and mentally sound."

Isabella seemed to retreat inside herself. She let Gabe check into the facility for both of them and roused only to accept the second key he handed her. Her first response of any kind came in the form of a gasp when he unlocked the cottage and stood aside to let her enter.

"Gabe, this is impossibly luxurious! There must be a mistake. We can't be getting all this for the amount you told me."

"I qualified for frequent flyer upgrades. I traveled a lot for SOS."

Isabella stepped to the middle of a central living space where light flooded in from clerestory windows. Turning slowly, she surveyed the thick gold carpet, the pale yellow walls, a beautiful brick fireplace surrounded by comfortable, inviting furniture.

Gabe pointed out a fair-sized kitchen and two couches that converted into beds before he led her to one of two bedrooms set on either side of a large, shared bath.

"I can't stay here." She grabbed the suitcase he'd set on her bed and started for the door.

"Wait! Why not? I've arranged to have the kitchen stocked while we're out. I thought you'd like to have some meals here. The place offers hiking, horseback riding and indoor swimming. You'll need to unwind after sitting all day in court."

"What if someone reports that we're…uh…staying together?"

"Who'll know except us, your family and James Hayden? I was assured the resort staff is very discreet. The registry is kept under lock and key. It'll be fine, Isabella. Or…is it…that you don't trust me?" Gabe confronted her with fists on his hips. He tried not to show how much her answer mattered.

"I trust you." As she walked past him, taking her suitcase back to the bed, it crossed her mind to wonder if she ought to trust herself. She alone knew how difficult it had been last night, watching him laugh and dance with her sisters. She'd cautioned herself a hundred times not to be jealous—he and she were nothing more than friends. But her heart refused to accept the truth that kept rearing its head.

He gazed at her stiff back for a few seconds, until her clipped statement sank in. "Well, good. Since that's settled, why don't you unpack. I'll do the same. We have twenty minutes before we need to leave."

Isabella sensed more than heard when he left her alone. Her knees had gone so weak, she finally turned and sat on the edge of the bed, clenching her shaking hands. Accepting these arrangements probably wasn't smart. Definitely wasn't smart. *What harm can come of it?* argued another part of her brain—the part Isabella chose to hear. *You're a big girl. The cottage is almost as big as the house you shared with Julian. You managed to avoid him for weeks after you filed for divorce.*

Feeling calmer, Isabella rose and hung her things in the closet. Storing her bath items in drawers and a cabinet where Gabe had already left his soap and shaving kit almost sent her running again.

She picked up a new bar of soap and sniffed the wrapper. A light, woodsy aroma, which Isabella recognized as Gabe's, was discernible for only a second, as if his ghost had walked by. It was far superior to anything her brothers wore. Keenly aware of the fact that she couldn't pass any counter displaying Julian's aftershave without gagging, she wondered if her brain had drawn her to Gabe because she found this tangy scent so appealing.

Replacing the shaving kit where she'd found it, Isabella bent over the sink and splashed cold water on her face and wrists. She fluffed her hair and applied some fresh lipstick, refusing to let her eyes stray again to Gabe's personal belongings.

"Ah, so you've finished," Gabe said when she emerged from the bathroom. "Rather than take any more time, let's stop somewhere on the way for coffee. I checked the phone book, and found a place near the courthouse."

"I'd love a coffee with cream." She slung her purse over her shoulder and advanced to the door. "I've got a beautiful view of snow-capped peaks from my bedroom window."

"The clouds have disappeared. It may turn out to be a nice day."

"I don't know about nice, but not so gloomy at least."

"I'm sorry, Isabella. It's easy for me to look around and pretend I'm on vacation. You constantly live with the truth of why we're here."

"It's a relief to finally get to this point. As the days and weeks passed, it was as if other people forgot what happened. Oh, not my family, but others. Whenever I go home at night, I still expect to see Toni and Ramon coloring at Mama's table or playing with my brothers' and sisters' kids. Over Christmas, I wanted to die.''

"God, Isabella." Gabe reached out and clasped her hand.

"God is why I'm still here. My beliefs would never allow me to take my life or anyone else's. Part of what's so incomprehensible to me is that Julian and I were raised in the same faith. We rarely missed attending church.''

Gabe puzzled over her remarks. If she had all that figured out, why was it so difficult for her to accept that Julian's mind might simply have snapped? Considering how defensive she always got, he didn't say what he was thinking.

They picked up coffee before parking in one of the lots near the courthouse. As they entered the building, Gabe noticed that Isabella seemed to have trouble catching her breath. No wonder—a bailiff was coming down the steps leading a group of prospective jurors. "Are you okay?" he whispered near her ear.

"Silly, isn't it?" she whispered back. "Julian's the one who should have problems breathing. It's just…these people look so ordinary, and they wield such power.''

"Guess I never thought of it that way. Keep in mind that most jurors take their responsibility very seriously.''

Isabella nodded as they entered a courtroom already filling up with people.

Hayden spotted them right off and motioned them up front. Gabe would've preferred to observe from the back of the room, although he knew James would want Isabella front and center.

"You can relax, Isabella. Neither Julian nor anyone

from his family is sitting in on the selection of jurors,''
Hayden said after introducing them to his team of
three.

Isabella frowned. ''How will that work in Julian's
favor?''

James unloaded his briefcase. ''I don't know that it
will.''

''Are you kidding? Every move Julian makes is calculated.''

The junior prosecutor no doubt thought he was helping when he told her the opposing team had presented
the judge with a doctor's certificate stating Julian's
health precluded his attending anything but the actual
trial.

''Bullpucky,'' was Isabella's succinct response. She
sat then, revealing an odd mix of anger and dignity.

Frustrations mounted on all sides as the day wore
on. The judge, who apparently liked the sound of his
own voice, lectured prospective jurors on trial rules ad
nauseam. When he finished culling out those he
deemed unsuitable, it was lunchtime.

''I'm not hungry,'' Isabella said, even though she
went with Gabe, James and his associates to a sandwich shop a few blocks from the court.

''If you don't want a sandwich, then have soup,''
Gabe said.

''My stomach already feels like a churning cement
mixer. Throwing food in there isn't such a great idea,
Gabe.''

''Eating something may take the edge off your headache.''

''How did you know I have a headache?''

''I'm not psychic.'' His grin spread slowly. ''You've
been rubbing your neck for the last hour.''

The lawyers trooped to the table. James made room for all their plates and cups. "You two had better eat. I know Judge Weller. This phase could take days."

Isabella steepled her fingers. "I thought you said you and Julian's lawyer would be asking the questions."

"We may get a crack at the potential jurors he passes on this afternoon. No one ever said this was going to be a simple case, Isabella."

"No. No, it isn't. But I never imagined convicting him would take so long."

James Hayden stopped with a sandwich halfway to his mouth. "Isabella," he cautioned, "I warned you about making those kinds of remarks. Julian is innocent until proven guilty in a court of law."

"Not in my book. He's guilty as guilty can be," she bit back with such fury that Gabe looped an arm around her shaking shoulders.

"Have you ever been on a jury?" one of the assistants asked.

Isabella shook her head as she sank against Gabe. "But if I were called, I'd never be wishy-washy like some of those people. Anyone who's read the paper or watched TV can't doubt Julian's intent. He ran a hose from his tailpipe into the car. James, you said you only have to prove intent."

Gabe felt the muscles along her neck and back tighten. He wished there was some way he could ease the terrible pain she seemed determined to inflict on herself. "The lunch hour is half gone. Come through the line with me and pick out a soup."

She rose and followed him without enthusiasm. "You said James had a passion for his work," she murmured dully as Gabe thrust a tray into her nerveless hands.

"He does. The system demands he try his best to seat twelve unbiased people. They do exist. It takes time, but the teams will get there, you'll see."

"I'll pray for biased people, Gabe. Ones willing to avenge Toni and Ramon."

"There's no point in arguing, Isabella. Our soup choices are broccoli-cheese or minestrone."

"I'll have a toasted bagel, plain."

Gabe gave their order before she could change her mind and come away with nothing. He was glad to see James and his assistants tossing their trash in the waste cans, getting ready to leave by the time he and Isabella sat down again.

"Chris spilled catsup on his tie." James pointed to the splotch. "We'll run back to the hotel so he can change. See you two in court at one o'clock."

Gabe had ordered the broccoli-cheese soup. He checked the paisley tie he had on and muttered to Isabella, "If I spill any of this, we won't have time to go back to the cottage."

"You're lucky. There's yellow and green already mixed in with the blue. The soup will blend right in," she said, which told Gabe she wasn't all nerves and no humor. If only he knew how to help her reach beyond the hatred she'd stored up. Maybe he ought to admit he'd once been consumed with hostility, too. He'd remained miserable until he learned the only road out was to let go of his anger at his parents. Mostly Russ, but then he had discovered he was also furious at his mother for dying. Ultimately he decided Isabella didn't need his old troubles heaped atop hers.

The first half of the afternoon was a repeat of the morning. A second pool of twenty-four would-be jurors trooped into the room behind a bailiff, only to be subjected to the same scrutiny by Weller. Midway through the afternoon, James and Julian's attorney were finally given the go-ahead to ask questions of those Weller had okayed.

Isabella stopped fidgeting and leaned forward in her seat.

Back and forth the teams hurled questions, one after another. Isabella nearly jumped out of her skin when the judge banged his gavel.

"May I advise the court that these proceedings are suspended until 9:00 a.m. tomorrow." Weller rose in a rustle of black silky robes. His clerk hurriedly asked everyone to rise.

"What's happening?" Isabella asked Gabe, who'd pulled her out of her chair.

"It's five o'clock. Time for us to go."

James shut his folders and approached Isabella and Gabe. "The last hour went well, don't you agree?"

"Well?" Isabella gaped. "The day's gone and you've only selected one man and one woman to be on the jury."

"Which only gives us ten to go. Isabella, I explained this phase would likely be long and drawn-out. If you'd rather conserve your energy for the competency arguments, then by all means, do so."

"Absolutely not. I'm not missing one minute."

"Suit yourself." He aimed a slight shrug toward Gabe.

"Before you go—is there a back door? I saw several eager-beaver reporters out front. I'd like to duck them for Isabella's sake if we can."

He shook his head. "Just hustle on by those jokers or they'll hound you to death. It's way too early to make statements to the press."

Gabe did his darnedest to shield Isabella from having notepads, microphones and flashing cameras shoved into her face. The two of them were out of breath when they reached the Lexus.

"Are you okay?" he asked, stripping off the glasses he'd worn in court.

"To tell you the truth, I don't know." Closing her eyes, she cupped both hands over her face. "They all ask how I feel. How do they *think* I feel, for pity's sake?"

Gabe fastened their seat belts. "News is their job, and this trial is news," he said matter-of-factly. He motioned for two particularly pushy reporters to get out from behind the SUV. "I'm backing out," he warned, lowering his window a crack.

They scattered at the last moment and he drove away.

"Gabe, some of them are following us." Isabella had grown panicky.

"It's their turf. No sense trying to ditch them. We'll rely on the resort's security to keep the wolves off our doorstep."

"Why are they so interested in knowing your name?"

"They smell a sidebar. I'm a new wrinkle," he explained. "Reporters are always on the lookout for a scandal."

"What?" Her voice rose shrilly.

Gabe slowed to go through the resort gate. He had the electronic key card in his hand, but couldn't resist bending over and planting a kiss on Isabella's lips in order to silence what would surely lead to another disagreement.

She pressed a hand to her tingling lips, never realizing they'd passed through the gates and left the reporters outside.

"We'll change clothes. You can phone your folks and catch them up. Then let's take a horseback ride through the pines before I toss a couple of steaks on the grill. Wait—do you ride?"

"Yes. I owned two horses. Julian sold them. He hated the way I smelled when I came in from a ride. Or that was his excuse. He didn't like to ride, but disliked even more that riding got me out from under his watchful eye."

"I proposed a ride as a way to relax. If it brings you bad memories—"

"You know, it does sound inviting. Gosh, I hope I haven't forgotten how. It's been ten years."

"I don't think you forget how." He winked at her. "It's like riding a bike."

"All right. Please make the arrangements. And Gabe, thanks. I feel less tense already."

He smiled as he unlocked the cottage. Once they were inside, he reached up and released the clip holding Isabella's braid. When the hair didn't at once tumble free, Gabe threaded his fingers through the strands.

She grabbed his hand. "Why did you do that? It takes me an hour to fix a nice French braid."

He teased the soft ends of her hair between forefinger and thumb. "All day I've been watching you rub your head. Can you honestly tell me this doesn't feel better?"

"Of course it does. But if I wear it loose, it falls to my waist and takes years off my age. I need the jurors to see me as a woman, not a girl."

"No danger of missing that, Isabella." Gabe's eyes

darkened appreciably. His fingers inched up to her neck, and he leaned toward her lips again.

She sidestepped his touch and massaged her upper arms briskly. "We're, uh, just friends, remember?"

Gabe brushed back a lock of his own hair, which had fallen into his eyes. "Right! Friends. So." He blew out air. "Do you want first crack at the bathroom?"

"Go ahead. I'll, ah…phone Mama. She'll be anxious to hear from me. Then you can call the stable while I change into jeans."

An hour later, their ride went off without a hitch. Afterward, the steaks were grilled to perfection, even if Gabe did say so himself. Isabella refused to share the wine he'd carefully chosen to go with the meal. He regretted making that earlier move on her; it had left her wary of being alone with him in the cottage.

"You have a lock on your bedroom door," he felt compelled to point out when she made excuses to flee there the moment dishes had been dispensed with.

"Rick's coming tomorrow. Just for the day. He'll probably have a lot to say about our accommodations. I'm sorry, Gabe. My brother's a nice man. He's only gotten this way after Julian—well, Rick's afraid I'll be hurt again."

"You have my word I'd never hurt you, Isabella. I can handle Rick, okay?"

She nodded, but it didn't stop her from shooting home the dead bolt on her door.

COURT WAS MORE UNCOMFORTABLE for Gabe the next day, Rick Navarro's hulking presence being the largest contributor. "I rented the cottage for security reasons," he told Rick after lunch. They were waiting for Isabella to return from the ladies' room. "There are two hide-a-beds in the cottage. You're welcome to use them. Same goes for any member of your family. Move in tonight. I'll get you an extra key.''

''You know damn well I can't take more than a day at a time away from the orchards. All of us are in the same boat.''

''I can't help that.'' Gabe straightened his tie. ''This isn't about us.'' He looked directly into Rick's eyes. ''You helped stave off the mob of reporters earlier—you saw what it's like. Isabella's beyond their reach at the resort.''

''But not beyond yours.'' Plenty of heat dripped off Rick's words.

''No. Not beyond mine,'' Gabe said flatly. ''Can't you see I care about her?''

Rick reared back to study his adversary. ''Hurt her, Poston, and we'll settle this in a different way.''

Gabe rattled around the cottage alone that night. Rick took Isabella out to dinner and didn't invite him. Needing to release some energy, Gabe ambled off to swim laps. He missed Isabella's arrival home. She'd left a note on the kitchen counter saying Joe would pick her up in the morning. *Fine!* He'd take Wednesday off and run home to see how the carpentry work was coming.

It was while he was there that he learned Manny planned to be in court the following day. ''Here, take my key card to save explaining to security. And this card gives my cell number. Someone can let me know when or if I'm needed in Bend again. I'm glad we all agree Isabella shouldn't go through this trial process alone.''

''Look, Bella's five years my senior. I think Rick's gone overboard, but—hey, we're family.''

"I have no experience in that quarter, Manny. But I'd never get between Isabella and her family. Just keep me updated, okay?"

Early the next morning, at daybreak, Gabe's cell phone rang. He'd spent half the night tearing out kitchen cabinets and felt as if he'd barely gotten to sleep. "'Lo," he croaked.

"Gabe, it's Manny. Manny Navarro. Christina went into labor about an hour ago. I'm at the hospital. The doctor thinks she may need a C-section."

Scrambling in the dark to find his clothes, Gabe asked what he could do to help. "Do you want me to bring your mother to the hospital?"

"She's here. Most of the family is. I'm calling because it leaves Bella alone. Joe said they still have three jurors to go. And Bella's a bundle of nerves. Joe says she's worried sick about the outcome."

"Plus now she'll have Christina to worry over. Damn, it's almost six o'clock." Gabe stroked his unshaven jaw. "I worked on the house till three. Did Joe say what time court reconvenes?"

"Ten."

"If traffic's with me, I may get in before they close the doors. Phone Isabella and have her take a cab. Tell her I'll meet her at the courthouse. And Manny, call me on my cell to let us know how Christina makes out. Good luck, man."

After the fastest shower and shave in history, Gabe was on the road in sixteen minutes. He'd left extra clothes at the cottage, so he didn't need to pack. Surely they ought to be able to agree on the last three jurors today, he thought. That would let Isabella come home to be with her family during this crisis. She'd have a few days to spend with them before the hard part of the trial began.

He dashed into the courtroom with mere minutes to spare. As Gabe slid into the empty seat next to Isabella, he tried not to show his shock at her pale, drawn appearance. She looked a wreck.

"Gabe! Manny said you'd be here. I'm so torn about staying or going home."

"Any word on Christina's condition?" he asked, not caring who saw him rub life back into Isabella's cold hands.

She gave a shake of her head. "Not a word. Manny sounded frantic."

"If they'd get this show on the road, with luck we'll be done early enough to get you back to Callanton to see your new niece or nephew. Unless—will that be too hard on you, Isabella? To see a baby, I mean."

She squeezed his fingers. "It will, but not as hard as if Christina lo-loses this baby. Her first. God, Gabe, I couldn't handle another funeral. I couldn't."

"Whoa! Manny didn't even hint that was a possibility."

Members of the defense team whirled and glared at them. Gabe belatedly realized everyone else was standing because the judge had entered the room.

They'd been wrong in assuming the final jurors would be seated quickly. Five o'clock rolled around, after a grueling day of first one lawyer dismissing a juror, then the other throwing out the next one. Everyone left in a snit.

"James is concerned," Isabella said as Gabe shut them both into the Lexus. "He's determined the last three slots on the jury should go to women."

"It's apparent the defense team knows and intends

to block him. Here's my cell. Phone Manny and find out what's going on. I think we should head back to Callanton tonight."

"And not see who the last jurors are?" She bit her lip. "I want to stay. I hope they can complete the jury selection on Friday."

The phone rang then, and Isabella almost dropped it.

"Manny, thank heaven," she cried. "How's Christina? You have a girl?" She covered the phone. "They have a daughter," she informed Gabe. "She didn't need a C-section?" Turning, Isabella spoke into the phone again. "So, everything went slow but fine? You named her Manuela. Well, that's original." She rolled her eyes at Gabe. "Actually, it didn't wind down today. No progress. Hopefully tomorrow. Either way, I'll be home for the weekend. It's okay, Manny. Tell Rick to get a life. Hug Christina and the baby for me." She said the last brightly. Too brightly.

Gabe knew that both the ordeal in court and the shaky birth of her niece had rattled Isabella. "What's there to eat at the cottage? Do you want to go out somewhere instead? Somewhere nice where we can toast Manuela's entry into the world?"

"What about those blasted reporters?"

"I was thinking of the resort dining room. From what I saw, it's pretty posh."

"How posh? I packed one dress, raw silk, but nothing out of the ordinary."

"You could wear a laundry bag and still be the most beautiful woman in the room."

Isabella snorted in disbelief and averted her eyes.

It pleased Gabe to see some pink appear in her cheeks. She'd looked like a damned ghost.

And he'd been right on the mark, he saw an hour

later when she emerged from the bathroom wearing a sleeveless black dress that hit her mid-thigh. He could barely keep his eyes in his head and didn't even attempt to stifle a growl of pleasure.

"Stop. You're too good for my ego, Gabe."

"It's about time someone is. Do you want to walk or drive?"

"Walk. It's cool, but I brought a coat. It's not far."

Gabe hadn't expected her to agree to a glass of wine. He ordered a bottle after they were seated and handed menus. She surprised him as she often did.

"Remind me to tell Louis I've found a red wine better than his." She licked her lips and Gabe felt rooted to his chair. He fumbled for words.

"How's the work going on your house?" she asked.

"It's humming right along," he managed after a few seconds. "The deck's half done. I tore out kitchen cupboards last night."

They were interrupted by the waiter and quickly ordered their meals—chicken for him, salmon for her.

"Gabe, I'm really sorry Rick's acting like such an ass." She poured them each more wine.

Taking her hand, he toyed with her fingers and was grateful she didn't pull away. "If I had a sister, Isabella, I'd probably be worse than Rick."

"I believe so. If I was in any position to be more than friends with a man, Gabe, well…" she cast down her lashes and blushed. "I'd pick you," she blurted.

Astonished, he groped for words that wouldn't slide past the clog in his throat. Luckily, their meals were delivered, and they spent the next hour eating and getting to know more about each other. He found out Isabella liked poker.

She learned he'd visited places in the world where

she'd traveled only in books. Gabe had such a vivid way of describing them, she believed she'd step out of the restaurant and find herself somewhere exotic. A place with white sandy beaches and swaying palms.

It was the most relaxed either of them had been in a while. They lingered over the last of the wine. Finally, since neither wanted coffee, they had no choice but to leave.

Isabella slid her arm through Gabe's as they sauntered through the crisp cool night. He paused, drew her beneath a pine, and kissed her softly. They kissed quite a few times before they all but fell, panting, through the front door. "Your perfume drives me wild," he admitted, licking his way from her ear and down her neck.

"Likewise," she murmured, shedding her coat, uncaring that it hit the floor even as she swayed forward seeking another of his lethal kisses. Her hands busily untied his tie. "You must own stock in a tie company. Do you know they all match your eyes?"

"A tie is a tie is a tie," he murmured.

Isabella's shoes hit the floor, one after the other. She dispensed with them at the same moment she slid her hands between Gabe's shirt and his jacket, which rapidly landed on the carpet, followed by his loafers and then his shirt.

Catching her hands, he walked her backward to his bedroom, all the while running a row of wet kisses from her ear to the round neck of her little black dress. Her zipper slid down with a hiss as he tumbled her onto his wide, soft bed. This time the hiss escaped Gabe's parted lips as the silk dress slithered between them, exposing Isabella's creamy skin and a nothing of a black bra.

She wiggled out of the dress. Then as he watched with blue eyes turning silver in the shaft of moonlight streaking across the bed, she slowly peeled off her sheer black panty hose.

He'd rolled to the side, allowing her room to complete her mission. He felt his heart slam up into his throat. When it dropped back, it beat in four-four time. Parts of his brain went numb with wanting her. He heard the snick of his belt buckle, and before every shred of good sense failed him, Gabe pulled her against his chest and asked in a roughened voice, "If this isn't leading all the way down the path, stop me now. Otherwise I don't think I can be responsible. But...I'm not prepared."

"Shh. I have an IUD." She wedged a space between them and covered his lips with two trembling fingers. "Don't talk. Don't think. Just...do."

Gabe was ready. More than ready. And she'd extended all the invitation he needed. He stripped off what remained of his clothes, only taking time to make sure Isabella was equally ready. *She certainly was.* Yet she looked so beautiful and so fragile lying there in the center of his massive bed. Imbued by a rush of tenderness, he bore most of his considerably greater weight on his arms as he entered her little by little by little. Even though his arms shook and sweat plastered his dark hair to his brow, Gabe maintained that position until he felt her open, submit fully and cry out in pleasure. He rolled off her then, letting her set the pace for what followed.

For several hours, the world receded as Gabe tasted the passion he'd always believed Isabella was capable of giving. And she gave without reservation, filling his heart with a joy greater than he'd ever known.

CHAPTER THIRTEEN

THE SUNLIGHT WOKE ISABELLA. She lay still a moment, disoriented and unsure of her surroundings. A strange but pleasant lethargy weighted her body, making it oh-so-tempting to nod off to sleep again.

Beside her the mattress dipped and shook a little. Suddenly, a shadow loomed above her, blocking the ribbon of sun. A man's chest pressed against her back. Isabella screamed.

"Whoa! Whoa, there." A scratchy masculine voice sent her diving frantically for the sheet, which had slipped to her waist.

Julian? Oh, God! For a panicked moment she fought to untangle her limbs. *Where was her nightgown? Gone!* Fear slammed through her as Isabella discovered she was naked.

"Isabella, stop! What is it? Are you having a nightmare?"

Gabe, groggy himself from a long night of making love, rolled toward her and attempted to soothe her with gentle hands. He strung soft kisses along the pulse thundering in her neck. Feeling her flesh jump crazily under his lips left Gabe hard, and left him wanting her all over again.

Practically tearing the sheet from the bed, Isabella moved back against the headboard. Once again large hands reached for her. A gruff but imploring voice asked what was wrong.

Gabe. Gabe. Not Julian. He hadn't come back to torment her. Dropping her head onto her knees, Isabella tucked them against her chest. She moaned as memories of a long, passionate night washed over her. "I'm sorry. Gabe, I'm so sorry." Lifting her head, she stared at his unshaven morning face. His thick, dark hair was endearingly spiked.

"Stop apologizing, dammit. If you and I remotely felt the same last night, there'd be no damned need for the word *sorry* to pass between us." Gabe flung off the rest of the sheet and stalked around the bed to face her.

She blanched. Last night she'd only felt Gabe's fitness as they rolled and tumbled across his bed. In daylight, his sculpted body, tanned except for a pale narrow strip starting low on his hips, left her mouth dry and her throat parched. "I'm...sorry," she breathed, unable to help herself.

He threw up his hands and strode to the window, where he stood with one arm braced against the frame to support his forehead. He said nothing, but the rigid muscles of his back shouted his feelings clearly enough.

"I'm not in the habit of waking up with a man in my bed," she said by way of explanation. "I don't know what's...correct."

He turned and drilled her with smoldering eyes. "A good morning kiss would've been nice."

She ran a hand through her heavy, disheveled hair. "What time is it? Court convenes at nine."

Gabe bent his head and stared through the door at

the kitchen clock. "If that clock's right, it's ten to eleven."

"What?" she shrieked, bounding off the bed. "My Lord, it is." She'd found her watch among the folds of her black dress and discarded underwear. "Why didn't you set an alarm?"

His slow sexy smile shook her. "The last time we made love, the clock said 4:00 a.m. Getting up—getting any part of me up—after that seemed a remote possibility."

Not responding to his provocative remark, she began to frantically gather her clothing. "If we hurry, we can be there for start of afternoon session. I'll shower first."

"Why don't we shower together and say to hell with the session?" Crossing the room, he lifted her, the sheet and the clothes she'd collected, and swung her around.

"Quit it, Gabe." She sounded so stern, he set her down at once.

"Last night was—" She broke off as his bright blue eyes narrowed.

"Go on." He crossed his arms. "Last night was…what?"

She angled her chin upward. "A result of too much stress. Too much wine after worrying about Christina. Speaking plainly—last night was a mistake, Gabe."

He wasn't able to cloak his pain fast enough. He recoiled as if she'd slapped him. Indeed, it felt as if she had. Reeling from the blow, he kicked the bedspread aside and searched for his suit pants and shirt. "Last night you began as a bundle of nerves. If you continue to sit in court day after day, you're gonna self-destruct."

"I thought I'd made it clear. Nothing is more important than this trial. Nothing."

"Yes. Well, the outcome's going to be the same whether you kill yourself over it or not."

"Julian has to pay. With prison time. I want him sentenced to a hundred years." Her face was white, her eyes stark, burning holes. "I thought you understood me."

Gabe yanked on his pants and gentled his tone. "One way or another, they're locking the bastard up, Isabella." He zipped his pants and slung his shirt around his neck. "Asylums aren't exactly the Ritz, you know."

"Javier and Elena chose a private sanitarium. It's like a resort. I won't have him lounging his life away among the birds and flowers. Antonia loved flowers. Julian took all that away. I hate him. I hate him." She clutched her clothing to her heaving breast. Her dark eyes were bottomless, and a bit wild.

"Isabella, hate is eating you alive. Listen to me. You're not going to heal yourself until you dig deep inside and forgive the man who's caused you pain."

"*Forgive* him? That's blasphemy." She was shaking all over. "If I live to be a thousand I'll never, ever forgive that man. A parent should protect his children from harm. Julian used them to punish me. I asked the family court judge not to give him unsupervised visitations. They didn't listen. I knew he was mean and manipulative. No one would listen. Well, I'll make them listen now. I'll *make* them listen."

If Gabe had ever doubted that Julian Arana was a bastard, a man who'd subtly abused his wife, he doubted no more. "I understand what you feel. I've sort of been there, Isabella. Not to this extent...but I know what it's like to hate. It can emotionally cripple you. Forgiving someone who hurts you isn't easy. It's tough. Damned tough. But I'm here to tell you, your life will stall where it is now if you don't get past the betrayal.''

"If I wanted psychobabble, I'd go to a shrink.''

"Maybe you should,'' Gabe said. "They make you see—''

"Get out! You'd no idea what I'm feeling. My heart is bleeding inside. Go. I never want to see you again.''

"Isabella…'' He said quietly, tentatively.

"Go. I'll phone Rick or Joe or Louis to come get me.''

Because Gabe feared he might have pushed her too far, too fast, he yanked his things from the closet, jammed them in his suitcase and after one last worried glance at her, he pressed his key into her limp hand. "The rent on the cottage is paid for a month. Get someone in your family to stay with you when they start the trial.'' Brushing a light kiss on her hair, Gabe made sure she'd come out of her catatonic state before he left.

Feeling anger spewing up from her toes, Isabella pitched the key across the room and knew satisfaction when it bounced off the wall. How dared he counsel her to forgive a man as purely evil as Julian! Who was Gabe, anyway? What gave him the right to spout off to her about forgiveness?

It was a question that nagged her on the cab ride to the courthouse. And bothered her enough to sow seeds of doubt during the trip back to Callanton with Joe, who'd come to take her home for the weekend.

"What happened to Gabe? Manny was pretty sure he said he'd be able to attend the rest of the jury selection process with you. But then, Manny's been a head case lately.'' Joe grinned the Navarro grin. ''You'd think Christina was the only woman in the world who ever delivered a baby. Sorry, I had to say that. So, what's with Gabe?''

''Something came up.'' Isabella curled into a corner of Joe's truck.

''You seem depressed, Bella. On TV, that prosecutor fellow acted real happy over who's gonna be on the jury.''

''Hayden managed to seat three more women. He says that's significant. Joe…has Gabe said anything about his background any time the two of you have talked?''

''Nothing that I recall. He's a good sport. Catches on to things fast. He's generous. I say that because of the lease terms he gave Papa and me on his pastures. He could've asked a lot more. Why? He say something to make you doubt him?''

She shrugged listlessly. ''No.'' She didn't want to tell Joe about the blow-up she'd had with Gabe. Being an older brother, he might think he had to defend her. But judging by the way he scowled at her now, she needed to give him some other reason. ''The other day Rick said we didn't know beans about Gabe. Not where he came from or why he suddenly appeared. Or why a *maketo* would buy land in a Basque community.''

''I guess technically he is a stranger.'' Joe scratched an ear. ''Gabe's savvy enough about land to know that the only other good piece that's been on the market was the Forked Lightning. His buddy, Colt, waltzed off with that prize. Say, if you want to check up on Gabe, talk to Quinn. Sounds as if they've been friends a long time.''

"Hmm. Maybe. So tell me about our new niece. Is she as cute as Manny claims?"

GABE HAD beaten Isabella to the punch. As she rode home with her brother, he sat, pouring his guts out over coffee in Summer Quinn's kitchen. Summer's son Rory was visiting Jesse Cook, a Paiute rancher who lived beyond the open range circling the Forked Lightning. Tracey Jackson, Marley's nephew and Summer's cattle manager, was off moving a herd to greener pastures. Summer's housekeeper and her husband had gone to Callanton for groceries.

"Everyone thinks I'm too pregnant to leave the house," Summer said, pouting just a little. "They can't seem to get it through their heads that I'm barely four months along." She set a mug full of coffee in front of Gabe and took the seat across the table from him.

"Four months?" That news jolted Gabe out of his own preoccupation.

"Bullpucky. Now I've shocked you. Coltrane will probably have my head."

"Isabella says that in place of swearing. She must've picked it up from you. Oh, you didn't shock me, Summer. I think it's cool. Colt's gonna make a fantastic dad."

Summer slouched in her chair. She rubbed her belly, part of which was exposed only because she could no longer snap her jeans. "Do I detect a sad note somewhere in that statement?"

Gabe cracked the knuckles on his left hand. Something he'd stopped doing after the Marine Corps shrink got hold of him. "I'll probably never have what Colt's found here with you, Summer."

"Why not?" She blew on her tea. She'd served

Gabe strong black coffee, but for the sake of her baby, she'd begun drinking herbal teas. "I happen to know John Campos's ranch is prime grassland. We hear you're going great guns renovating his house, too. Not that we heard it from *your* lips, my friend."

"Yeah. I've been kinda busy. I wasn't referring so much to the Forked Lightning itself, Summer, but to you and Rory—and this new baby." He shrugged. "That's unfamiliar territory to me."

"Coltrane said you had a crappy childhood." Summer pressed a sympathetic hand briefly to Gabe's wrist.

"Crappy sums it up, though I'm not complaining. It's more the other stuff I envy. Good folks, a loving wife. Kids," he said bleakly.

"If you went to town occasionally, you might find a woman who'd be a loving wife."

"Isabella is so consumed with hatred for her ex, I wonder if she'll ever open herself up to love."

"Isabella?" Summer's eyebrows shot up. "Gabe! I did warn you at the wedding reception. You didn't listen to a word I said, did you?"

He shook his head, staring miserably into the black depths of his coffee. "Her family hasn't been able to attend court with her during the jury selection over in Bend. They wanted to, but that freak hailstorm left them all in a bind. You probably know how it is with sheep and orchards."

"So you've been going with Isabella?"

"I rented a cottage at a gated resort. So she wouldn't be bugged by reporters. Last night we, uh…she, uh…today we had a big row. She tossed me out of her life."

"Ah. But you two—I mean, she let you get close

enough to…to…'' Summer groped for polite words to ask if they'd shared a bed.

''Dammit, that's not news a guy wants blabbed around. Not if he cares about the woman.''

Summer smiled. ''Why, Gabe. I believe you've fallen in love with my friend.''

''For all the good it does.'' Planting his elbows on his knees, he scrubbed his face hard with both hands.

''Did you tell her?''

''Like she'd listen.'' He shook his head. ''She said she never wanted to see me again.''

''You dope. All women want to know they're loved. Especially by the man they, uh, let into their bed.''

He just kept shaking his head.

''Then what you have to do is show Izzy how much you care. It'll have to be something grand, I think. Could you maybe skywrite *I love you* over top of the courthouse? Or spread ten million rose petals from your bed to hers.''

''Yeah, sure. I try that and her brother Rick will draw and quarter me.''

''I was kidding.'' Summer fluffed a hand through the air. ''I forgot she'd moved home. Well, you get the idea. I'm sure you'll think of the perfect gesture, Gabriel. Hey, do you want to stay for dinner? Colt's due home in an hour. Maybe he'll come up with a better plan.''

''I would stay, but I have to run a check over to my contractor's office so he can bank it tonight. He's ready to buy my kitchen cabinets. Going without cabinets wasn't an issue when I thought I'd be staying in Bend another week or so.''

''Okay, but don't be a stranger. I hope you don't

mind my telling Colt. We promised not to keep secrets from each other.''

"That's good. Secrets can be as damaging to a relationship as hate.''

Summer walked him to his SUV and bestowed a sisterly good-luck kiss.

Gabe mulled over Summer's suggestion on the way into town. He had doubts about some off-the-wall romantic gesture carrying any weight with Isabella. And stuff like that wasn't really him. His off-the-wall years were far in the past.

It was after Gabe had delivered the check to his contractor's office in Callanton that he chanced across an opportunity. A For Sale sign stuck in a plot of ground adjacent to the city park had caught Gabe's eye. Asking around, he discovered it was less than half the size of a city lot. Even the bank manager who had the lot for sale said it wasn't really buildable. It had come to him in lieu of a bad debt.

Excited, Gabe wrote out a check and took it off the banker's hands. He raced back to the builder's office and burst through his door seconds before the man closed up. "Jeez, I'm glad I caught you. I have a new project. You may not be the one to do it, but it takes precedence over my house. I bought property next to the park. I want to construct a public garden. A butterfly garden with flowers that'll bloom year-round.''

The builder stared at Gabe as if he'd taken leave of his senses.

"Look.'' Gabe grabbed a paper and pencil from the man's desk. "It's roughly this shape. These are the dimensions. I'll set up a fund for perpetual care. I also want mushroom and gnome statuary, along with shrubs and flowers. And I want pinwheels. Big, colorful ones that are light enough to catch a small breeze. And benches. Benches where people can sit and eat their lunch, or kids can curl up and read.''

''Anything else?'' his builder inquired dryly.

''One other thing,'' Gabe said solemnly. ''A large brass plaque dedicating the garden to Antonia and Ramon Navarro. They're—''

''I know who they are. In view of the trial starting next week, Gabe, I think it's a fine and noble gesture.''

''To hell with that. Is it possible? And if so, when can it be ready?''

Again the man pondered. ''I know an innovative landscaper who has a nursery in Burns. If you've got time, we can take a drive over there. I've seen this woman work miracles in a week.''

''Really? Hey, my time is yours.'' Gabe tucked his hands in his front pockets. A smile lit his formerly grave face.

ISABELLA'S FIRST ACT after she got home, changed clothes and brought her family up to date on the jury selection, was to visit her sister-in-law in the hospital. Christina had roomed in with her baby. Looking at the sleeping infant tore a chunk out of Isabella's heart.

''Bella, are you okay?'' her brother Manny asked.

She backed away from the bassinet. ''Manuela reminds me of how Antonia looked as a baby.'' Her voice ended up cracking.

Christina bit her lip. Manny rushed to put his arms around his older sister. ''Mama said that very thing. I should have forewarned you.''

''It's okay. I'm so happy for you two. Really.'' Because her chest felt too tight, Isabella pushed out of Manny's arms and dug through her purse. ''I had Joe stop at a shop in Bend so I could buy a gift. He said no one had bought you this yet.'' Pulling out a small jewelry box, Isabella passed it to her sister-in-law.

Christina untied the ribbon. ''Eighteen-carat gold stud earrings! Isabella, how thoughtful. I'm surprised no one did buy Manuela earrings, especially since it's a long-standing tradition in my family to pierce a baby girl's ears at four weeks. She'll love them. I love them.'' She raised her arms for a hug. ''Bella, Manny and I don't expect you to come around wanting to hold her. We understand you need time for your pain to subside.''

''This seems to be the day for people wanting me to get beyond my pain. I appreciate your concern, Christina. But I have to go now. Bye.'' Isabella walked to the door, then ran down the hall and down the stairs, finally taking refuge in her van. She wrapped her arms around the steering wheel. Her empty, empty arms. ''Damn!'' Her hands shook so hard she couldn't get the key in the ignition.

Isabella didn't want to go home, where the topic of conversation would be either babies or the upcoming trial. She needed time to prepare herself for both subjects.

Suddenly Gabe popped into her mind, although she didn't really understand why. Especially as his SUV hadn't been at his house when she left home. Anyway, she couldn't, *wouldn't,* go see him. But maybe a talk with Colt Quinn—to ask the questions that had nagged her earlier.

Stars winked in the sky by the time Isabella turned under the arch bearing the Forked Lightning brand. A yellow moon hung low overhead, dappling bright spots on the hood of her van as she drove along the peach trees planted by Summer's great-grandmother. Or was it her great-great-grandmother? Isabella tried in vain to recall—to think of anything rather than let the moonlight remind her of last night with Gabe.

Which turned out to be a lost cause. She hadn't felt this special in so long—if ever, she thought, remembering how carefully, reverently and fully he'd loved her. She wished he hadn't ruined it all this morning. Why had he? She brooded about it as she parked the van.

Summer and Coltrane were seated on the front porch glider. They rose the instant Isabella mounted the steps.

"Izzy, welcome." Summer hurried to hug her. "I'd just been telling Coltrane how the trial is all over tonight's news. It's finally going to happen, Izzy. Are you relieved?"

Isabella couldn't respond because the moment Summer turned her loose, Colt squeezed the stuffing out of her. "Here, sit on the glider with Summer," he said. "I'll drag over Virgil's chair. Unless you two have girl-talk and would prefer I took a hike."

"No, no," Isabella assured him. Now that she was here, she didn't know how to go about questioning him about his good friend. It seemed easier to start with another subject and work her way into that one. "I see you're getting rounder, Summer. It seems I can't avoid discussing babies tonight." She sighed without realizing she had. "I've just come from visiting Christina. Have you heard she and Manny had a girl yesterday?"

"That kind of news travels fast." Summer took Isabella's hand. "If you came here to get away from all the oohing and cooing, we can find other things to talk about."

"Not the trial, either. Although James Hayden is

pleased with the panel of jurors. Aside from that, there's nothing to say until next week."

"You have a new neighbor." Colt tossed that into the mix in spite of his wife's trying to telegraph him a squelching glance. Ignoring her, he kicked back in the chair and continued. "Of all the people I could imagine herding sheep, Gabe Poston's the very last."

"Oh? Why?"

"I've never seen anybody with a head for figures like Gabe has. He's got a mind like a damned calculator. When it comes to business, he knows all the ins and outs. And investment strategy—anything you want to know, ask Gabe. It wouldn't surprise me to hear he's got millions socked away. What really shocked the daylights out of me, Marc and Reggie was learning that Gabe paid above market value for John's ranch."

"Maybe John's ranch reminded him of where he grew up." Isabella dropped a fishing line and baited the hook.

"Hardly," Coltrane snorted.

"Oh. So, he grew up in the city?"

"On the streets."

Summer, who'd felt her friend stiffen at the tidbit Colt threw out, released Izzy's hand and plumped a pillow into one corner of the glider, where she then curled up. "Don't leave us hanging, Colt. Tell us what you know about Gabe's childhood."

"I don't know it all. He's pretty closemouthed."

Reaching out, Summer nudged her husband's knee. "Izzy's not the type to spread tales. At least tell her what happened with Gabe's mom and dad. She's Gabe's nearest neighbor, and you don't want her to accidentally say something that might upset him."

Colt shot his wife a puzzled glance. Their eyes

locked, and as if a light bulb came on, he suddenly nodded, expelling a breath. Over the next ten minutes, he told Gabe's story, from his erratic, lonely childhood to his mother's tragic death to his father's disowning him, then callously tossing him aside like garbage.

Every two seconds, Isabella cleared her throat in shock and sympathy. "I cannot believe a child's father could wash his hands of responsibility—without so much as making an effort to see if Gabe was his son. But then, I don't know why that surprises me," she said faintly. "Take Julian…" As she brought up Julian's transgressions, Isabella remembered what Gabe had said about digging deep and forgiving someone who'd transgressed against you. Had he forgiven a man who'd treated him worse than any decent person would treat a dog? Or his mother for shamefully neglecting him?

"What are you thinking now, Izzy?" Summer inquired. "I see the wheels turning round and round in your head."

"Nothing," she stammered. "I…he appears to have risen above his tragic life. While I…I find it impossible to accept the terrible things a person can do to those they ought to love most in the world."

Summer let Isabella's statement go without comment. "Well," she said, struggling to get out of the glider. "Enough morbid talk. Coltrane, your son or daughter is telling me it's time for a dish of the Rocky Road ice cream I saw you and Rory sneak into the freezer. Bring Izzy a bowl, too. As a matter of fact, let's retire to the kitchen. Even with the porch screened in, it's getting too nippy to sit out here."

"I ought to go and leave you two to your dessert."

"Nonsense." Summer linked arms with Isabella and

tugged her into the house. "If I'm going to pig out on ice cream and get big as a house, I'd like to know my good friends are going to gain at least a few ounces. You, my love, could benefit from rich cream and gooey marshmallow more than anyone I know."

Isabella came the closest to smiling she had in a long while. Well, except for the satisfied smile Gabe had left her wearing last night. She sank gratefully into a chair. Feeling unexpectedly ravenous, she dug into the generous bowl of creamy confection Colt sat in front of her.

Driving home an hour later, Isabella found that her stomach had calmed but her brain was working overtime. She'd been embarrassingly wrong in her judgment of Gabe. He'd spoken as he had out of true concern. She probably ought to apologize, if only to say she understood he'd spoken from his heart.

The need to do this preyed on her, so she decided to get it over with tonight.

Gabe's house was dark. She pressed the switch to illuminate the van's clock. Nearly ten. Half expecting to see his SUV parked in her parents' drive, Isabella felt disappointment as she pulled in between Trini's car and Joe's pickup. Louis and his family were climbing into their car. She stopped to chat.

"Where've you been?" Ruby asked. "Manny worried everyone, phoning us to say you'd freaked out over the baby."

"I didn't freak out. Okay, maybe I did a little. It's hard, Ruby. The baby looks so much like Antonia at the same age."

"We know, sweetie."

Drawn into her oldest sister's plump, comforting arms, Isabella sucked in enough deep breaths to regain her emotional balance before returning the hug and stepping back.

"Sylvia and I are taking turns helping Christina out next week. Mama's got her hands full feeding orphaned lambs. We agreed Maria will go to Bend on Monday. Rick said you have an extra bed so she can stay over for a second day?"

"Yes." Isabella's gaze darted to Gabe's pitch-dark house. "Gabe said he rented the cottage for a month. I'll settle up with him after the trial."

Ruby's kids were clamoring at her to go, and Louis revved the engine impatiently. She muttered in Euskera. Then in English, she said, "Phone Maria, okay?"

Slightly lighter of heart knowing she'd have some family support at the start of the trial, Isabella entered the house.

Several members of her noisy family jumped up and rushed toward her. "Bella, where have you been?" Trini helped her out of her jacket.

"I wasn't aware I needed to check in." Isabella realized she'd sounded impatient. "I visited Summer and Colt. They invited me to stay for ice cream. Time got away from us."

"Joe said you were probably with Gabe," Sylvia volunteered from where she sat knitting in the living room. "Trini knew that wasn't true. She saw him in town with some blond babe."

That information totally disarmed Isabella. He'd been angry when he left the cottage, but to go from her bed to another woman hurt more than she dared admit.

"She's no one local, either," Trini supplied. "I'd gone to town to make a night deposit for Papa. I saw them come out of the park. At first I couldn't believe my eyes. They turned and walked up Main past that empty lot, then I guess they must've decided they were hungry, because they retraced their steps, crossed the street and went into the Green Willow. He held the door for her, so I got a good look. Enough to know she's a natural blonde—the type guys go for. And she filled out her jeans and shirt in a way that appeals to their neanderthal brains, too.''

Angel and Joe both cuffed Trini teasingly on the back of the head. But Isabella had no reaction to their antics. The ice cream she'd had at Summer's home threatened to come up. She felt their eyes on her as she pounded up the stairs. On the landing, she stilled her galloping heart and called down, ''Please excuse me. I've had a long, trying week. A really, really trying week.''

GABE WALKED Jamie Kent to her mud-splattered Chevy pickup. He waited politely for her to unlock the dented driver's door. Something had caved in the painted garden scene below the name of her landscape firm. She noticed what claimed his attention. ''That happened at the quarry. A line snapped on a two-man rock they were loading. Our insurance companies are in the throes of settling our dispute.''

''I hope no one was hurt.''

''Only pride. The paint was barely dry on that logo.'' Laughing, she extended her hand. ''Thanks for your business and the down payment. My husband will have a crew in to clear the lot tomorrow. Monday, I'll send over topsoil while I select the plants, forest creatures and the fountain. I'm so glad you decided to let me work everything around a four-tiered fountain. The sound of water adds to the serenity of a garden.''

Gabe nodded absently, thinking of the woman he hoped could find a measure of serenity in this place he and Mrs. Kent had begun referring to as "the healing garden." "It's getting late. You still have to drive back to Burns. I told you about the trial, so I'll leave the project in your hands. You have my card if you run into any problems with permits or anything."

"I'll be here, although I'd rather be on that jury."

Gabe ran a hand down the tie he'd put on after leaving Isabella in the cottage. "That's interesting. Most people try to avoid jury duty at all cost."

"That's one guy who deserves to get back-to-back life sentences with no possibility of parole."

"I agree. On the other hand, if he's truly crazy…"

"Are you kidding? Watch him closely. My husband, Randy, and I had this same argument when we saw a broadcast of his initial arrest. The guy's crazy like a fox. Well, good night, and good luck to Ms. Navarro." Jamie Kent started her pickup and drove off, leaving Gabe looking after her, chewing a hole on the inside of his mouth.

CHAPTER FOURTEEN

MONDAY, AT SOME INDECENT HOUR, a raucous thumping, accompanied by what sounded to Gabe like squealing pigs, jolted him out of bed. Stumbling to the window, he saw Joe, Benito, Louis and Angel unloading white blobs down some kind of ramp. Throwing on his jeans, shirt and boots, Gabe raced out to see what they were doing.

"The new goats arrived," Benito announced. "Aren't they beauties?"

"At this hour, only a woman qualifies in that category," Gabe growled.

Angel rammed Gabe with an elbow. "Touchy, touchy. Or should I say oops? Have you left a beautiful blonde in your bed, Poston?"

"What the hell are you driving at, Angel? Spit it out."

Louis donned a smug smile. "No need to play dumb, man. Trini saw you in town Friday night with a blond babe. And you were decidedly scarce around here this weekend. We dropped over both Saturday and Sunday, hoping to tell you about today's delivery."

Gabriel nearly choked, he clenched his teeth so hard. He wanted Isabella to be first to learn about the garden. "Mrs. Kent's strictly business," he said, as they waited expectantly to be clued in.

"Missus, huh?" Angel muttered.

"Sounds like monkey business," Louis said.

"No way! Listen, Benito, I finally made a decision about the lease you and I discussed. I spent both days coming to an agreement with Larkin Crosley. With his coaching, he thinks I can pass the Oregon bar exam in July when it's given. If I succeed, I'll take over his practice in Callanton in August."

Gabe was glad to see that gave them something to think about besides Jamie Kent. He shouldn't have taken her to the Green Willow to discuss the project. Damn, he kept forgetting how fast rumors circulated in small towns.

"Are any of you going with Isabella to the trial today?"

"Maria," Benito said. "You're going, too, aren't you, Gabe?"

"I planned to. But Isabella and I had words on Friday. She won't be happy to see me."

"Bella looked rocky all weekend. I'm counting on you to be in her corner." Isabella's father's distress was never more evident. "We're getting a handle on lambing, but with adding these goats, it'll probably be next week before I can break loose."

"I'll be there, Benito. For my own peace of mind as well as yours. I'd better get ready to take off, then. Say, my kitchen cabinets are being delivered today. Will that cause you guys any problems?"

"Nope." Joe answered. "Do you need someone to sign for the shipment?"

"My contractor plans to be on hand, but thanks."

As Gabe showered, and even throughout his drive to Bend, he worried about what kind of reception he'd get from Isabella. He wished he'd been more discreet in his appointment with Jamie Kent, too. Had news of his meeting with Jamie reached Isabella?

Maria Navarro saw Gabe the moment he walked into the courtroom. He smiled. She didn't. Not surprising, considering how Isabella gazed through and not at him. Gabe chose a seat where he could see both the proceedings and Isabella. He took it as a slightly good omen that she still wore his angel pin.

Five minutes later, there was a stir at the entrance. Gabe was treated to his first glimpse of Julian Arana. An attendant dressed in medical whites, for effect no doubt, wheeled Arana slowly up the center aisle. *Brother! The defense lawyer ought to be in show business.* If Arana was faking, he'd been well coached. He never once lifted his chin off his chest. The forest-green velour robe and slippers he wore made him look frailer than he might be. Plain blue cotton pajamas covered his legs.

Julian's parents were seated in the front row on the other side of the aisle, opposite Maria and Isabella.

Isabella began to tremble all over. Gabe prayed she wouldn't lose it then and there. Ah, to hell with it. Let her get mad at him. Standing, Gabe strode across the room, past the Aranas, to claim the vacant seat on Isabella's right.

Leaning across her, he whispered to Maria, "It's clever staging. Judge Weller will instruct the jury not to pay attention to any theatrics played out by either team."

Isabella clasped her hands so tightly around a tissue, Gabe was afraid her narrow bones might crack.

"Why are you here?" she asked stiffly. This wasn't the time or place to throw what she knew about Gabe's girlfriend in his face, though she wanted to. Oh, how she wanted to.

"If you think hard enough about that, sweetheart, you'll figure out the answer." He might have said more, but they were instructed to rise for the judge. Gabe heard her hiss at him not to call her sweetheart.

Everyone in the room got to their feet except for Julian.

The defense attorney, in his opening statement, alluded to the reason Julian didn't stand. "The defendant suffered severe memory loss due to inhalation of carbon monoxide. I have statements here from three independent physicians, your honor."

After copies had been distributed to Hayden's team, the defense added increasingly more documentation. "These reports are from psychologists who have examined my client. Their findings support our contention that Mr. Arana is simply not able to understand the charges the state's brought against him. His brain is in a vegetative state, to put it bluntly." The wily old attorney ran his gaze over various members of the jury as he delivered his proclamation.

Gabe feared Isabella had slid into a vegetative state. She sat without moving, her hollow eyes rarely blinking. Maria was the opposite. She fidgeted. First crossing her ankles, then uncrossing them, then shifting from one hip to the other.

By noon, James Hayden had yet to make a peep. Gabe wouldn't have believed the defense could dredge up and present so much pure crap. But then it'd been a long time since he'd sat through a criminal trial. Back in law school, as a matter of fact. And he hadn't paid much attention, since he wasn't planning to practice criminal law.

After Weller called a lunch recess, Gabe took it upon himself to direct Maria and Isabella out a side door of the courtroom, to save them passing either Julian or his parents. They were still mobbed by reporters, so Gabe sheltered both women as best he could.

"Mrs. Arana," a pushy woman with a TV camera shouted. "Tell us how your lawyer hopes to refute Thomas Meyer's brilliant defense. Don't you think Meyer has all the cards in his hand?"

Another also referred to Isabella as Mrs. Arana. "How did you feel seeing your husband sitting like a zombie in a wheelchair?" a third one asked. "Is Meyer right? Should you share responsibility? Was your husband distraught because you kicked him out of the house for no good reason?"

Isabella stopped as though struck and would have buckled had Gabe not had a firm grip on her arm.

He deflected the microphone none too gently and shoved aside the menacing TV camera. "Ms. Navarro took back her maiden name in the divorce. And she has no comment while this trial is in progress."

He literally ran—with the women under the protective covering of his suit jacket—to where he'd parked. The more insistent reporters followed. Gabe managed to shepherd the women into his vehicle and climb inside, in spite of some press members still knocking on the smoke-toned windows.

Isabella shivered in her seat, as did Maria. "I've seen people hounded by the press on TV. It's far worse when you're actually involved," Maria whispered shakily. "Why didn't they leave us alone when you told them Bella had nothing to say?"

Gabe stripped off his suit jacket and draped it around Isabella for warmth. His suit today was the color of dark chocolate. A shade that only emphasized the deep circles bruising the skin around her eyes.

"I don't have a problem with them asking questions, Maria," he answered. "There's fierce competition between print and visual media to get the top stories. Most of these people are just doing a job. I resent the smug ones who get overly aggressive. Are you both okay?"

"I am." Maria, who'd climbed into the rear seat, leaned forward and pressed a hand to her sister-in-law's bony shoulder. "Bella, I had no idea how bad this trial would be. No wonder you're having trouble eating and sleeping."

"Speaking of eating," Gabe said after he started the engine. "I don't foresee getting any peace at a restaurant in town. Since Judge Weller's given us a two-hour break, it'd be best if we went back to the cottage and maybe heated up some soup."

"I'm all for that." Maria spoke up at once.

Isabella barely nodded. She was grateful for Gabe's intervention. On top of all the mixed emotions she had about seeing Julian for the first time since that horrible evening, she was plagued by a need to apologize to Gabe. Which she could hardly do in front of her sister-in-law.

Taking her brief nod as assent, Gabe zigzagged through the streets, trying to shake as many reporters as possible. Finally they cleared the security gate at the resort, once again successfully leaving behind two tenacious reporters whom he hadn't managed to dodge.

At the cottage, Isabella stood inside the living room, still clutching Gabe's jacket around her bowed shoulders.

"I'll put on water for tea and see what kind of soup

you have in the cupboard." Maria cast a worried glance toward Gabe on her way to the kitchen.

"Come and sit down, Isabella," he urged, leading her to the couch.

An audible sigh wracked her thin frame.

"There's sun on the patio. Would you rather sit outside?"

Heavy-lidded eyes flashed her gratitude. She allowed herself to be led out into the sunshine. Taking a seat in one of the padded wicker chairs, she raised her face to receive the sun rays and sucked in a deep breath. "Fresh air. Do courtrooms always smell bad? Stale and fusty, I mean."

"There's a certain sameness to them. Isabella, I didn't mean to upset you the other day. I'll take another stab and hope I do a better job of explaining what I was trying to say. Forgiving someone who's caused you unspeakable harm doesn't mean they get off scot-free if they've committed a crime. My point is that it's what *you* have to do to free yourself from the hold they have on your life."

"I'm sorry I lost control that day, Gabe. I know you meant well."

He noticed she didn't agree with him, though.

Isabella fixed her gaze on something beyond his shoulder. "Our…uh…getting involved at this time is still a mistake."

"A kiss or two might be blamed on hormones gone amuck, Isabella. Our marathon night in bed took mutual agreement, wouldn't you say?"

"No. I can't think what came over me."

"Seems simple enough to me," Gabe growled. He broke off what else he might have added when Maria stepped onto the patio bearing a tray filled with a tea service and soup bowls.

"The soup is ready. I hope tomato's okay. It seemed the best I had to choose from. Of course, I'm used to the homemade variety."

"None for me, Maria," Isabella said, though she did accept a cup of tea from the bustling woman.

"Bella, you're going to fade away if you don't eat. Tonight I'll fix leek and potato soup for tomorrow's lunch. I know it's your favorite."

Gabe, who'd dragged the low, glass-topped wicker table to the center of the patio, ladled tomato soup into three bowls. "I almost forgot. Luisa sent a loaf of home-baked bread with me this morning. It's in the Lexus. I'll go get it."

"And I'll nab the butter." Maria hurried into the house behind Gabe. "Bella's got to eat," she whispered, catching up to Gabe.

"She won't if we make too big a deal of it. If we fix her a plate and set it in front of her, maybe the aroma will entice her to take a few bites. Or if not the aroma, the guilt over letting it go to waste."

"You know her well, I think." Maria crossed her arms, all the while eyeing Gabe as if waiting for him to admit just *how* well he knew Isabella.

He'd left his cell phone in the SUV. It beeped, notifying him of a missed call. Stopping to check, Gabe saw that both Marc and Moss had left messages within the space of fifteen minutes. Wondering what could be urgent enough to shake them both loose in the middle of the week, he dialed Marc as he rummaged around for the sack that held the loaf of bread.

"Hey, Marc, what's up? Did the old geezer reconsider selling his land to SOS?"

"No. What have you been up to since you left Utah? Seeing that you were the one so concerned about all of us not staying connected, you've been awful quiet."

"I've been tied up, buddy. It's a long story. I'm about to eat lunch. Can I call you back tonight?"

"Sure. You've got my number." Marc clicked off.

Gabe turned around and punched in Reggie Mossberger's number. "It's Gabe. Do you need something, Moss?"

"I hear from Coltrane that some woman's got her hooks in you."

"*What?* What are you talking about?"

"Aren't you buying property all over town hoping to win the heart of that caterer who's too traumatized to love you back?"

"Did Coltrane say that?" Gabe felt his anger flare.

"He said you have his blessing and to cut you some slack. Marc and I can't figure out what these Oregon women have that's turned two good men's brains to mush."

"So you and Marc have been discussing my love life? Is that what's behind his call, too?"

"We're worried about you, Gabe. And neither of us can get away to come there in person. Hell, the way we left it after Colt's wedding, Marc and I thought by now you'd be back in Sun Valley."

"Marc knew better. I tried to tell him about Isabella when I went to Utah. He was too wrapped up in Lizzy to hear."

"So tell me."

"Okay. Meeting her…was like nothing I can describe. Being run over by a Sherman tank is the best comparison I can give you. Maybe I can't make things better for her, Moss. All I know is I've got to try."

"Sounds like love to me. Hey, I guess this means I should've sent my tux jacket to the cleaners, right?"

"Yesterday morning I might've said yes. Today I'm not so sure," Gabe admitted miserably.

"Hey, I've got a patient mooing out back. And one barking its head off in my waiting room. You make her treat you right, okay buddy?" Reggie said with a decided catch in his voice.

Gabe closed his phone, feeling lucky to have such good friends—and feeling more hopeless than ever about his shaky footing with Isabella.

He grabbed the bread and went back inside.

"Bring the bread out onto the patio," Maria called. "I already brought the cutting board and knife."

"Sorry to be so long. I had a couple of messages on my cell phone."

"Anything to do with the trial?" Isabella raised her head.

"No. Personal business," he replied, passing the loaf to Maria.

"Oh. Not bad news concerning Papa's goats, I hope?" When Gabe looked surprised that she knew about the goats, Isabella explained. "Maria just spoke with Rick. He said the hills behind your house are no longer green but white with this new breed of goat Angel talked Papa into bringing up from Texas."

"They showed up so early this morning, the hills were almost littered with their fluffy white carcasses."

Maria laughed. She handed Gabe a thick slice of buttered bread to go with the fresh soup she'd dipped for him.

Isabella broke a chunk off her slice. "Gabe, are you really buying out Larkin Crosley's law practice? Uh…Rick also told Maria that."

"Rick covered a lot of ground. What else did he say?"

"Nothing much." Isabella reacted to Gabe's sharp tone. "Well, nothing Maria repeated. I didn't talk to him. Um, were you hoping to keep that news a secret?"

He shook his head. He did, however, hope to keep news of the garden he'd commissioned a secret—from Isabella, at least. Until the majority of the work was done, anyway. "It didn't seem right to burden you with the details of my decision. You have enough on your mind at the moment."

"True, but a few weeks ago you bought a ranch and hired Papa to teach you to raise sheep. Then practically overnight you lease him your pasture. Now, you're suddenly going to study for the Oregon bar?"

"You could say it came as a revelation on one of those cold mornings as I lay face first in the icy mud. This was after a ram took offense at what he saw as my interference." He grinned wryly. "I'm not cut out to be a rancher, Isabella."

His self-deprecation bought a slight curve to her lips. Maria snickered. "Don't let my husband hear you say that. Rick's positive he ran you off."

"I'm here to stay, and everyone had better get used to that fact." Gabe answered Maria, but his gaze bored straight through Isabella.

She tapped her watch, not wanting anyone to see how her pulse leaped at Gabe's declaration. "Shouldn't we start back soon? We've been gone over an hour."

"We'll go as soon as you make a dent in your bowl of soup." Gabe dug a spoon into his own.

Isabella stuck out her tongue at his bent head. However, she picked up her soupspoon. "Isn't it too cold to eat?"

"Nutrition in it's the same hot or cold, isn't that right, Maria?"

She nodded enthusiastically, so Isabella wrinkled her nose and ate.

They arrived back at the courthouse with ten minutes to spare. Again Gabe escorted them through the blockade of reporters. The ones he'd been rude to earlier were even pushier, until a harsh glare from him had them falling back to let his party through.

Once Judge Weller took his chair, James Hayden presented affidavits from the doctors and psychiatrists he'd hired to examine Julian. If Arana was found competent to stand trial, the medical experts themselves might be called to testify. His arguments continued for slightly less time than the defense had used to plead their case. Hayden wound down his argument, saying, "It is the contention of the prosecution that we have proved Mr. Arana is well aware that his children died the day they were in his custodial care. He's also cognizant of what charges will be levied against him if he's found sane and competent to face those charges. Therefore, the prosecution rests. We reserve the right to call our witnesses should the defense call theirs."

Thomas Meyer huddled with his team a moment. "Your honor, we believe the jury has only to look at Mr. Arana here today to make the right choice."

Weller banged his gavel and proceeded to instruct the jury.

"That's it? They're going off to determine my children's fate based on one day's input from the lawyers?" Isabella whispered to Gabe, but failed to keep her voice low enough. Weller smacked his gavel. "I'll have order," he demanded.

Gabe leaned very near her ear to murmur, "Honey, it's really Julian's fate in their hands. Each juror heard the arguments. They'll study both packets of medical affidavits. Weller is sequestering them tonight. Sometime tomorrow or the next day they'll decree whether Julian's fit to stand trial for the murder of your children."

The jury had filed out and so had the judge. The crowds in the courtroom were dispersing under the watchful eye of court security. Isabella jumped to her feet. "So you've come around to my way of thinking? You agree Julian should be charged with murder in the first degree?"

Gabe diverted them toward a different exit than the one they'd used at noon. "Is it enough that I'd like to believe it for your sake?"

"No. No, Gabe, it isn't. If you cared as much for me as you imply, you'd believe Julian's lying. Go. Just leave us. Maria and I will ask James for a lift to the cottage."

Gabe touched her hair to maintain contact, but she tore away from him. He stood helplessly by, watching her drag Maria down the hall to catch Hayden. Dammit, at this point none of them knew if Arana's brain was actually fried. Could he carry off such an elaborate charade?

Gabe drove back to Callanton with a knotted stomach. He swung by the site for the garden, to see what progress had been made. A great deal for one day, which pleased him. The land had been cleared and spread with topsoil. Part of the rockery was already set.

Work on his own house had progressed, too. After

changing clothes and before he tackled cleaning the fireplace brick, Gabe popped the top on a beer and sat on his patio to enjoy it, gazing out at the goats who frolicked in his pastures. He had to admit they made an idyllic picture.

He stewed, too. Over whether he should go back to Bend and ask James Hayden to add him to the call list when the judge was ready to reconvene. Or simply forget about showing up unless they entered phase two of the trial. He hadn't fully decided, although he leaned toward going and contacting James, when a hulking shadow cut off what was left of the fading sunlight.

Rick Navarro sauntered onto Gabe's patio and helped himself to a chair. "I'll take one of those if you've got another."

Gabe stared at him. Rising, he stomped into the house and returned with what was left of a six-pack. "If you're planning to get me drunk and then beat the crap out of me, two beers apiece isn't nearly enough."

Rick pulled the tab and stuck it in his shirt pocket. "I suppose you have a chip on your shoulder because Bella sent you packing today." Tipping his head back, Rick took a long pull from the can. After wiping a hand across his mouth, he said, "Maria told me. Now you know Bella's got the Navarro temper. I assure you, she's gonna be happy when she sees the garden you're having done in memory of her kids. Or else she'll blubber. Navarro women are good at that, too."

Gabe stopped with the can halfway to his lips. "Did you tell Maria about the garden?"

"I'm not stupid," Rick shot back. "I talked to the woman—the blonde directing the work. She said you want the garden finished right down to a dedication plaque before Bella sees it. So, I guess you've already invited the mayor to give a speech and present the plaque.''

"The garden's not about presentations by self-aggrandizing politicians. I just hope it'll relieve some of Isabella's pain. That's all it's about.''

"Right answer, Poston.'' Rick took another swig. "Know what? You're okay. Now tell me what happened today. I can't make heads or tails outta what my wife said.''

Gabe talked in brief spurts and ended by gesturing with his can. "If you've got spare time to spend in town talking to Mrs. Kent, why weren't you in Bend for your sister? Why isn't your whole family there? Dammit, she needs her loved ones around her.''

"And that includes you?''

"What if I say it does?'' Gabe thrust out his chin.

Rick grinned and crushed his beer can. "I went to town on business, but you're right, Poston, we should be there for Bella. Where and what time tomorrow?''

"That's the thing. Hayden will be notified what time court reconvenes. He'll call Isabella. It may not be tomorrow. But if you go, please go prepared to stay a few days. Tell you what, I'll rent a second cottage. The one next to Isabella and Maria is vacant.''

"You'll rent another—so are you rich?'' Rick demanded bluntly.

"What's money? Wouldn't you spend every cent you had to help Maria?''

"Rather than throwing your money around, big shot, maybe Bella would rather hear you say you believe Julian Arana is scum of the earth.''

"That's a low blow, Rick. I've never doubted the man is bad to the core. I've only said I'm not qualified to judge if he's sane or if the gas didn't leave him too debilitated to understand his rights. I've also said that if Isabella can't get past the hate corroding her emotions, then no matter what happens, Arana's won. Especially if destroying her is what he hoped to do.''

"Spoken like Callanton's soon-to-be newest lawyer." Rick clapped Gabe on the shoulder. "I'll collect the family if you'll help transport them. Shall we be on the road at six o'clock in the morning?''

"Tell Luisa to expect me for breakfast.''

Gabe knew the road to Bend so well, the next morning he was able to keep one ear open to the chatter going on around him while he planned what he'd say to Isabella.

She was so ecstatic to see her family, Gabe got no opportunity to even speak to her until everyone else had finished crying and hugging her.

"Come, take a short walk with me,'' he said, cornering her after the men went to unload the cars and Maria took Luisa, Sylvia and Ruby to check out the second cottage.

"Gabe, I can't even begin to thank you. But—'' she hesitated "—shouldn't someone stay in case James phones?''

"I have my cell phone with me.'' He tapped the case looped onto his belt. "I already spoke with James. He's not expecting word anytime soon.''

"Why? What's so hard? Julian would run over his grandmother to achieve his own ends.''

Gabe opened the front door and called to the others that he and Isabella were taking a short walk. He slipped an arm about her waist and deftly maneuvered her out the back way, across the patio. A trail that led through the pines blocked them from view of the house. "Isabella…''

Slowing her steps, she turned and drew her fingers over his lips. "I like the way you don't shorten my name. Everyone else either shortens it to Bella or Izzy."

Capturing her hand, he pressed a kiss into her palm. He liked that his kiss flustered her and brought traces of pink to her colorless cheeks.

"Rick said something last night that started me thinking."

"I'm surprised and pleased to see that you two apparently resolved your differences."

"Because I managed to convince him you're significant to me, Isabella. The question is, why can't I convince you?"

She clutched her stomach and stared at Gabe with big, tragic eyes. "You think I'm lying about Julian."

Taking her hands, Gabe kissed her knuckles. "I have no doubt that Julian physically and mentally abused you, and hid the fact from everyone who knew you both. He's a terrible man. His crimes are heinous."

"Then, how can you believe he's insane? Or that he shouldn't go to prison for what he did to Antonia and Ramon?"

"I've always agreed he should be locked up. Isabella, do you know what was in Julian's head? Did he plot a cold-blooded murder-suicide, or did he snap and do it on the spur of the moment? Or did he simply think he could scare you into coming back, and something went terribly wrong?"

"What difference does it make? Doesn't it all add up to murder?"

Giving up for the moment, Gabe pulled her into the crook of his arm and walked out of the trees into a field of flowers.

Isabella rested her head on his shoulder. When he stopped, she rose on tiptoe and kissed him lightly. "You're a good, caring man, Gabe. But all men aren't like you."

Caught in a spell cast by her nearness and her humbling assessment, Gabe crushed her in his arms and delivered a long, satisfying kiss. Who knew where it would've led, considering the inviting bed of wildflowers and soft green grass, had a couple strolling with a boy and a dog not interrupted them?

Gabe recognized that the moment was lost, especially as Isabella, blushed, grabbed his hand and began pulling him back the way they'd come.

He regretted that he'd let kissing her get in the way of finishing their argument. And of course, once they reached the cottage, the boisterous Navarro family filled the rooms, negating any opportunity for private conversation.

It pleased him immensely, though, to watch Isabella bask in her family's unconditional love. Before night fell on a day that was otherwise upsetting—since James had phoned to say there was no verdict yet—Gabe knew one thing without reservation. Isabella owned all of his heart. Right or wrong, just or not, he wanted Julian Arana to spend the rest of his natural life in prison for no other reason than that he'd hurt the woman Gabe loved.

In spite of the revelation, he left Isabella without telling her and went to spend the night in the second cottage with all the men. That was how it had been decided. Men in one cottage. Women in the other.

The following morning, Gabe had even less opportunity to find time alone with her. Breakfast, as always with the Navarro clan, bustled with energy and chatter.

Halfway through washing dishes, the phone rang. Isabella answered. "It's James," she said, shushing everyone. "They've come to an agreement. We're to meet in courtroom C at one o'clock." All her fears, doubts and worries sapped any trace of light from her eyes as she dropped the receiver in the cradle with hands that visibly shook.

CHAPTER FIFTEEN

AT FIFTEEN MINUTES to the hour, they sat shoulder to shoulder in the first and second rows of the courtroom, all of them grim-faced. The Aranas sat squarely behind their only son, who still exhibited no sign of life.

Judge Weller swept into the courtroom at one on the dot. He issued a stern lecture aimed at reporters. "I won't tolerate outbursts of any kind, is that under-stood?" he said, letting his hot gaze run up and down the rows. Apparently satisfied he'd gotten through, he asked the bailiff to summon the jury.

"Have you reached a verdict in the competency case of the state of Oregon versus Julian Arana?"

Gabe, who'd finagled a seat next to Isabella, automatically reached for her hand.

A jury spokesman rose. "We have, your honor. This jury unanimously determines Julian Arana to be of sound mind."

The courtroom erupted in a jumble of voices as reporters scrambled for their cell phones to call their offices. The judge pounded his gavel to no avail.

While most eyes in court were locked on the man reading the verdict, Gabe's had swung to Isabella's ex. It was ever so slight, but Julian raised his head the moment the decision was read. Gabe witnessed an instant of unfiltered malice—aimed squarely at Isabella, who'd just been yanked into her happy parents' arms.

Short but stunning in intensity and portent, the look of pure hatred had lasted long enough for Gabe to know he hadn't imagined it.

He tried unsuccessfully to gain Isabella's attention. He needed to tell her about this discovery. As she was passed from brother to sister for hugging, the most he managed was to be on the receiving end of one of her grateful kisses.

Judge Weller surged to his feet and roared, "If the visitors to this court aren't seated at once, I'm citing each of you for contempt."

Of course they sat. "Well, now," Weller said, "that's better. We'll recess for one hour to give both teams an opportunity to collect themselves and contact witnesses. The jury will remain in quarters, where they'll have no access to the press."

The judge gathered his calendar and sheaf of papers. Julian's lawyer addressed him. "Your honor, the defense respectfully requests that we recess until one tomorrow. My client is not a well man, and he's been dealt a terrible blow."

"Mr. Meyer, with all due respect, this court has just determined that your client is perfectly fit. I recognize, and so should you, that because the trial was moved from the area where all parties reside, time presents a hardship. One hour stands."

"What shall we do for one hour?" Joe rolled his shoulders.

Rick got up. "I'm going to phone Manny." Their youngest brother had stayed behind with the brothers-in-law. To help at home, but also because his new baby had developed colic, and he'd gotten little sleep the previous night.

James Hayden moved into their circle. "A lawyer I

know has offered us the use of his office. Isabella, I'd like you to stick close by. Meyer indicated to me that they may want to dicker.''

''What does he mean?'' Isabella asked Gabe.

''Plea bargain. He means they may want to plea-bargain a lesser charge. Don't do it, Isabella. You were right, and I was wrong. Julian is play-acting.'' He filled her in on what he'd witnessed. ''I'm sorry for ever suggesting you forgive such a dangerous man. He's not crazy.''

''But Gabe. You've made me see how pathetic Julian is. I really looked at him when his attendant wheeled him in and thought I should try not to hate him so much.''

Gabe massaged her slender neck. ''Right now you're riding the euphoria of success. Let's all go have a cup of coffee and wait to see what Meyer proposes.''

They had less than half an hour to wait. Hayden strode into the room and found Isabella. ''I know what a strain the wait and then this phase of the trial has put on you and your family. Tom Meyer approached me with an offer. Julian will plead guilty to Man One if we withdraw our request for his sentence to include no chance for parole.''

Isabella edged closer to Gabe, even going so far as to clutch his hand. He thought it significant that she gravitated toward him and not her father or brothers. Personally, he doubted she'd rest easy with Man One. ''What sentence does Man One carry here, James?'' Gabe asked.

''Twelve to fifteen, eligible for parole in five to seven. We could get lucky and the judge could give him fifteen per child.''

"Which won't matter much if he makes parole in seven," Gabe pointed out.

"Seven years? No," Isabella said with finality. "Even thirty is too little. James, you promised we'd ask fifty years for each child and request they run back to back."

"That's what I thought you'd say. All right. We'll turn them down. I'll see you inside in twenty minutes. Be prepared for this to get ugly."

Isabella turned her face into Gabe's shirtfront. He slid his arms around her and rocked her ever so gently as she murmured, "I'm really trying not to hate his guts, Gabe. But he has to pay. He has to pay for what he did."

"I agree wholeheartedly." Gabe rested his cheek on the intricate braid that had first caught his attention and caused him to take a second look at Isabella. He felt so attuned to her now that he suffered when she did.

During the remainder of the day's session, the trial seesawed back and forth.

At the end of a long afternoon, the family returned to the cottages, strangely dejected in spite of their earlier triumph.

The next day, two of Julian's friends from work testified they'd only heard him speak highly of Isabella. The second salesman with the company told how Julian always flashed around pictures of his children.

Isabella leaned over to Gabe. "I'm sure he did. Julian took care to come off as the perfect husband and father to everyone he met."

James was frustrated because he wanted to call the priest who'd counseled the couple on their failing marriage. The judge denied Hayden's request. "Priests and clergy are exempt from testifying against parties they counsel in good faith.''

That afternoon, the prosecution saw their first real break. One of the psychiatric witnesses for the defense admitted under James's cross-questioning that he'd picked up patterns of erratic behavior in tests he'd administered to Julian. Tests showing that Julian was capable of lying without remorse.

The following morning, witnesses were recalled and cross-examined. James held off putting Isabella on the stand.

On day four, he admitted he didn't want the defense ripping her to shreds. ''Anyway, Weller threw out possible testimony regarding anything you observed or experienced at his hands while the two of you were married.''

''Why?'' Isabella and Gabe asked together.

''Weller is limiting your testimony to the time between the divorce and when you opened the garage door. He has that right, Isabella. So I'm going to lean on the defense's experts some more. I think the jury is already bending toward us.''

For two more days, the defense called physicians, nurses, neighbors and minor acquaintances of Julian. All the way down to his car mechanic. None really shed any light on the case. The neighbors who said Julian seemed like a nice guy couldn't bring themselves to look at Isabella when they testified.

It did come out that Julian was a loner throughout most of elementary and high school. It was generally agreed he had no close friends after he married Isabella.

''What's wrong with the people who knew Julian well?'' Isabella fumed once the whole family had congregated again in the largest of the cottages at the end of yet another trying day. "Now we're reduced to hearing so-called medical experts expound on what Hayden and Meyer already summarized in an hour at the end of the competency phase. It's like Meyer's still hoping to have Julian declared insane."

Gabe smiled at her. "Sweetheart, that's what defense lawyers do. Meyer wants sympathy for his client from the jurors. Trust James to cut through the bull. He knows juries. He's biding his time for the right moment."

Joe leaned forward, clasping his hands between his knees. "And this is what you want to do with your life, Gabe? You could be out with sheep, breathing fresh air."

"Oh, sure. Wet wool and sheep shit smell so great."

Luisa Navarro rapped Joe's knuckles. "Don't pick on Gabriel. He's a genius with numbers. Already he's drawn up a computerized budget for you and Papa. We're lucky to have him join our family."

All talk ground to a halt. Songbirds could be heard chirping through an open window. Outside of that, there was no sound for a drawn-out period.

Ruby, the outspoken sister, broke through the silence, rattling off a question in Euskera.

Only Gabe remained in the dark as Isabella launched out of her chair. "Why would you even think Gabe had asked Papa for my hand? First off, I'm not Papa's to give or keep. Secondly, Gabe and I are not involved…uh…like that."

But he *was* involved, and some present knew it. Seven pair of eyes stared at Gabe. Only Isabella's remained glued to Ruby. He felt like an unknown blob slithering under a microscope. Though no one accused him in so many words, Gabe had the awkward feeling that the women in particular were aware he and Isabella had made love.

He had no experience of standing up against a family unit. Still, he wasn't about to let Isabella take the heat alone. "I realize you're all close and I'm a *maketo,* but I suggest you let Isabella and me handle whatever's between us."

Her gaze flew from Ruby to Gabe. "Didn't I just say there's *nothing* between us?"

Gabe left the couch. "They don't buy it. And I don't, either. Which makes you a majority of one, honey. But I think at our age, the timetable for buying rings, booking a church and ordering a cake," he said, tongue in cheek, "should be left up to us."

"Exactly. We're way past the age where—good grief!" Close to apoplectic, Isabella turned red. Then white. Then sort of a sickly gray.

Gabe directed her to the spot he'd vacated and breathed a deep sigh of relief when she sank down on the couch.

"Did…ah…you…just propose to me?" Isabella, feeling woozy, put her head between her knees.

"Yeah. Yeah, I did, as a matter of fact."

Isabella heard Gabe's voice as though from afar.

"Well, I did if you've got no objection to this being such a public announcement," he muttered, wishing she'd say something in response.

"I don't. Object," she eventually squeaked, obviously close to hyperventilating.

"That's good. Hey, did you all hear? She said yes…I think." Gabe frowned down at her bent head.

"Oh, but the timing stinks." She raised her face, then bounded up from the couch. "It'll leak out. Julian's lawyers will have a field day trying to make me

out as the town slut. Forget it. We must all be deliri-
ous.''

"It won't leak." Gabe stared stonily at each member
of Isabella's family, leaving them in no doubt that he'd
hammer anyone who dared breathe a word.

Luisa wiped the grin off her face. She clapped to
gain everyone's attention. "Insurance is always best,
yes? While some of us must go home tonight as formerly agreed, someone will stay. Always Bella and Gabriel will have a chaperone.''

Gabe muttered in disbelief. And yet, Luisa's plan
made sense, given the current climate.

Since no one else had a better solution, the Navarro
family drew toothpicks that Benito broke and shuffled
in his hand. Sylvia held up the short stick. She elbowed
a confused Isabella. "Well, big sister, at long last the
tables are turned. After all the years you bossed me, I
finally get to make sure that *you* behave.''

"I don't believe this. None of this. I'm dreaming.
Or else it's a nightmare." Isabella hung back, still reeling from all that had taken place. The majority of her
family started packing to return home.

"If the judge doesn't think the trial is near winding
down, he'll probably recess for the weekend. Either
way, we'll spend Saturday and Sunday at home." Gabe
helped carry suitcases out to Joe's truck. He waved as
the two vehicles drove off.

He nabbed Sylvia before she returned to the cottage.
"I'm taking Isabella for a horseback ride. Just the two
of us.''

"Sure. For the record, Gabe, I think you're a good
sport. Mama and Papa and well, Rick and Ruby, too,
are old-fashioned. I was twenty-three, yet Angel had to
ask Papa if he could marry me.''

"I like your family, Sylvia. I had folks who didn't give a damn. I want to fit in."

She glanced uneasily toward the house, where Isabella was still in seclusion. "Easy does it talking about the future, Gabe. She's grieving. That takes time."

Nodding, he ran ahead to ask Isabella to join him on the ride.

A strong moon practically turned night into day as they rode; after half an hour Gabe thought enough time had passed in silence. "Let's stop here a minute and walk along the lake. Then we'll go back," he said, stepping out of his stirrups.

Isabella slid off her horse, a trim roan mare with a white face. Gabe's gray gelding was taller, rangier. He adjusted his hold on the bridle and slowed his longer stride to match Isabella's shorter steps.

"It's a beautiful night. Surreal. I—Gabe…"

He broke in. "Isabella, I'm guilty of keeping things from you. Time was, I hated the night and would never have gone this near water. My mom got into drug use when I was a baby. She drowned in Galveston Bay when I was a boy. Suicide, some said. Others thought she'd dropped a needle and went in after it, and was caught in an outgoing tide."

"I'm so very sorry," Isabella said, reaching up to stroke his face.

"I…I just thought you should know."

"There's more, right?"

"Yes. The man I called Dad claimed I wasn't his kid. The night after Mom died, he threw me out, bag and baggage. I ran away to the East Texas hills and slept in the woods until someone reported me to Child Services. For years I hated dark nights and the smell of pine."

Isabella rose on tiptoe and found Gabe's lips. "I have to confess I asked Colt about your background. It was the night after we argued," she said, dropping back down. "I know I'm not the only one who's suffered at the hands of someone evil. We have a lot in common. Maybe that's why I've always felt...I don't know...*comfortable* with you. It's just that I'm a mess with the trial and all. I said yes to your proposal, but...but what if I don't deserve to be happy?"

"It's an inalienable right, Isabella. The right to pursue happiness."

"I've never told anyone, not even my family, Gabe. I live with the fear that I didn't present enough facts in family court. I divorced Julian over his growing abuse. He never should've been awarded joint custody of Toni and Ramon. I should've done more to make the judge see that."

"You aren't to blame," Gabe assured her. "James nailed it when he called Julian a chameleon. A clever skunk who hid his stripes. Isabella, I won't pressure you to set a wedding date. I'll leave it for you to let me know when you're ready." Smiling, he boosted her back into her saddle. "I think we've probably stirred up enough ghosts for one night, don't you? We'd better get back to the cottage before Sylvia calls the cops."

"She won't. My family adores you, Gabe."

MIDMORNING OF THE NEXT DAY, the judge called for summations. Meyer went first. He sang the same old song for half an hour. James spoke eloquently and briefly on behalf of Isabella and her children.

"No one could have advocated with greater passion," Gabe reminded her and Sylvia as they watched the jury file out for the second time.

"What happens now?" Isabella seemed terribly on edge.

"Now we go to the cottage and wait. Hopefully this decision won't take as long as the first one that found him fit to stand trial. In essence they've heard the same evidence twice."

Still, it was a somber threesome who sat around the cottage trying to pretend interest in television or reading. They all checked their watches frequently.

Sylvia went into the kitchen to fix a lunch no one wanted. She managed to corner Gabe alone. "Angel is coming to get me. He should be here soon. We'll both go back into court for the reading of the verdict. No matter how it turns out, I think you and Bella need to be alone during the drive home. Oh, and Angel said your garden's done, Gabe. He said to tell you Mrs. Kent phoned. According to her, the place is even more than you dreamed. I know from Rick that you planned on the family attending a simple dedication. Take my advice, Gabe. Show it to Bella without anyone else there."

"I think you're right. I can't believe they finished it so fast."

During lunch Isabella didn't eat a thing. Gabe and Sylvia nibbled.

Angel blew in on a cloud of dust. "I'm hungry enough to eat a horse," he said two seconds after he stepped out of his pickup. He scarfed up everything they hadn't touched.

At two-twenty the phone rang. Sylvia, Gabe and Isabella jumped to grab for it. They pulled back and let Isabella pick it up instead.

"That was James," she said, seemingly unable to

return the receiver to the cradle. "This feels like déjà vu. We're to be back there at three."

Gabe took the phone from her fingers. "I think we should go pack our things. I don't see any need to come back here."

"What about the sentencing?" Angel asked.

Isabella gave him a hollow-eyed stare. "They'll only sentence him if we won. If his team won, he'll go quietly to a private sanitarium and stay there until Javier and Elena can convince some doctor to declare him cured."

"Here, now. Let's have some positive thinking, shall we?" Gabe urged everyone again to pack their things.

He'd seen Isabella nervous before, but never like this. No longer caring what Julian's lawyer might make of it, Gabe slid a bracing arm around her shoulders the moment they sat.

The ritual of seating the court secretary and those in attendance being asked to rise for the judge had become commonplace. Yet the process seemed to drift by in slow motion this time.

Gabe held Isabella tight when the jury filed in. All eyes swung to the rows of jurors.

Weller let the group be seated before he requested the defendant's team to ready themselves for the verdict. Meyer wheeled Julian to the table and the team rose. The judge asked the foreman of the jury to stand. "How finds the jury in the capital offense case, the state of Oregon vs. Julian Arana in the wrongful death of Antonia Maria Arana?"

"The jury finds Mr. Arana guilty, your honor."

Isabella slumped against Gabe. He tightened his grip. "How finds the jury in the capital offense case, the state of Oregon vs. Julian Arana in the wrongful death of Ramon Benito Arana?''

"The jury finds him guilty, your honor."

Gabe expected Isabella to burst into tears at the joyous news. She remained dry-eyed as the judge brought order to the buzzing courtroom.

Weller struck his gavel five times, drawing all eyes back to him. "The defendant will be remanded to the Deschutes County Jail until such time as his sentencing will take place. In looking at my calendar, I see thirty days from today is free. All parties will be notified as to time and exact location."

Gabe congratulated James, while Isabella remained in some kind of a stupor.

They were together in the SUV driving home before she spoke. "I thought I would feel better. More relieved. I feel as empty as ever. What's wrong with me, Gabe?"

He squeezed her hand, wishing he could stop and take her in his arms. "Give it time to sink in. You've lived with this hanging over you for almost a year."

"I heard James say Judge Weller isn't known for giving harsh sentences. So it's not really over. Not until I know Julian's off the streets for good."

They sank into silence again, Gabe wondering if Isabella could ever move beyond this day. Even after the sentencing, would she forgive herself?

"I have something I'd like you to see," Gabe said, rousing himself when they neared the outskirts of Callanton.

She stirred. "Oh, Gabe. I'm exhausted. I just want to go home and sleep for a week. Maybe a month. Until the sentencing, at least."

"This won't take long." He turned onto Main Street

and parked a hundred or so yards from the garden. As they approached the spot, he saw Jamie Kent attaching a pinwheel to what appeared to be the final stake. She glanced up and noticed them at almost the same moment.

"Gabe," she exclaimed, stripping off a glove to extend her hand. "I—oh, gosh, is this Isabella?"

Gabe made the introductions. The lovely blond landscape architect murmured an excuse and slipped away soon after.

Taking Isabella's hand, Gabe led her up a cinder path that wound among a fairy garden. A stiff breeze propelled pinwheels of all sizes and colors. "I'm calling it a healing garden," Gabe said, urging Isabella to sit on a stone bench, where she could read the simple brass plaque embedded in a rock.

"In memory of Antonia and Ramon Navarro," she whispered. "Oh, Gabriel, it's exactly the kind of place they would've loved." Falling to her knees to trace a finger over their names, she gazed up at Gabe through a sheen of tears. Tears she couldn't seem to shut off, even though he lifted her up and sat her on his lap. People walked by on the street and still she sobbed. The sun had begun to sink in the west when Isabella finally mopped away the last of her tears.

"I love you, Gabe. I've…been too afraid to admit it." Sitting up, she took his face gently between her hands, rubbing her thumbs restlessly over his lips. "You understood from the beginning that I haven't been able to say goodbye to Toni and Ramon. Maybe now… I thank you with all my heart. This truly is a healing garden."

He kissed her, letting the warmth from his lips slowly absorb the frost that had permanently invaded hers. ''Healing doesn't happen all at once, Isabella. I'm happy the garden pleases you. I love you. You say you love me. It's enough for now.'' He carried her to the car, not giving a damn about the stares of passersby. He was content thinking they'd spend the next thirty days getting to know each other. Although, even now, when he looked at her huddled in the corner, Gabe felt Julian Arana's shadow standing between them.

EPILOGUE

THIRTY DAYS WHIZZED PAST. Neither Isabella nor Gabe could believe it was time for Julian's sentencing. But Isabella received a letter from the court, naming the date, time and place. The final phase had arrived at last.

The night before the event, they discussed it under a star-studded sky as they relaxed in Gabe's newly installed hot tub.

"It's hard to imagine I've been able to put Julian completely out of my mind since the trial," Isabella murmured, nestling her head on Gabe's bare shoulder. "I hope the sentencing doesn't end up bringing the whole horrid nightmare back to me."

Gabe kissed her temple. "You've come a long way in thirty days, sweetheart. Ask anyone."

"I have you to thank. For so many things," she said hesitantly. "I'm feeling less and less guilty—I've almost stopped thinking I played some part in what happened to my children. Now I'm feeling guilt of a different kind. Not a day passes that someone in my family doesn't bring up weddings. Rick gives me a certain look when he knows I'm sneaking home after leaving your bed. And you, Gabe. You've been more patient than I've got any right to expect."

He drew her closer, well aware of how much time Isabella spent wandering through the healing garden. Not that he minded her stopping there after work. It was, after all, why he'd commissioned Jamie Kent to build it. Besides, studying for the bar kept him occupied.

What bothered Gabe was the idea of Isabella stealing across the road in the dawn hours. But he'd promised that he wouldn't pressure her to set a wedding date. And he'd keep that promise.

"What time do you want to leave for Bend in the morning?"

"Six o'clock. Are you sure you can afford the time off to take me?" she asked, rising as Gabe reached to shut off the jets. "I know how hard you're studying."

"The whole family's going. Even Trini, our new M.A. Believe it or not, Christina found a baby-sitter she trusts, so she and Manny will be backing you, too."

"That's good. I need all the support I can get right now."

"It's only eight. Shall we dress and run over to the church to light a couple of candles? Or is that overkill?"

"Oh, Gabe. That's perfect. I should've thought of it myself."

They went. Gabe almost wished he hadn't suggested it since Isabella became once again the brooding woman he'd first met. They parted later without kissing. Gabe tried not to attach a whole lot of importance to that fact.

She didn't look any calmer the next morning when he picked her up, and they led the Navarro caravan on the highway to Bend. His concern deepened.

"Do you mind if we don't talk, Gabe? I didn't sleep at all. I'm too edgy to concentrate. I hope the judge gives Julian a hundred years. A hundred years, or life without parole."

Once they disembarked at the courthouse, they went in search of the courtroom. A different, smaller one than last time. And it was packed. There didn't seem to be good air flow, and for May, it was hot.

"I almost forgot to tell you, Isabella. Colt phoned last night. He and Summer wanted to come, but she has her ultrasound today. He's excited about finding out whether they're going to have a boy or a girl. I think he wants a girl."

"She's brave, having another baby. I'll never go through that again." Her eyes weren't on Gabe when she made the announcement, but were locked on Julian, who'd abandoned his wheelchair to sit next to his attorney.

Gabe froze. He wanted a family like the ones her brothers and sisters had. Having kids was something they hadn't discussed, and now he wondered why.

As before, everyone in the room was asked to stand for Judge Weller's entry. As before, he got right to it. "I've given this case my full attention," he said, letting his eyes roam from prosecution to defense and back to prosecution. "The prosecution requested life for each child. The defense argues for leniency, given that Mr. Arana's health has been compromised by his exposure to carbon monoxide."

Weller adjusted his glasses, and Gabe found himself doing the same with his. "After much consideration," Weller said, "I'm ready to sentence Mr. Arana. Will the defendant please rise."

Julian shuffled to his feet, helped by Tom Meyer.

"Mr. Arana, I sentence you to thirty years for the wrongful death of Antonia Arana, and a second thirty years for the wrongful death of Ramon Arana. Both shall be served without option of parole. Do you understand what I've said?"

Julian nodded once.

Isabella turned to Gabe. "A paltry sixty years is all he's getting?"

"Sweetheart, it's without parole. He'll be ninety-six by the time he's released—assuming he lives that long. He doesn't appear in the best of health."

"Right. When you put it that way, it seems long enough...."

The judge spoke directly to the prosecutor. "Mr. Hayden, in accordance with a new protocol, this is the time the children's mother can address the guilty party if she so desires."

The last thing Gabe had imagined was that Isabella would be willing—or able—to face her ex-husband. She shocked him and everyone in her family when she stood and walked straight to where Hayden sat. She cleared her throat a few times, but once she began speaking, her voice rang clear enough. "Our innocent children had no idea how evil you were, Julian. Antonia and Ramon loved you. It was your responsibility to protect them from harm. You violated a beautiful and sacred trust. I hope you live every day of those sixty years, and that you begin and end each one seeing their faces in your warped mind."

Spinning abruptly, she returned and sat beside Gabe. He realized she'd pulled a five-by-seven photo of the two kids out of her purse and now held it crushed against her heart.

That part of the sentencing left Gabe shaken. He had difficulty following the family out of the building.

"Well, it's over," Benito exclaimed. They'd all reached the parking lot after shaking hands with Hayden and his team. "Time to move forward," the Navarro patriarch said. "Are you two going straight home from here?" He stopped, aiming his query at Gabe and Isabella.

"I ordered flowers," Gabe muttered, thinking now it was probably a bad idea. "I thought we'd pick them up and drive out to the cemetery. But if Isabella would rather not, she can go with you and I'll make the trip alone."

Stepping close, she linked her arm through Gabe's. "That's not something anyone should ever do alone."

Gabe recognized his own words, spoken to her only a few months ago, although it seemed a lifetime.

Midafternoon they arrived at the cemetery. Gabe collected the two vases of flowers, then remembered that the previous time he'd been here, Isabella had preferred to go to the grave site by herself.

"Come with me," she pleaded, her eyes shimmering with unshed tears.

Gabe blinked a few times. His cheeks were wet, he noticed as he set the vases between the pinwheels. There were already fresh roses lying on the ground in front of each small mound.

"I drove out here before dawn," Isabella said, kneeling to set the picture of two smiling children between Gabe's bouquets. One was tied with a pink satin ribbon, the other with blue. Taking off the angel pin she always wore, Isabella crossed the ribbon tails. "Someone to watch over Toni and Ramon," she whispered as she pinned the filigree angel to the ribbons.

Raising a hand, she let Gabe help her to her feet. She automatically slipped an arm around his waist. "There's no wind today. No turbulence at all. I think, as Papa said, it's over. Justice has been served. For them and for me.'' Pressing her left hand against Gabe's chest, she raised her face for his kiss. His heart beat firm and strong beneath her fingers, although his cheeks were as damp as hers.

Once the kiss came to a natural end, they stood for several moments with just their heads touching. ''In a way, we're both wounded souls, you and I,'' she murmured.

''I'd rather think we're broken souls who have become whole over time.''

''Yes. Me, too. But I'm not sure I'm ready to say we'll never face any struggles in the future. For instance…if we decided to have—or adopt—a baby. Or babies.''

Turning slightly, Isabella gazed directly into Gabe's blue eyes. ''But I *am* ready to travel down the road of life with you. If you still want me,'' she said shyly.

What struck Gabe most as he scooped Isabella into his arms and swung her around was her eyes. Because there was life there now. Life and happiness and hope. And love.

HARLEQUIN *Super*ROMANCE®

presents a compelling family drama—
an exciting new trilogy
by popular author Debra Salonen

THOSE SULLIVAN SISTERS

Jenny, Andrea and Kristin Sullivan are much more
than sisters—*they're triplets!* Growing up as one of
a threesome meant life was never lonely...or dull.

Now they're adults—with separate lives, loves,
dreams and secrets. But underneath everything that
keeps them apart is the bond that holds them together.

MY HUSBAND, MY BABIES
(Jenny's story)
available December 2002

WITHOUT A PAST
(Andi's story)
available January 2003

THE COMEBACK GIRL
(Kristin's story)
available February 2003

HARLEQUIN®
Makes any time special ®

HARLEQUIN *Super*ROMANCE®

Two brothers—
and the women they love.

Nate Hawkins. He returns to Colorado to attend his father's unexpected second wedding—and runs into Laurel Pierce. A woman he fell in love with ten years before. A woman who was his best friend's wife. A woman who's now pregnant with another man's child....
Another Man's Wife,
coming in February 2003

Rick Hawkins. He comes home for the same reason his brother did. Then he meets Audra Jerrett, a woman he didn't expect to like. After all, she's the first cousin of his father's new wife. But she's just suffered a devastating trauma—the kind of trauma Rick understands.
Home to Copper Mountain,
coming in May 2003

**Two of Rebecca Winters's trademark larger-than-life heroes.
Two of her passionate and emotional romances.
Enjoy them both!**

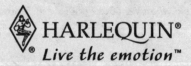

HARLEQUIN®
Live the emotion™

Visit us at www.eHarlequin.com

HARLEQUIN SUPERROMANCE®

HSRAMWRW

Welcome to Koomera Crossing,
a town hidden deep in the Australian Outback.
Let renowned romance novelist Margaret Way take
you there. Let her introduce you to the people of
Koomera Crossing. Let her tell you their secrets....

In **Sarah's Baby** meet Dr. Sarah Dempsey and
Kyall McQueen. And then there's the town's
matriarch, Ruth McQueen, who played a role
in Sarah's disappearance from her grandson
Kyall's life—and who now dreads Sarah's
return to Koomera Crossing.

Sarah's Baby is available in February
wherever Harlequin books are sold.
And watch for the next Koomera Crossing story,
coming from Harlequin Romance in October.

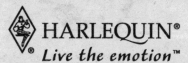

HARLEQUIN®
Live the emotion™

Visit us at www.eHarlequin.com

HARLEQUIN SUPERROMANCE®